THE
LONG ROAD
BACK

Roxanne Gail Hodge

THE LONG ROAD BACK
Second Edition

ISBN Perfect Bound Paperback 978-1-0879-1861-7
ISBN Case Wrap Hardcover 978-1-0879-1823-3
ISBN eBook 978-1-0879-1871-6

Printed in the United States of America

Published by Author Enterprise, a Publishing Partnership Company

Murphy, TX

www.AuthorEnterprise.com

AUTHOR
ENTERPRISE

Other Books Written by Roxanne Gail Hodge

Thistles & Blossoms

My Journey Through Poetry

Dedication

I want to dedicate this Novel to Laurie Munden, and her ministry "99Behind – because the ONE Matters". She helped me start this writing journey and has been with me every step of the way, encouraging me as I stumbled through all of my drafts and wanting to give up. Without her selfless mentoring (because the One Matters), I would probably never have realized the thrill of completing and publishing a novel!

Thank you,

Roxanne Gail Hodge

Acknowledgements

I have a list of people to acknowledge, and if for some reason your name does not make it with this book, see me for the next one! You will be on it.

First to Rebecca Nietert: Author Enterprise, NetLits.com, Lone Star Writers club, Renowned Author, and a courageous overcomer of a life that most of us would never have survived. A friend to struggling authors, tirelessly makes the writing journey less daunting for the beginner, always ready to provide wise counsel and honest feedback, even when it hurts. Graciously interacts with everyone she meets. Thank you so much for all of your hard work on behalf of me! Without you, I would still be re-writing this book.

Thank you to (Sarah) Janet Vangemeren for the wonderful content and grammar editing during a time I had no resources for a professional. So glad we met!

To Caputo Studio, and Alyssa for the polish edit.

For my Sister, Rhonda and her husband Ted, the first two people to read my book and praised and encouraged me to "go for it" and they didn't even get the benefit of the best versions yet!

My Sister-in-law Cassie, for taking time out of her busy life and doing editing for me along the way, and her continued encouragement.

For the ladies in my Bible Class at First McKinney Baptist; the Naomi Blossoms, the first people to purchase my book.

My two daughters Tonya and Tamra, who loved me through the tough times I had during their formative years, and they remain my cheerleaders still today. They increased my cheerleader section with four beautiful grandchildren, Cameron, Tamina, Kaylee, and Zacharia.

Can't forget my good friend Marilyn, who has been my anchor for over thirty years!

To my greatest fan Barbara McAllaster. When I need an upper (not the drug kind, the lasting kind), I go to her.

To Jennifer host of the Jennifer Sheehan Show who encouraged me with her words.

A special thank you to Theresa for her wise counsel and ability to keep me moving in the right direction.

To the writers in the writing club, Tiffany, Melanie, Veronica, Kristina, Patti, Rox, Rich, Kaveri, Peter, and editor, Addie.

All the credit for what I write, must go to God the Father, Lord and Savior, Jesus Christ. Without His care, direction, and unconditional love, I would not be possible.

Chapter One

Monique walked into her bungalow and laid her keys onto the countertop. *What an evening!* Before she reached the bathroom to start her bath, there was a knock on the door. *Who could be at my door this late?* But even before she thought the last word, a sense of foreboding washed over her and increased ten-fold when she looked out the window and met Connor's hostile eyes. Monique paused a moment to decide how to play this and concluded that innocence was the best strategy.

"Connor!? How good of you to drop by. I thought you had a play to see or something. Come in."

Connor stepped into the door and quietly shut it.

"Hello, Monique. You've been busy this evening, haven't you? I want you to give me what you took, and I want it now."

Connor did not speak loudly, but Monique heard the menace in his tone.

"I don't know what you mean. I just got home from work. What makes you think I took anything?"

Monique took a step back as she saw Connor approach. She knew he would stop at nothing to appropriate the evidence. It was time to change tactics.

"Connor, I don't know what you are mixed up in, but you are in way over your head."

Connor did not stop his forward trajectory.

"All I want is what you took. You haven't had time to make copies, so you and I are the only ones who know what you have."

"No, really. I don't have anything. I dropped it off at the bank in a safety deposit box before I came home."

Monique's mind frantically searched for a way to diffuse Connor's anger before he became violent, but she realized it was too late. Connor charged and grabbed for her shoulders. The young woman was too quick for him and dodged his grasp. Connor quickly regrouped and attacked again, forcing Monique into the living room against the fireplace. Her body tensed as she made a move to counterattack, but at the same time, Connor reached behind her head for an object. Before she could kick his feet out from under

1

him, a sharp pain pierced through her fear. Then everything went black.

Connor stared at the lifeless body and in a panic, knelt to check her. *Thank goodness she had a pulse, faint but steady.* He didn't see any blood from the wound. Monique was knocked out cold and wouldn't be giving up information anytime soon. The best way to make this go away was to get rid of her, but he had to act quickly in case she regained consciousness. His mind raced trying to find a way to finish her off where he didn't have to take responsibility. The only option that came to mind was a violent one-car accident. *Think Connor, is there another option?* He decided that the accident would be perfect. The night was cloudy and there was a new moon, a combination to make a perfect storm for stealth. The best place to simulate a one-car accident was Gipper's Gully, a remote, dark stretch of highway with a hairpin curve. Monique had parked her car in the spot right outside the bungalow apartment. That would keep unwanted eyes from inspecting his activities as he carried an unconscious woman.

Connor grabbed Monique's keys from the counter and quickly moved to unlock the passenger side door. He didn't think there could be any evidence of a struggle because their confrontation was brief; however, he made a cursory look around the apartment to make sure. Nothing looked out of place. It wasn't as easy as he thought it would be to carry Monique out the door and put her into the car. She may be petite, but carrying dead weight was hard. Before he hurried back to close the apartment, Connor made sure no one could see the unconscious woman. He was ready to lock the apartment, when a horrifying thought rumbled through his mind. *How was he supposed to get back from Gipper's Gully? It was impossible to drive two vehicles at the same time.* Connor was a runner, but even at his best speed, it would take hours to get back. *Perhaps Monique had a bike.*

He rushed towards the patio in search of transportation. There was her bike. Not as fast as a car, but it beat walking or running. Connor wrestled the Schwinn onto the bike rack and calculated the time to complete his caper. Ten o'clock right now. The trip to Gipper's Gully would take thirty minutes. It would take about fifteen minutes to take the bike off of the rack and push the car over the edge. He wouldn't have time to drive to his home in the suburbs, which meant staying at his apartment in town. Even then, it would be close to four o'clock in the morning by the time he got back to Monique's place to put her bike back and retrieve his car. He would get to the apartment with just enough time to shower and get ready for the day. Hopefully, the adrenalin would keep him going.

Connor squeezed into the driver's side and moved the seat to accommodate his long legs. Monique remained slouched out of sight in the passenger's seat. He had to take a deep breath to steady his nerves before he turned the ignition and cleared the parking lot. "Monique, this is all your fault!"

Chapter Two

I wake to the pleasant sound of water as it cascades over the rocks. I see birds fly and hear their melodious songs. Where? Someplace I don't know, but it's peaceful. I'm too tired to move, why? I drift away with questions and no answer—where am I? How did I get here, and for how long…?

The Intensive Care Unit at Mercy Memorial Hospital was quiet for the moment. It was after seven in the evening, and the shift change activity was over. Constance sat in a not so comfortable recliner and prayed for some movement or sign from her daughter. It had been weeks of waiting and Constance was losing hope. Torrie abruptly interrupted the silent plea when she burst through the door.

"Mom! How is Monique?"

"Goodness, Torrie. You surprised me. I don't know. The doctor was just here and didn't say much, except…"

Constance burst into tears.

Torrie ran to her side as she rescued a box of tissues from Monique's bedside table.

"Here, please don't cry,"

Constance gratefully pulled a Kleenex from the box and wiped her tears. Her daughter observed the scene.

"You look exhausted."

"No, I'm all right. What I am tired of is sitting here waiting for something to change."

Torrie had a different thought on that statement.

"I know one thing for certain; nothing will change in the next few hours. The best thing for you to do is to go home and sleep in your own bed."

"No, I can't leave her; what if she…"

"Stop it. Monique is in a hospital and exhausting yourself is not going to make her better. If you would just go home, I'll stay with Monique tonight."

Constance stared at her beautiful youngest daughter as she lay lifeless, not sure what to do.

"But Torrie, you hate hospitals, and besides..."

"Mom, go home."

"Okay. All right already. You don't have to push me. Are you sure it isn't too much for you?"

"I said I'd stay. Now go."

Constance gathered the rest of her stuff and, with a half-hearted wave, left the room. Torrie turned her attention to Monique. The doctor encouraged active communication with coma patients, but how was she supposed to make conversation to someone who wouldn't talk back? Besides, even on a good day, she never knew what to say to her sister. Still, if it could help.

"Monique"—*I can't talk to someone who doesn't talk back. But okay.* "Um, how was your day?" *Oh, that's just lame, Torrie!* "I mean—what I really want to say is you have put us in a hell of a spot, and I'm angry with you right now. Dammit, Monique, wake up! How can you put us through this hardship?"

Chapter Three

I wonder why it's dark. The birds take flight with angry, accusatory shrieks! A deafening roar replaces the stream's soft bubbly hum. What happened? Why did everything change? —so, so tired. I want to—I will just—close my—rest...

Alarms blared, and Torrie jumped out of the chair at the same time the nurse rushed in the door.

"What happened!"

The nurse's arrival eased Torrie's panic.

"Nothing. I mean, I talked to her like the doctor said—and..."

Nurse Sally Barrington didn't expect an answer. She concentrated on tasks to stabilize Monique's vital signs, and the first order of business was to silence the alarms. Sally rubbed Monique's arm and murmured to the young lady until her vital signs settled, then turned her attention to Torrie.

"Goodness, girl, you are white as a ghost. Sit down before you faint!"

"Are all of those alarms necessary? They can scare a person, and If something happened to Monique with my mom at home—it would not be pretty. What did I do?"

"What makes you think you did something wrong? Look, we don't understand what the mind does when in a coma. What happened is Monique's heart rate changed slightly, which triggered one alarm, which sparked a rise in her blood pressure that set off another alarm. Your sister is fine now. I must say, though, her reaction to the sound is a good sign. It means her mind hasn't shut down."

"I don't understand what you mean. How can you tell her mind isn't shut down if she isn't talking or responding?"

"Unresponsive does not mean unaware. The word coma is a simplistic term for an unconscious person. There are different levels of comas and unresponsiveness. The fact that the alarms caused a

6

reaction suggests some awareness of her surroundings. The chances of her coming out of her coma are greater."

"I just wish it would happen faster."

"Hang in there. It'll happen. Your sister is okay for now. I'll check on her later."

The nurse left Torrie to the overpowering silence of the tiny room. She paced to alleviate the stress. Why did she offer to stay with Monique? Too restless to hang out in the small room, Torrie rationalized a reason to leave in search of a TV. As she cleared the doorway, her phone chirped, prompting her to fumble through her purse to retrieve it.

"Hello?"

"Torrie? This is Mom. I know how much you hate being cooped up, especially in a hospital. I shouldn't have made you feel obligated to stay with Monique. It's okay if you go home now. As you said, she is in the hospital and is closely monitored. It's not going to make any difference if someone is with her or not at this time."

"But you said—Are you sure you won't worry?"

"Of course, I'll worry. To be honest, though, I won't worry any less with you there, or even if I stayed. Just go home, only make sure you tell the nurses no one will be there tonight and to call me if Monique's status changes, no matter how small."

For a moment, Torrie felt guilty for her desire to escape but not enough to reject her mom's offer.

"Thanks, Mom. I'll make sure the nurses have both of our phone numbers. And Mom?"

"Yes, sweetheart?"

"Don't come back until late tomorrow morning."

"I'll do my best."

Torrie took a quick detour to the nurses' desk.

"Excuse me, Sally?"

"Yes?"

"I'm on my way out now, and my mom will stay home tonight, so no one will be in the room with Monique. Do you have both of our phone numbers handy, so you can call us if you need us?"

"Sure, we have them in her patient records. I'm glad..."

Torrie walked away before nurse Barrington finished her statement. She stepped into her sister's room one more time for the night.

"Monique, I love you, sis! Please forgive me for what I said earlier; just rest up and get well. We miss you."

Torrie left the hospital for the more familiar outside world.

I awake slowly to discover this strange world has reset. There is the sun again, and color. The birds sing in harmony, and my exhaustion is gone. I still have no memory, though. This world is peaceful. Probably because there isn't anyone else here. I have times of conscious thought but no reference point of a beginning or end. Do I exist? Of course, I do; I'm here and aware, even if I don't know where here is. I must believe time will bring clarity. I close my eyes; the lead is back in my body.

Chapter Four

Constance tossed and turned the entire night. She looked at the clock, surprised to discover it was five o'clock in the morning. The last time she looked at the clock, it was two-thirty. To get up or not. Weariness had forced her to bed by eleven, but her mind wouldn't stop. She couldn't keep from ruminating on the police report from Monique's accident. The report said Monique fell asleep at the wheel and missed the curve, but mother's intuition refuted that statement. Unfortunately, a mother's instinct isn't enough evidence to change their conclusion. *"On the night of the accident, the roads were dry; there were no apparent skid marks and no indication of mechanical failure. What else could it be?"*

Sleep was no longer an option, so Constance thrust off her covers. She wanted to call the hospital before the shift change.

"Hello, ICU, Nurse Barrington speaking.

"Good morning. I'm Constance, Monique's mother. I want to check on my daughter."

"Good morning, Ms. Yorkshire! We had a quiet night, and Monique slept well."

"Great! I'll be back at the hospital at nine-thirty."

"Thanks, I'll make a notation for the day shift. I won't be here when you get in, and I won't be back for the next three nights."

"Really? I'm glad you told me. Do you know who her nurse will be until you get back?"

"No. The assignments aren't made until the night shift, but Nurse Dooley will be here."

"Yes, I've met her. I guess I can go to her for any questions."

"Of course, you can, but all the nurses in ICU are perfectly competent."

"I know. You're right; it's just, well—oh, nothing—goodbye, and have a good weekend."

Constance showered, dressed carefully, and put on make-up. She poured herself a cup a coffee, and to honor Torrie's request, waited to leave until nine o'clock. Sleeping in her own bed and not rushing off to the hospital was a good plan. The day was brighter,

9

and she was energized, ready to meet the challenges of whatever came. Little did she know how short-lived her optimism would be.

I must figure out who I am, yet there isn't a soul to help me. Why? I don't even know my name. Oh! Strange sensation. Goodness, the sky is dark again! My head! My head hurts! Oh, God, please help me! Please make this pain go away!

The minute Constance stepped out of the elevators, she knew something was terribly wrong, but as she made a beeline to Monique's room, a nurse intercepted her.

"Good morning, Ms. Yorkshire. I need you to come with me."

"No, I want to see Monique!"

"Let's go talk in the conference room."

"Tell me what's going on?!"

"Look, Monique is stable..."

"Stable! From what?"

"Please, let's go to the conference room, and I will explain everything."

Constance realized resistance only delayed the answers she sought, so she complied. The two women entered the conference room, and the nurse closed the door.

"Please have a seat. Thank you. Now, Monique's blood pressure spiked, and she became agitated and restless, all symptoms of extreme pain. We stabilized her and called Dr. Kabra, who called in another neurologist, one who specializes in long-term coma patients. The doctors mutually decided to order a CT scan and bloodwork to rule out complications that may have been dormant since the accident."

Constance nodded.

The nurse observed the dazed woman and continued.

"She is on her way to radiology as we speak. Do you want me to call Torrie?"

"Huh, oh, Torrie. I don't think so. You said she isn't in any danger now, and the tests are merely precautionary?"

"Yes."

"Then, don't call her. She's at work, and it's a busy time for her business. She doesn't need to be bothered."

"If you're sure."

Constance didn't reply, so the nurse continued.

"My name is Nurse Chapel. Monique is my patient until the end of the shift. You can stay here, or if you want, wait in her room. She won't be back for at least an hour or two, maybe longer."

Nurse Chapel attempted to reassure Constance with a pat on her hand as she left.

Chapter Five

Time passed, though Constance wasn't aware of how long. A lone person quietly entered the room and settled into one of the chairs. She was oblivious of his presence at first, then...

"I'm so sorry! I didn't hear you enter."

"No worries, Ms. Yorkshire. You may not remember me. I'm the chaplain, and I visited you a few times early on. I've not been too good with my follow-up visits."

"Of course, I remember you."

"May I buy you a cup of coffee?"

"I don't know about—I can't. I have to be here when Monique gets back."

"You've got time. I spoke to Nurse Chapel and confirmed your daughter won't be back for at least another hour."

Constance sighed.

"I guess I might as will go then. Thank you, Father."

"Oh, no, I'm not a Father. Catholics aren't the only clergy who wear collars. I'm non-denominational. Please call me Steve."

"Steve? Sure, then you can call me Constance."

"Okay – Constance, shall we go?"

Steve held out his hand to assist Constance to her feet, and they headed toward the cafeteria. Neither one spoke on the short trip. The chaplain got the coffee and guided Constance to a table at the back of the cafeteria.

"Let's sit over here."

Constance gratefully sat down with a big sigh.

"Thank you. Goodness. Forgive my fuzziness; I'm slightly shell shocked."

"Understandable."

The two sipped on their coffee before Steve continued.

"You and Torrie appear to be alone in this tragedy, and I want to offer my pastoral services."

"That is so sweet of you! – You know, your offer made me realize that I've been so focused on circumstances that I've left God out of the equation. There's this verse I like— something like raising my eyes to the mountains?"

"Of course, that's a good one, Psalm 121:1-2, 'I lift my eyes to the mountains. Where does my strength come from? My help comes from the Lord, the Maker of heaven and earth.'"

"That's it."

Constance meditated briefly on the words. She glanced at the chaplain.

"Thank you for your generous offer, and the answer is yes. It's been years since I've been to church, and now, well, I'm out of touch with everyone."

Steve gave Constance another moment before he spoke again.

"May I pray with you?"

"Uh, sure, yes, I guess that will be okay."

The two bowed their heads, and Steve gently took Constance's hands.

"Our Heavenly Father, thank You for every provision You give us during the times we are in the deserts of our life. You have Constance surrounded by Your love, and You have the answers she seeks. I pray for supernatural revelation and confidence in the path she is on.

"Lord, we know Monique is in your arms. You are the best doctor, and You have the power to heal. Your time for her to come back to us is perfect. I pray for grace and the patience to wait.

"Also, we ask that You be with Torrie, and I ask for Your best angels of reassurance to minister to Constance and Torrie.

"One more request, Lord. Please show me how I can be Your arms and legs to help this sweet family. All of this, we ask in Your great and powerful name. Amen."

Constance smiled through her tears.

"Thank you. I feel so much better and not so alone. Now, if you'll excuse me, I need to get back to Monique."

"Sure, let me walk back with you. Later tonight, when you're ready, ask Nurse Chapel to page me. I'll come to take you to my office so we can discuss options and ways in which I can assist."

"I will, and Steve – I can't thank you enough."

Constance and Steve arrived in the ICU.

"Here we are. You are quite welcome. I look forward to our visit."

I keep my eyes closed against the intense pain. A loud noise as disturbing as a bass drum intensifies my agony. I peek through my lids and see a gray world, which frightens me. I fade. Now I'm back in a world filled with suffocating quiet and insufferable torture. Darkness returns, and with darkness comes relief. The hurt leaves me, at last. I am tired. I relax into oblivion.

Constance arrived in Monique's room, but no Monique. Surprised, she sought Nurse Chapel.

"Excuse me, Nurse Chapel...."

"Please, Ms. Yorkshire, call me Candy."

"Sure, Candy, why is Monique still gone? Shouldn't she be back by now?"

Candy looked at the distraught mother.

"There's no reason for alarm. The noise of the CT machine agitated Monique, and the technician delayed the scan to ask for a tranquilizer. I checked her status just now. Monique will be back in her room in about thirty minutes."

"Oh. Thank you. Do you think I can stay in her room until she gets back?"

"Absolutely! No one will bother you."

"Thank you..."

Chapter Six

Torrie sat in her large corner office and stared out her window with a panoramic view of the mountains. Her dark thoughts blocked out the loveliness. Even in her jumbled mind, she knew she needed to prioritize the marketing deadline for the company's most significant client. Her team worked efficiently; however, this client over-demanded and challenged the best.

"Hey, Torrie! What's the matter?"

Torrie was annoyed with the intrusion.

"How dare you barge into my office unannounced! I've told you before, knock first and wait for an invitation."

"Excuse me! I knocked— many times. What is wrong with you?"

Connor was beyond exasperated.

"What do you mean? I'm perfectly normal."

"No—no, you're not. You're distracted and irritable. It's to the point I'm afraid to say anything. Something's definitely wrong."

Connor walked into the room and double-checked to make sure he locked the door behind him. He wasn't ashamed of his attraction to Torrie, but there was no need to provide fodder for the office grapevine. If only Torrie would open up about the status of Monique's condition. He couldn't believe she was still alive after Gipper's Gully.

"Please, tell me what is going on. Is it the job or this client? Don't shut me out. I want to help."

Torrie took a deep breath. She never brought her personal life into work and adamantly discouraged private conversations, but today Connor's attentiveness and empathy proved to be her undoing. She let go of her pent-up emotions, and they crashed through their long-standing barriers. Tears flowed, disrupting her words.

"It's been two months, and my sister is still in a coma. I am so angry because it looks like she is just being stubborn. I told her I was angry and..."

Torrie dissolved almost to hysterics.

Connor's ears picked up on the words. Had Monique finally succumbed to her injuries? If so, he wasn't sure he could pretend

15

to be sad.

"Torrie, honey, come here; let's sit down. Now, tell me what happened."

He wrapped Torrie in his arms and led her to the loveseat. Connor intended to exploit Torrie's vulnerability to coerce information from her.

"I am so s-s-sorry."

As soon as they began, Torrie's tears dried up.

"This is so not me."

She disengaged from a perplexed Connor and returned to her desk. Once again, Torrie was in control. She sat down and returned to her business persona.

"Now, what can I do for you?"

Connor sighed. The Torrie he knew and loved was back; well, maybe it was love. Trouble was, he loved his wife and two daughters equally. Falling for Torrie was never his plan, plus it made his life more complicated. The only reason he got this job without the proper credentials was due to his handler's leverage with the company. He had orders to use his relationship with Torrie to keep track of Monique's activities. Things were not working out the way he intended.

The window of opportunity passed, and Connor resigned himself to the change in conversation.

"The team is ready to update you on the presentation, but I suggest we wait until after lunch. I'll tell everyone you had a meeting and won't be available until this afternoon. We can go to my apartment and unwind with a glass of wine."

The hidden invitation in Connor's voice disgusted Torrie. She accepted partial responsibility for his brashness and resented the day her boss gave her an assistant. She never worked with a partner and had no desire to start. Why her boss insisted on inserting Connor into her life, she had no idea. At first, it was easy for Torrie to maintain a professional relationship and overlook Connor's invitations to enhance their connection, even during necessary late-night consultations. What Connor lacked in imagination, he overachieved in persistence and patience.

Torrie always suspected his motive for leasing an apartment in town for a place to crash after late-night meetings extended beyond convenience, and her suspicions were confirmed not too long ago. One evening after they completed a tough project, Connor convinced her to join him for dinner and drinks. Torrie's weariness, along with the alcohol, deadened her reserve. She always admired Connor's good looks with his dark brown hair, deep brown eyes that sparkled when he laughed, tanned skin and athletic body, but during dinner, she discovered his talent for conversation. Connor used her exhaustion and charmed his way into her personal life. After that night, they became an item.

"Earth to Torrie—where did you go?"

"Huh? Oh. No, tell the team they can have an extended lunch, but I want to check in with Mom at the hospital."

Connor stifled his objection. Torrie protected her family as fiercely as a mother bear does when her cub is in danger. Once, during a conversation, she made a negative comment about her sister, and he agreed. But that was the last time because Torrie had turned violent in an instant.

"Okay, babe, but I think you're making a mistake going into a stressful situation when..."

"Quit!"

"Hey, I'm just saying!"

Wisely, he changed tactics. If Torrie refused to discuss Monique's condition, maybe he could manipulate his way to an invitation to go with her.

"Why don't you let me go with you to the hospital. I bet I can get some answers for you."

Torrie was rankled. Connor pretended he wasn't chauvinistic, but then his true nature was revealed with his inane remarks.

"Thanks, but no thanks. I can drive myself to the hospital, and we don't need your manliness to intercede for us."

"Ouch! I'm sorry. I get the message; you don't need me. I'm going to go now. I plan to reserve the large conference room from two-thirty through the rest of the evening. Will that work?"

"Sure, fine. I'm sorry I snapped at you, and also, thank you for dealing with the team."

Chapter Seven

"Hello, Ms. Yorkshire, we have your daughter back intact. Do you mind stepping out for a minute?"

Constance was startled by the technician's booming voice.

"Finally. Let me see her first. Then I'll run down to the cafeteria."

She looked at Monique and gave her a quick kiss. Stepping out of the elevator, Torrie nearly collided head-on with her mom.

"Mom? Goodness, that was close. What's up?"

Constance gave Torrie a brief hug.

"Hello, dear, I'm on my way to the cafeteria. Are you at lunch?"

"Yes. I took an extended lunch to catch up on Monique's status. I see you put on some make-up."

"A little—I'm glad you came. There was an incident earlier with..."

"What? An incident? What incident? Why you didn't call me?"

"It's Okay. I didn't call you because it was over before I knew about it. When I arrived this morning, Monique was on her way to radiology for tests. The nurse explained about her blood pressure spike, which indicated symptoms of extreme pain. She told the neurologist, and he ordered the tests to rule out anything significant."

Torrie was perturbed.

"You mean she went this morning, and they just now brought her back? This is absurd; we have got to get some answers—they can't..."

Why did she yell at her mom?

"Sorry. I'm so ready for her to wake up so we can put this nightmare behind us."

Constance agreed but determined she had better change the course of the conversation.

"Why don't we go down to the cafeteria and visit. I may even get me something to eat."

"Sure, I'll tag along but only for a few minutes. I have a meeting at two-thirty."

Neither one spoke as they walked to the cafeteria together, each lost in their reflections. Constance chose a chicken salad sandwich, while Torrie took a yogurt, and both settled for iced tea. Torrie pointed to a deserted spot at the back of the room, unloaded the trays for both of them, and sat down. After a couple of bites of her sandwich, Constance proceeded to discuss Monique's status.

"The nurse said the neurologist planned to review Monique's test results with us this evening. She wasn't able to give me an exact time, just between five and nine."

"Between five and nine. That's four hours. There's no way I can be here that long."

"I never expected you to."

"I know, but I want to be here. Maybe if I get here by seven, it will be soon enough. Is it the same neurologist that's been on her case since the accident?"

"No, Dr. Kabra called in another neurologist. The nurses tell me this one specializes in long-term coma patients."

The two ladies were so intent on their conversation, they didn't see the chaplain approach.

"Good afternoon, ladies..."

Torrie's and Constance's identical startled expressions tickled him. He was able to suppress the chuckle but failed to hide his smile.

"Why the snicker?"

"Forgive me, Torrie. You both looked up with the same expression, and, well, it struck my funny bone. I am so sorry I surprised you. I guess you didn't see me wave."

"Apparently not, and last I looked, we did not invite you to interrupt our conversation. Mom, I have to run. I'll be back tonight."

Torrie gave her mom a peck on her cheek and left without a word to Steve.

"Is it all clergies or just me?"

"Please excuse her. Torrie keeps a tight rein on her emotions.

19

Thg combination of the pressure of her job, her sister's continued coma, plus her personal issues has her stressed. I worry she'll snap."

"I know these are stressful times. I may not be able to make Torrie's life easier, but I am here for you. Since you hadn't called me, I decided to get some lunch. Did Monique get back to her room?"

"Yes, just. The nurse asked me to leave until they got her settled. Torrie and I came here to get out of the way, and, as much as I hate to abandon you, I'm sure they are finished by now. I'm anxious to get back, but I promise I will contact you later."

Steve watched yet another member of the Yorkshire family rush away. These two suffering women whom he wanted to assist were a mystery to him. *Dear Lord, please give me the wisdom to understand how to best serve this family.*

Chapter Eight

My eyes are heavy, and I feel drugged. I remember the pain and then nothingness. Right now, the pain is gone. I urge my eyes to open and notice yet another change in this world. The gray is now white. A shadow passes overhead and then silence. I panic; there's no air. This colorless world is suffocating—and, now I can't breathe! Help! Somebody! Anybody—Can't, no air—p...!

"Code Blue! Code Blue! ICU-24! Code Blue!"

The ICU disrupted into a flurry of activity. A rush of bodies ran into Monique's room. During the pandemonium, no one noticed a solitary person slink into the shadows. He waited to make sure everyone was occupied with a task, then, unhurriedly and silently made his way to the elevators and out the door.

Constance heard those dreaded words. Monique's room was ICU-24. She stopped in front of the nurses' counter and ached to rush to her daughter's aid, but wisdom arrested the urge. She didn't want to get in the way. *What happened? Monique had been stable until yesterday. What happened to make everything go wrong?*

Meanwhile, still in the cafeteria, Steve heard the code blue and recognized Monique's room number. His first reaction was to rush to Constance but instead, he said a silent prayer. When he finished his petition, he felt peace; Monique was out of danger. The best option for him was to go back to his rounds and wait for Constance to contact him.

How much time passed? The color is back in my world. I consider it my world because there isn't anyone else here. Wait! There is something, or maybe someone looming on the horizon. Something—another person? No, actually— well, maybe not. I want to summon up enough energy to take a stroll through this strange world of mine to no avail. I'm sure I can speak— I yell, but nothing registers with my ears. Maybe I'm deaf—No, I can't be deaf because I hear the birds and stream.

All right, Monique, start...hey! My name is Monique. Wow, it just came to me just like that. Monique. My name is Monique, and I am—I don't know.

Thoughts bombard my mind until the pain once again interrupts. At least I can breathe this time.

I look at something on the horizon and notice it's closer. So, it isn't an inanimate object then because it moved. I close my eyes to rest. Yea, right as if you worked so hard! But—rest is—good— I will—aft—er I uh— rest—

Chapter Nine

Torrie walked into the Premier Towers where McGregor, Bright & Anderson had their offices. The name sounded suspiciously like attorneys instead of a prestigious marketing firm. There hadn't been any McGregors, Brights or Andersons for several years, but the reputation of the firm was based on those names, so it stayed.

Despite her hateful attitude regarding the reverend, Steve walked up at an opportune time. Torrie was happy for any excuse to vacate hospitals. His presence gave her the reason she needed to leave and, at the same time, appeased her conscience for abandoning her mom.

The elevator doors opened and brought Torrie out of her mindless internal chatter. She had yet to understand why she generated absurd, random thoughts. Maybe it was a defense mechanism to keep her sane from the extreme pressures prevalent in her life. *Good grief, now I'm thinking like a therapist! Ugh!*

Torrie arrived for the meeting only a few minutes late, took a deep breath, and made her entrance. Her team was all present.

"Good afternoon, everyone. Are you ready to get some work done?"

The next few hours the team collaborated on making necessary changes to clean up their campaign.

"Okay, people. You have done great last-minute work. We've met the client's expectations, and our meeting isn't until Friday. Let's all go home for now. We can complete the changes in the morning. I don't want anyone to celebrate tomorrow night because I want all of you rested, bright, and alert for the meeting."

A stunned silence pursued.

"Wait, Torrie. Do you mean you want all of us at the meeting?"

Reed was the newest member on the team, but he was brave enough to voice everyone's incredulousness.

"Is it unusual that..."

"Yes!" The entire team spoke at once.

Torrie was momentarily confused. Either she entered the twilight zone, or she completely lost it. Her hesitation lasted only a moment.

"This is a particular client, and I think it practical to be proactive. Each one of you worked on a different component of this campaign. In the event the client voices concerns, it's logical to allow the one familiar with the process to be present and available to address those concerns. I don't want to go back to the drawing board on this one. Any questions?"

She gave them little time to respond.

"Good, see you tomorrow."

The team left. Everyone except for Connor. His attention bordered on obsessive. All she wanted right then was to be left alone.

Connor, on the other hand, wondered what Torrie was up to. Her attitude was distant, and almost—he wasn't sure what the almost was, but he feared the worst. Breaking up would be disastrous, and it was essential to keep close to her so he could monitor Monique's status. The best plan was to give her some space.

"Torrie, I think I'll go home early for a change. I haven't seen Bonnie or the girls for a while. Good-bye until tomorrow. Oh, and have a good evening; get some rest; you look beat."

That was a turn of events.

"Sure, okay, then, see you in the morning."

Torrie remained where she was and thought about home, the rarely used Jacuzzi, silk pajamas, quiet time with TV and a glass of wine. Unfortunately, the hospital beckoned. Monique's recent complications concerned her, and Torrie was anxious to learn the results of the tests. She suspected the doctor found some overlooked damage. Why was it taking the doctors so long to figure out what was wrong? She understood the difficulty her mom had sitting with Monique.

On the other hand, Torrie was sorry for herself. She had a problematic client, an affair she suddenly wasn't happy about and then an obligation to put going to the hospital into her already full schedule! *No use sitting here feeling sorry for myself. Nothing is accomplished with self-pity.*

Chapter Ten

The activity in the ICU had lessened. Monique was once again stable. Constance vacantly stared at her daughter, wondering what to do next. There was no reason to contact Torrie and get her upset. She looked at her watch for what seemed like the hundredth time. Three-thirty. Another hour and a half before her mandatory vigil for the doctor. Time for a reprieve.

"Candy, excuse me, Candy?"

"Yes, Ms. Yorkshire, what can I do for you?"

"Can you please page the chaplain for me?"

"Absolutely."

For lack of anything better to do, Constance paced between the nurses' station and Monique's room while she waited for Steve. She didn't have to wait long.

"Constance, hi. How are you holding up?"

"Not so good. I feel helpless and restless and—and..."

Constance's words trailed to nothing as the tears threatened to erupt. Steve gave her a moment before he spoke.

"Why don't we go to my office to talk."

"Yes, sure. Your office has privacy, which means no one will be around to see me if I lose it again. I've already embarrassed myself enough in front of you."

"Au contraire, Madam. You have demonstrated exceptional courage in a tragic situation. And here we are. My most humble office, and I mean that in every sense of the word."

Constance followed Steve and sat in one of the chairs he offered.

"May I get you anything? Coffee, soda, water?"

"Yes, I think I'd like some water, please."

"Be right back."

During his absence, Constance took a moment to survey her surroundings. She had to smile because Steve did not exaggerate his description. The room was only slightly larger than a janitor's closet, and that was a charitable account. There was room for his small desk and two chairs, which were comfortable enough if one didn't have a wide girth.

"Here. It's bottled water. I didn't have anything already cold; I hope you don't mind."

"Thank you. This is fine."

Steve settled into the second chair.

"Let me open this meeting in prayer, may I?"

Constance sighed.

"I suppose."

Dear Heavenly Father, thank You for being a God who cares. Though I'm surrounded by tragedy of catastrophic proportions, I remember your Son, Jesus, and how You, in all Your love, asked Him to perform the ultimate sacrifice for a sinful people, and He said, 'Yes.' The love displayed in that sacrifice puts everything into perspective. Your promise to us is that You are always with us. You go before us, walk beside us, encourage us from behind. You even carry us at times. I ask for wisdom, not to attempt to explain what I don't understand, but rather for guidance to do what is best for these precious people. In Jesus's name, Amen.

Constance reached for the box of Kleenex that Steve discreetly put within her reach. She took a deep breath to gain control of her emotions.

"Thank you for that prayer; it helped."

Steve observed the difference in this remarkable woman's countenance.

"You are in a tough situation right now. In fact, I daresay, this is one of the greatest challenges of your life. What can I do to help?"

"I've got quite a list and jotted them down so I wouldn't forget. First, I want someone to tell me the truth about Monique. I think the doctors are unsure of something. Maybe they don't have all the information; I don't know. When I think about the accident, I feel we've missed something. I've gone through several scenarios in my mind, but nothing seems to fit.

"Another thing, I know if she doesn't wake up soon, I'll have to move her to a long-term care facility. Actually, with what's happened in the last few hours, I probably won't have to worry about that one for a while. However, if that time comes, how do I find a long-term facility? Where do I go for assistance, so I can even put her somewhere? I am not poor by any means, but I don't have an endless cash flow either.

"Let's see, oh, and yes, I've talked to Monique's employer, and

26

her secretary helped me apply for disability on her behalf. Thank goodness Torrie had the foresight to insist that all of us get our legal paperwork in order. Because of that, Monique named me first and Torrie next as her medical power of attorney, so I can act on her behalf.

"I also have to consider Monique's apartment. We haven't paid any rent, so I suspect she will be evicted. Plus, I have no idea what other bills she has, but they will have to be paid somehow."

Steve mentally reviewed the extensive list. Okay, let's take this one step at a time, starting with the last item. That is something I know I can take off your shoulders. Why don't you give me the keys to Monique's apartment? I will speak to the leasing office about her past rent and find out what options are available. Also, I have an accountant friend whom I trust. He will be happy to work with your daughter's financial affairs, and his fees are reasonable. He'd write letters to creditors, arrange payments, and keep track of what monies come and go. I'll be glad to make an appointment for you two to meet in my office."

Steve noticed a funny look on Constance's face and realized precisely what she thought.

"Well, maybe I'll reserve a small conference room." "Yes, a conference room is a much better idea. I like the idea of an accountant, thank you. You know? It's kind of nice to have someone to talk through things with me."

Constance was happy to confide in this man, but her thoughts quickly went to the time.

"Goodness! It's after five! The nurse said the doctor made rounds between five and nine. I must get back to ICU. With my luck, he's already been and gone, and I won't get another chance to talk to him until tomorrow night!"

Steve diffused her urgency to flee.

"Relax, I gave Candy explicit instructions to page me the minute any of Monique's doctors stepped into the ICU. She hasn't paged me, so all is good."

Steve opened the door for Constance.

"After you. Here is my card. You can call me directly or have one of the nurses page me at any time."

Constance gratefully accepted the business card.

"Thank you, Steve."

Chapter Eleven

I am aware again and rested. The moving object is more substantial. Yes, I see it's a person, probably male. He is engulfed in a cloud.

"Hey, Monique."

"Hello. Do I know you?"

"Let me introduce myself. I'm Gabriel."

"Gabriel? Really? An Angel? Why would an angel be visiting me? If I remember correctly, you are the announcer or proclaimer. I certainly hope you are here to proclaim my identity and what is going on here."

"You are correct; my purpose, dear Monique, is to proclaim and announce. I have information for you, though not everything you want to know, of course. You are only in this world for a short while, and I'm here to assist you. In time you will figure most things out by yourself."

"First, I can assure you, you aren't dead. You were in a serious one-car accident, and now you are in a coma at Grace Memorial Hospital. However, your doctors have discovered inconsistencies in the initial determination, and soon you're going to be the focus of an intense investigation, which will change your circumstances. I'm here to guide you through the changes."

"I didn't have to be a genius to figure out the 'I'm not dead' announcement on my own. A coma? I guess the fact that I remember my name is an accomplishment."

"Indeed, it is."

"Now what? Will you be here until this is over?"

"Sorry, no. You will see more of me later. Right now, though, I'm waiting for instructions before I take leave of you."

"Oh. Wait. Before you go, please tell me about the person in the cloud."

"Ah, yes, the reality you're not ready to face. Don't attempt to force details. As you get better and stronger, so will your memory."

"Are you sure? It seems like I've been here forever, and I don't like being in this state."

"I know, Monique. Might I remind you, the Father knows your past, your present, your future, and He has you. Nothing happens until it first passes through Him. Rest in that knowledge.

"Hello, Ms. Yorkshire—and you are?"

"Torrie Yorkshire"

"I'm Dr. Nevarez, Monique's neurologist. How is she?"

"Actually, doctor, we kind of expect you to give us some answers."

Dr. Nevarez studied Torrie for a moment.

"Please, let me rephrase my question. How has my patient been since she coded this afternoon?"

Constance quickly interjected before Torrie could make additional comments.

"Of course, Doctor. She's been quiet this afternoon. Though I might add, there has been more activity than I'm comfortable with around my daughter today. I have several questions for you."

Constance reached into her handbag and pulled out a rumpled piece of paper.

"Excuse me. I can't remember anything unless I write it down. Okay, these are the questions I have.

- Why subject Monique to tests which upset her?
- Since you did the tests, what are the results of those tests?
- I also want to know and understand what your prognosis is.
- Lastly, can you please tell us what you are going to do to help her come back to us?

"I wish more of my patients and family members were more like you. I get emails and voicemails all the time with people telling me they forgot to ask—whatever it is they didn't ask.

"Your questions are well thought out, and I intend to answer everyone. Let's go to the conference room across the hall. I want to use their image viewers to show you the CT films."

"Certainly, doctor."

The doctor began his monologue as they walked.

"Dr. Kabra asked me to accept Monique's case. My specialty is the treatment of patients suffering from long term comas. I won't agree to take on anyone until I've examined the medical reason for the trauma. Then I order my own scans from different angles to get a unique perspective of the condition. In Monique's situation, we repeated the previous scans as well, to compare with the original images. Additionally, I reviewed the notes from the last few hours and noticed several times she displayed evidence of a high level of pain. The initial test results don't justify heightened pain this far into her recovery period."

The doctor paused for a moment to put some film on the screen. When he finished the display, he looked at both women.

"These are the initial scans. The scans show slight swelling around the brain. Swelling, no matter how slight, concerns me. Compare this scan to this one, an image of a normal brain. Notice, there is no shadow on the normal brain scan. Now, look at Monique's brain scan. You see the shadow here?"

The doctor used a pen to guide the Yorkshires to the spot he indicated.

"Notice this fracture located toward the top of her head? Everything you see is consistent with an automobile accident, such as your daughter experienced. The first scans did not include a small space at the base of her skull. I requested additional shots to include all angles of the head and neck area and noticed a bruise and another fracture not consistent with an automobile accident."

This new development surprised Constance. "Doctor, what do you mean? Monique's accident was not an accident?

Torrie's mind was processing as fast as her mom's.

"Mom, I think the doctor means Monique may have injured herself earlier in a fall, and the injury didn't show up until she was driving. But Doctor, wouldn't that still be considered an accident?"

"I agree with both of you. Torrie, your theory is logical, but because of the location, I can't make a case for the fall scenario. The angle of the injury is such that it could not have been caused by a fall. The only conclusion which fits the injury is an intentional blow to the head with a blunt object. I say a blunt object because there isn't evidence of a cut. I'm not a detective and can't determine intent, but it appears suspicious to me. I already sent a report to the police. A detective will contact you soon, no doubt."

"Goodness! What a bomb!"

Constance couldn't think of anything more intelligent to say. Dr. Nevarez gave the shocked women time to absorb his weighty news. Constance was the first to surface from her thoughts.

"This news is a complete surprise, but the look on your face tells me you have more."

"Yes, I do, but before I continue would you like a break? We can even wait until tomorrow morning. The overnight break will give you time to process all that I've told you so far."

"No, I want everything now—unless, Mom, you need the break?"

"I agree. Let's hear all of it now."

"Good, now look at the swelling from the original scans again. Compare them to these images from today's scans. See, it's increased significantly, and this shadow right here? It concerned me, so I requested a contrasting CT scan and confirmed it is a blood clot consistent with the trauma she experienced at the base of her skull. I started aggressive treatment to dissolve the clot. If it dislodges, Monique might have a stroke or heart attack. I was actually afraid the clot caused her emergency this afternoon. The cardiologist thankfully reassured me that didn't happen. However, he plans to order additional tests on her heart in the next day or two to rule out any permanent damage.

"I want to dissolve the clot as soon as possible. We will do another CT scan early morning. Hopefully, it will be dissolved, or at least reduced.

"The fluid around her brain concerns me, so I have prescribed a diuretic. If the medication doesn't work, we may be forced to insert a shunt. If we have to, putting in a shunt is better than waiting for the fluid to absorb.

"Now the good news! Monique is healthy and young. The tests

show that her injuries are severe, but nothing significant enough to keep her in a coma indefinitely. Her brain waves tell me she is more active than she looks. Definitely not in a vegetative state. If we saw pictures of what is in her mind, we'd be astonished."

As the doctor removed the film from the viewer's screen, he asked if they had additional questions.

"No doctor, at least not now."

Torrie hesitated a moment, then made up her mind to continue.

"Dr. Nevarez, may I say something?"

"Sure, what is it, Ms. Yorkshire?"

"First, my name is Torrie, not Ms. Yorkshire. Second, I want to apologize for my childish behavior earlier. I reacted based on a preconceived notion that you were an egotistical and arrogant doctor who would breeze in, make a few comments, and rush away."

Constance was astounded with Torrie's words. She hardly apologized, and on those rare occasions she did it was only, 'I'm sorry,' nothing elaborate.

Dr. Nevarez was as surprised as Constance but had the good grace not to show it.

"Thank you, Torrie. There is no reason for an apology because I didn't notice any hostility. I think it's because I am egotistical and arrogant and can't imagine anyone not liking me."

Torrie was appalled by the doctor's remark and almost lost her temper again. Thankfully, she noticed his grin before she reacted. After a few additional words, the three said goodbye and went their separate ways; the doctor to finish his rounds, Constance to Monique's room, and Torrie home.

Chapter Twelve

I hope Gabriel dropped into my world to help me regain my memory. The figure in the distance hasn't moved. From Gabriel's attitude, and words, this person is responsible for my car accident. But what could I have done to cause someone to do something to me? Someone is here, and I figure its Gabriel, so I turn to him with another question—

"Oh, Hello. You aren't Gabriel."

"Yeah, you're correct. Last time I looked I wasn't an angel."

"Do I know you?"

"Ah me, Monique, I was hoping you would remember me."

"Don't be offended. I have a brain injury and can't remember much. You do look familiar. Keep talking to me; maybe I will hear something that will tell me who you are."

"I would love to talk to you. It has been a long time since we were together. I like this world of yours. It's calm, uncluttered, and simple. I'm afraid I have some bad news though. There is a storm coming, and no matter how much I want to protect you, your mother, and sister, I can't.

"I must say that I'm pleased to see that you and Torrie grew up to be beautiful young ladies."

"Yes! That's it. I remember! I have a sister named Torrie. She is my older sister— let me think. She's the only sister, no brother—and—oh, let me remember. Dad! That's why you look familiar, you are my dad!"

"You do remember. Don't get overexcited or try too hard to remember anything else. If you get another headache, I'll be in trouble. Close your eyes and rest."

"No, I don't want to rest. I just found you – well you found me – and I want to talk to you about my life. At least as soon as I can remember."

"I know, sweetums, but you won't remember anything more if you don't rest. Rest is important, so you will be ready for the future."

"You always called me sweetums when you tucked me into bed. You'd say 'goodnight, sweetums. Remember how special you are to your mom and me, but more importantly, you are a special princess in your Heavenly Father's eyes.' I felt loved when you said those words and was able to stop my mind from thinking and sleep. Daddy will you, please tuck—me—in and g—"

"Goodnight, sweetums."

Constance sat in the dark room and reflected on the doctor's report. Much of what he said changed the perspective of Monique's situation, but Constance wasn't sure what to do with it.

Nurse Dooley interrupted her thoughts.

"Good evening, Ms. Yorkshire, how are you this evening?"

"I'm good. At least as well as I can be."

"I've come to check on Monique one more time before I leave. I put some pillows and blankets in the small waiting room for you."

"Thank you so much. I think I'll use them right now. I'm ready for this long day to be over."

"Rest well."

"I plan to. Good night."

Nurse Dooley almost knocked Dr. Nevarez down when she left Monique's room.

"Oh my! Pardon me, doctor. You're here awfully late."

"Good evening. Yes, I just finished with my last patient and decided to look in on Monique. How is she?"

"Her heart rate was erratic for a moment, and her blood pressure started to rise, but she's calm now, and resting quietly."

"Good. I've ordered a CT scan for early in the morning. I want to make sure her blood clot goes away. See you tomorrow. Goodnight, Nurse Dooley."

The nurse was surprised anytime a doctor remembered her name, but the fact that Dr. Nevarez was new to the hospital, and he still. . . *Good grief Nelda you have a name tag. It doesn't take a genius to read a name tag."*

At about the time Constance retired for the evening, Torrie arrived at her condo. She couldn't wait to leave this hectic day behind. The first thing she did was to open a new bottle of wine and pour herself a glass. She turned on the rarely used Jacuzzi. While she waited for it to heat up, she laid out her silk pajamas. Classical music from her favorite station was the final touch before she could get into the jacuzzi with her glass of wine.

What a day. Torrie's mind drifted through the events. She couldn't believe how she acted today. The tears, the change in her attitude toward Connor, yes, and even her team? She couldn't understand her hostility towards Conner. And what possessed her to include her team in the meeting with the client? Her policy was, and had always been, the fewer people in the room, the higher the chances for success. Torrie liked to be in control of all meetings with clients, and she didn't have control over anyone but herself. All of that plus the curve ball the doctor threw them. No wonder she felt beat up.

The wine and the Jacuzzi helped dissipate all the pent-up stress of the day. Ninety minutes later, Torrie decided she had better exit before she was relaxed past the point of no return. She imagined how the headlines would read:

"High-Powered Executive Found Drowned in Her Jacuzzi!"

What is death like? Do we just die, or is there something more? The doctor said Monique's brain is active. Does that mean she knows what is happening to her? I wonder...

Chapter Thirteen

Steve looked up Monique's address before he left for the day. He decided to go to the leasing office and request entrance to her apartment instead of bothering Constance for the key. The office didn't open until ten o'clock. Nothing urgent waited for him at the hospital, so he decided to meander through the morning for a change. After breakfast, Steve read the paper, put a load of laundry in the wash, and tidied his apartment. No one had ever quantified him as an immaculate housekeeper; neat and tidy was enough. His small apartment was sparsely furnished, with a recliner that often served as his bed and a love seat for those rare occasions someone paid him a visit, and a barstool at the counter where he ate.

A longstanding widower, Steve lived a simple life with little drama. He didn't claim to be a contented widower, but the social scene left him dissatisfied, which left only his ministry to keep him busy. His offer to assist Constance with Monique's business affairs was more likely motivated by his need to stay in motion than his aspiration to perform a selfless act. The only reason he remained single was simple. He didn't want to marry again. Doreen was a once in a lifetime love and a perfect pastor's wife. Nothing stopped her concern for his congregation, even when cancer siphoned away her energy. Steve regretted the fact that they never had children, but in retrospect, the disease took Doreen so young he would have been left to raise young children on his own. It took every ounce of strength to take care of himself. After she died, he resigned from his church and drifted through life, doing nothing living off the savings they had.

The Lord finally kicked him out of his funk when he ran out of money. Steve did not want to pastor another congregation without Doreen by his side, which led him to consider alternative forms of ministry. He utilized a website that listed non-traditional opportunities for pastors. A small listing, so tiny he almost overlooked it, caught his attention. *"Grace Memorial Hospital seeks to fill the position of Chaplain."* Initially, he read the job description and rejected the idea. He had no desire to spend his days in a hospital surrounded by sickness and death where he would be reminded of his wife's illness daily.

Days later, Steve still thought about the chaplain position. The Lord reminded him of how the hospital staff had ministered to him. Right before Doreen passed, Steve kept up an all-night prayer vigil in the chapel of the hospital. This one chaplain, whose name he never knew, came and sat down beside him for the duration. He never spoke a word, but his mere presence was the source of unsurpassed comfort. Who better to minister to others who suffer through severe and terminal illnesses than someone who's experienced those same tragedies? Weeks later, he noticed the position was still posted and made the initial contact. The rest is, as they say, history. He called, had a phone interview, and made an appointment with HR the next week. The interviewer was gracious, liked what Steve had to say, and hired him on the spot. Later, Steve found out they had already filled the position and were about to remove the listing. The person they hired changed his plans and decided to take a different job. Ten years later, he was still here and never once regretted it.

The chaplain turned his reflection to the Yorkshire family. He wasn't sure why this little family intrigued him. Maybe because they were a small family without a father. Though Constance projected endurance and strength, underneath her appearance, Steve saw through the façade. He recognized isolation and sadness when he saw it. Then there's Torrie and her hostility. A beautiful, accomplished young lady, brilliant and well respected as a businesswoman. Without examining too deep into her psyche, Steve surmised her antagonism stemmed from a desire to protect herself from hurt. Strip away the disguise, and there was nothing left but a sad, lonely, lost little girl.

The clock chimed ten times. *Thank goodness. I can stop analyzing life and get busy.* Steve got into his not so gently used Volkswagen and drove the fifteen minutes to Monique's apartment complex. There was a flurry of activity in the leasing office. No one acknowledged his presence for a full ten minutes. He was about to do something to draw attention to himself when a young lady invited him to an empty chair.

"How may we be of assistance?"

"Good morning. My name is Steve. I'm the chaplain at Mercy Memorial Hospital. We have a patient there, and I think you know her. She's Monique Yorkshire, and..."

Steve stopped mid-sentence because the agent turned chalk white and gasped.

"Just a moment, sir, my manager should talk to you."

Without another word, she was gone.

Steve had little time to reflect on this strange turn of events before he was approached by another person.

"Sir, please come with me to my office."

He felt like a little kid being summoned to the principal's office.

"Be seated. My name is Angela, and I am the leasing manager. May I ask why your interest in Monique?"

"As I tried to explain to the young lady, I am the chaplain at Mercy Memorial Hospital. Monique is a patient in ICU and has been for several weeks. I've offered to assist the family, and a major concern of her mother is Monique's failure to pay rent—for obvious reasons—and her probable pending eviction. My mission here is to let you know Monique's status and discuss what we can do to make her contract right and move her stuff out."

Angela nodded and waited for more, but Steve decided to delay any additional information until he discovered the reason for the secrecy.

"So, that's it? You didn't come for any other reason?"

"No, of course not. What other reason would there be?"

Angela paused and looked at the reverend. She appeared to weigh her response, and Steve became alarmed.

"Has something happened to Monique? The hospital hasn't called me."

Steve pulled out his pager as he continued.

"I left specific instructions to page me if...and I wasn't paged."

He looked at Angela expectantly.

"I suppose I can tell you what's going on. This morning, a police detective contacted me and requested a meeting. When I arrived, he asked me where Monique's apartment was located, and of course, I had to tell him. The police officer told me her apartment is a crime scene and put up those yellow barricades. In all my years of apartment leasing, I've never seen anything remotely serious enough for the police to be here all of the time. I asked the officer what happened, and he more or less told to mind my own business without saying those exact words."

Angela's information distressed Steve.

"I know less than or at least no more than you do. Is the detective still here?"

"I have no idea. Right now, we're busy calming our other residents. When police and police barricades come around and up, residents tend to panic."

"I guess my mission is a moot point. Are you going to evict Monique?"

"This week is the week to distribute thirty-day eviction notices. I stalled Monique's notice because, honestly, in the five years she's been here she has never been late on her rent. I hate to hear that she was involved in an accident, but Reverend, why did she wait until now to contact us, and why you?"

"I'm here to help the family, and the accident that Monique had was serious enough to put her in a coma. The tragedy happened so fast, and her injuries were so severe that the family didn't have time to think of anything except her care. I had a conversation yesterday with Monique's mom and offered to help her in anything I could. We decided that taking care of her rent and belongings was a priority, so I said I could do that. Of course, with everything that is going on, I don't think I can get approval to remove anything from her apartment. I think I'll go see if the officer is still at her place to find out if there is anything I can do. Can you give me her apartment number without a written authorization from someone?"

"Well, considering the circumstances and there are police on the property, I suppose I can tell you. It's apartment 1511.

"Thank you. Here is my business card. Please call me, instead of the family if you have more questions."

Steve sauntered back to his car. He wondered what had happened between the time he left Constance and now. Constance mentioned aspects of the accident, which didn't make sense. It appears her intuition was correct.

Monique's apartment wasn't far from the leasing office. Sure enough, yellow tape warned of the crime scene. A police officer stood guard outside for added security. Steve walked under the first tape. Not unexpectedly, the officer stopped Steve.

"Sir, this is a crime scene; no unauthorized entry is allowed."

"Of course, I understand. Is the detective in charge available?"

"Hey! McPherson! Someone wants to talk to you!"

Steve stepped back from the door and waited. Soon a tall, burly man, smartly dressed in Khaki pants and a button-down striped shirt, stepped through the door. The detective looked at Steve for a moment.

"Good morning. My name is Detective Mike McPherson. How may assist you?"

Steve was taken aback by the detective's politeness and formality. He expected an attitude of a TV detective: curt, forbidding, and suspicious. McPherson was more non-committal than anything; however, Steve suspected his demeanor could change in an instant.

"I'm Steve Robinson. I represent Monique's family; may I ask a few questions?"

The detective's eyes became hard, and his demeanor changed to suspicious,

"You mean you're their attorney?"

"Oh, no! I'm Reverend Steve Robinson. Monique, the resident of this apartment, was involved in an accident about two months ago. I came, on behalf of her mother, to clear out her apartment. Considering everything, is that even an option?"

The detective's attitude reverted to his original polite and professional demeanor.

"No, it isn't. We received information from the doctor earlier this morning, which reclassified the accident as suspicious. Monique's apartment, her car, and the accident site are now crime scenes and off-limits until we've gathered all of the evidence. We'll interview family and friends after I complete the analysis. That's all I am prepared to discuss at this time."

Chapter Fourteen

McPherson watched the reverend leave, then went back to the apartment and continued his search for answers. His partner, Eve, was in the bedroom. He rummaged through the desk in the study. The room was designed to be the eating area, but Monique had turned it into a makeshift study.

"Mike! Hey, Mike!"

"What's up?"

"The jackpot! I found journals, and she recorded nearly every day. The entries are random, but I've seen enough to warrant additional inspection."

Mike waived an officer over to the stack of journals.

"You! Over there! Bag and tag these journals and take them back to the station."

He turned back to Eve.

"Go talk to the leasing office staff. I'm going to talk to a few neighbors, not that it will do any good. Most people in apartment complexes tend to keep to themselves. Let's meet at the station after lunch. We should have news from forensics and the accident site by then."

Eve and Mike had been partners for several years and were an efficient team. They were the Mutt and Jeff of the department. Eve was petite, light complexion, with long, naturally blond hair tightly coiled at the back of her head to Mike's tall, muscular, cocoa brown with a shiny bald perfectly- formed head. One only needed to look at Mike to notice his police aura and understand his ability to avert violence. Eve's looks, on the other hand, deceived everyone, Mike included. She liked to dress stylishly. Today her outfit was a skirt with sensible but classy flats, and a jacket over her red cotton turtleneck. Only her badge indicated she was a police officer. Mike's surprise came the first time they competed. To his chagrin, the petite officer put him down with her Martial Arts Black Belt expertise.

Angela greeted Eve at the front door and quickly led her to the private office.

"What can we do for you, detective?"

"I want to ask the staff some questions; is there a place I can talk with them individually and privately?"

"Sure. You can use this office. I'll sit at one of the empty desks. Who would you like to speak with first?"

"What about you? Since you're here and all..."

"Oh, uh, sure."

Angela hoped to escape the questions, which, of course, was unrealistic.

"How long has Monique been a tenant here?"

"Five years."

"Was she a good tenant?"

"Yes."

Eve sat back in her chair and observed Angela for a minute.

"Look, Angela, I understand you don't want to be involved. No one wants to be involved in a police investigation. Hell, I don't want to be involved, and I'm a police detective! However, there is a young lady near death who appears to be a victim of a violent crime. Don't you want your other residents to know you co-operated fully with the police to assure this property is a safe place to live?"

Angela breathed out and visibly relaxed.

"Okay, detective, you're right. The best thing for me to do is to talk to the police, although I think you are happy to be involved in this investigation. What do you want to know?"

Eve smiled at Angela's astute observation. In fact, nothing energized Eve like an excellent elusive mystery. She loved to investigate and locate the puzzle pieces of a crime to reveal the truth.

"Why don't you tell me what you can about Monique."

"Sure. About five years ago, Monique came to lease an apartment, her first. She had just graduated from college at the time. We had a bungalow available, and I remember how excited she was. It's rare to find an apartment where there is no one above or below you. The bungalow is as close to a house as you can get. Monique was—is a dream tenant. She doesn't' complain about every little thing and is always on time with her rent. Her neighbors don't have any complaints with her either. I know she is a private person because she keeps her personal life to herself. That is, if she even has one. Her job has her traveling extensively, and she works long hours. I've never met her friends, male or female.

That's about the only thing I can tell you about her."

"Now, that wasn't too painful, was it? Here is my card; if you think of anything relevant to the case, no matter how small, please contact me, day or night. Now, if you will show in the next agent ..."

Eve received the same story with little variation from everyone in the office.

Meanwhile, Mike struck out. He gave up and went back to the apartment for another look. Eve's excitement about the journals interrupted his investigation. Unlike Eve who expected the journals to reveal valuable details, Mike held no such predictions. He discovered long ago that diaries, and especially journals revealed feelings and abstracts rather than facts. Emotions and ideas didn't solve crimes.

Mike stepped into Monique's apartment and stood still so he could view the rooms from the angle of the entrance. The coat closet right in front of the door almost blocked the access. To move big furniture with the closet door that close could challenge even the best movers. He turned to his right and spotted the bedroom. To his left was another wall, and immediately to the right of the wall was the living room with a fireplace. On the other side was the converted dining room. Next, Mike walked through the kitchen with a nook for a small table. The tiny laundry area was off the kitchen next to the back door.

According to the doctor, Monique's injury resulted from a blunt force trauma to the back of her head. The apartment was undisturbed except for the disarray the forensic and the CSI teams caused. Mike had years of experience as a detective. Tidy scenes rarely deceived him. He trained himself to look beyond the obvious. His co-workers observed, more than once, occasions he located clues others hardly ever found, causing them to swear he had psychic abilities. Contrary to their beliefs, Mike was not supernatural. He simply used all his senses, not just the eyes and ears.

A shiny object shoved under the couch caught his attention. He lowered his bulky body onto the floor and noticed the indentations on the carpet where the sofa used to be, indicating the couch was disturbed recently. He donned his latex gloves and used his pencil flashlight to locate the object of his interest and gingerly pulled it forward.

Mike prided himself on his agility despite his large size, but to rise from a prone position on the floor challenged his skills. He took a moment to inspect the object in his hand. It looked like a giant silver egg, heavy enough to be made of solid lead. This certainly fits the blunt object theory, but what purpose did this odd egg-like object serve? His eyes surveyed the room to locate the site which would have stored this strange trinket. Ah, the flat circular object on the fireplace mantle must go with the egg.

Mike laboriously extracted his body from the floor, and one short step took him to the fireplace. He studied the flat object and noticed an inscription that said, "Given with gratitude to Monique for helping with the annual Easter egg hunt for underprivileged children." The two pieces definitely went together. Mike picked up both pieces and deposited them into his evidence bag. He roamed around the little apartment. If Monique was attacked here, whoever hit her with the egg was not a small person and had the strength to transport an unconscious person into the car. The accident occurred at about ten at night, so the perpetrator had the cover of darkness to aid him in his mission. Mike walked outside and looked around the parking lot. Monique had the end apartment with no other buildings beside hers, which was probably the reason no one heard anything.

There was a parking spot right beside her front door, so this person wouldn't have had to take her too far before he reached the car. Mike walked to the curb, and his eyes picked up something shining in the corner. He pulled out a smaller evidence bag, reached down with his still-gloved hand and lifted the object. Interesting, a cufflink with an initial "C." Mike dropped the cuff link into the bag, went back to the apartment, and closed and locked the door. He wanted to get back to the precinct and go over all the information they had so far. The next step was to put together a list of witnesses and set up interviews. Mike wondered if Eve had been able to gather anything from those journals.

Chapter Fifteen

"Dad— Dad? Dad! Where are you?"

I wake in a panic. My last memory is a talk with Dad, then nothing, but how long ago?

"DAD!"

"Shhhh—hush Monique; I'm here. Look— see? I didn't leave."

"Yes, you did too leave me, and I'm afraid you will leave again."

I look around. My world is not empty anymore. I want to go back to when I didn't know anything, even before I knew my name.

"The person in the fog is closer. I'm not good with that."

"I know, pumpkin. Listen, I'm going to have to leave soon. Your memory is clearer, and the more you remember, the more you have to fear. You are in the arms of your true Father. He loves and cherishes you. He fills you with the courage to face what comes. The person in the fog is someone you know, and you'll remember at the time you gain full strength."

"Dad, please don't go. I don't want to be alone again. I remember now. One day you left, and I looked out the window every day for over a year expecting you to walk in the door. You never came back!"

"Sweetheart, didn't you hear me? You are never alone. God the Father has you."

I look at the man in the cloud and think of something I want to say to dad, but he's gone. Dad told me I'm not alone, and God has me covered. Then why do I feel so alone? Okay, think Monique think. I want memories.

I need memories. I have an older sister, Torrie. My mom's name is — uh — Constance, right. I know my dad died. A fleeting thought. I remember something, then it's gone. It was nothing. At least nothing I know I remember. No one else comes to mind. So far, nothing scary.

God is my Father. What do I remember about God?

"Well, hello, Gabriel. You snuck back!"

"I don't like the reference that I snuck back, but yes, I am back."

"What news do you have for me?"

"Monique, you are at a crossroad, and you have a decision to make."

"That sounds pretty ominous."

"Not ominous, but it is serious."

I don't know what to say to Gabriel. I'm tired. I don't want to think anymore.

"Gabriel. I'm just — going — to — close my eyes."

"Everything looks good, Ms. Yorkshire. I have orders for another scan to check on that blood clot. Just let the nurse know if your daughter begins to show the slightest difficulty. Do you have any questions?"

"No—wait, yes, actually I do. What did the police say?"

"Ah, yes, the detective began an investigation. I'm sure he will be in touch with you soon."

"Okay, thank you for your time, doctor."

Constance went back into Monique's room. The clock on the wall showed nine. The morning dragged, and Constance was concerned about Torrie because she didn't call before she went to work.

"Oh, Monique, please tell me what's going on inside that head of yours. Dr. Nevarez said your mind is active. I'm not surprised.

You were never able to unwind mentally or physically. Remember the time you dressed in your father's raincoat and hat with the blow dryer? I asked who you were supposed to be, and you told me you were James Bond's understudy. It took all of my willpower to keep from breaking out in laughter right then.

"You loved to play James Bond. I figured you would choose one of those dangerous careers. When you told me, you chose business as your major, I was surprised but relieved.

"Dr. Nevarez found evidence your injuries are more sinister than a car accident. What in the world did you get yourself mixed up in? I think your sister was impressed with the doctor."

I'm aware Gabriel is still with me. How Long? I wish I had a watch. In and out of awareness has disadvantages.

"Gabriel, you said something about a crossroad. I suppose I have to decide to either let go of life or get back Into It."

"Eventually, Monique. However, there are smaller steps to take before you can even entertain a decision about life in general. The Image In the distance is closer. Soon you will Identify him. With recognition comes a difficult decision or crossroad, what will you do?

"What are the choices? If you know about the crossroad, then you must know what choices I have."

"You're correct. You can choose to either let the knowledge destroy you or make you stronger."

"Gabriel, come on now! What kind of answer Is that? I make that decision almost daily. What's so special about this time?"

"You have never been in a coma before."

Gabriel says those words so kindly and gently that I feel foolish for being angry.

I just want this to go away. I don't like this un-world. The person in the distance is closer. I'm tired. I close my eyes to rest.

Chapter Sixteen

Torrie woke up confused. Her watch showed ten, but morning or night? She recognized she was home but didn't understand her sluggish brain. Last night—she had gotten into her Jacuzzi and the wine—that was it. Instead of the one or two glasses she typically allowed herself, she had finished a newly opened bottle. Torrie heard her phone and reached to retrieve it from the charger to no avail. Now, where did she leave it? Her head hurt too bad to remember much about last night, not even getting into bed. Ugh, why would she do this to herself!

The phone continued to ring—no, it stopped and went to voice mail. Someone had decided to call back again. Torrie struggled to get out of bed and stumbled into the living room from where she thought she had heard the phone. There it was, under the couch. She bent to pick it up…

"Hello?"

"Torrie! What in the world is wrong? We have all been worried; you are never late, and my goodness it is after ten!"

Connor had answered her question about night or day.

"Connor—Connor—CONNOR!! Shut UP!"

Torrie was finally able to break through Connor's hysteria.

"I'm sorry. Okay, I stopped but please tell me what's wrong."

Torrie plopped down in her recliner and closed her eyes to the brightness of the sun that streamed through her picture window before she responded.

"Connor, I'm fine. I pampered myself too much last night and went to bed way too late. I'm sorry I've concerned you. Since we meet with Global Resources tomorrow, I want to take the day off—at least most of it. I may try to go in later this afternoon."

Connor was dumbfounded. He didn't understand Torrie's erratic behavior or how to react. Maybe she had finally cracked under the added pressure of her sister.

How can Monique be alive? The crash was violent enough to finish her off immediately, or at least shortly afterward.

"Fine. I'll tell those who are on a need-to-know basis, that you won't be in today."

"Thank you."

"Uh, Torrie; I know how upset you've been about Monique. I wonder—uh—I mean, I want to —well, uh—okay, do you want me to go with you to the hospital?"

Torrie was flabbergasted.

"I don't understand. You don't even care about my family! Why the sudden interest in Monique? What are you up to?"

"Gosh, Torrie, all I want to do is help you. So, I haven't shown much interest in your life, but your sister is in a bad way."

"I'm sorry, of course, but no, you at the hospital is not an option. Thank you anyway. My head hurts too bad to think, so I'll talk to you later."

Connor disconnected. When would this nightmare go away! After the accident didn't finish the job, his employers recommended someone to help him, but the name escaped him. This person was supposed to dress in scrubs and sneak into Monique's room to give her a high dose of potassium. If he did what he was supposed to, Monique would appear to die of a heart attack. Obviously, he either chickened out, or it didn't work.

It was time to contact his employers. Connor had avoided their calls all along, but now decided they could help him. Connor locked the door to his office to eliminate interruption, pulled out his unregistered burn phone, and made the call.

"Why, hello, Connor. We wondered when you would call us. It seems you are in a, how do you say, pickle?"

Connor wasn't happy to hear that his handlers had anticipated his call, but then again, why was he surprised? They had eyes and ears everywhere.

"Yes, I thought I had taken care of the package, but I discovered it was still in my possession. If you have any suggestions, please..."

"I'm sure you will come up with something. Oh, a bit of information. Your package is now under investigation. Please don't call again as this office will closed for two weeks. We are on our way to an extended conference."

Connor felt like a doomed man as he grasped the enormity of his situation. He was cut off, no support, and on his own to figure things out.

"I understand, really, but, uh, is there an emergency contact while you're away?"

"Oh, I don't think that is necessary. We plan to monitor the situation and contact you if an occasion calls for it."

"But..."

"I must disconnect now, Connor, late for a meeting. Good day."

Damn, how had he gotten into this situation? More importantly, how was he supposed to get out? He was sure any in-depth investigation of Monique's accident pointed straight to him. From there, it got worse. The accident led to Global Resources, and that investigation led directly to their ties with black-market arms sales and his name connected to all of it! A nightmare!

"Connor! Connor, are you in there?"

Clearly, it wasn't a nightmare. Reed's persistence slowly penetrated Connor's paralysis.

"Yes, yes, of course, Reed! One moment."

Connor deposited his burn phone into his safe, re-adjusted his suit, and smoothed his hair. He took a deep breath, put on his work look, and opened the door.

"Hello, I apologize for my delayed response. I was deep in concentration on some paperwork and was lost in thought. What can I do for you?"

Reed noted there were no papers on Connor's desk or on the small conference table in the office.

"Where's Torrie? We want to go over our presentation one more time since we made the changes discussed last night. No one wants unforeseen glitches during tomorrow's meeting with the client."

"Yes, well, Torrie won't be in the office this morning and maybe not at all, but you have a point. A final meeting is a good idea. Have the team hang loose and be prepared to stay a little after hours. Torrie wants everyone to be fully rested and alert tomorrow, so the meeting will end no later than seven or seven-thirty. I'll get back with you this afternoon."

Connor made his way back to his desk and took some papers out of his desk drawer. He had seen Reed's suspicious look when he came into the office and didn't see documents.

"Sure. I'll relay the message to the rest of the team." Reed didn't turn around and leave as Connor expected. If he ignored Reed, perhaps the young man would go. When that didn't happen, Connor was forced to further acknowledge him.

"Reed, do you have another question? Ok. I get it. Obviously, you are observant and intuitive, excellent qualities for a successful career. I'm going to tell you something, but it goes no further, understand?"

Reed nodded.

"These last few weeks have been stressful for Torrie and in turn for me. Torrie's sister was involved in a near-fatal car accident and was—and still is in a coma. Torrie has been stretched thin, and her loyalties divided. She's extremely private, so I don't have details or updates. So now you know. Go back to work, and I'll let you guys know when to expect the meeting."

Reed stood there for a moment or two as if he had something else to say but thought better of it and left.

Connor was disconcerted with the conversation. Something seemed off, and if he didn't know better, he was sure Reed was about to say something about— but no, he couldn't have any knowledge of anything. Connor had to stop his ruminating and come up with a plan of some kind. He looked at his watch, noon – lunch. Another hour before Torrie's call. Meanwhile, he had to think of a way to correct his mistakes.

Chapter Seventeen

I wake up in my created in-between world and remember my conversations with Gabriel and my dad. Did I really talk to them? The conversations seemed so real. The good news is that since I remembered my name and my family, my brain fog is lifted. My history plays through my mind like a movie, or a novel. I remember everything except why I am in the hospital in a coma. My name is Monique, and I work for the CIA.

I attended a local college as a business major, which bored me to death. My reason for choosing a boring job was to protect my mom. One semester on a whim, I enrolled in Criminal Investigation. The course got my adventurous juices flowing. My quite elderly instructor took an interest in my abilities of observation and reasoning. During one of our many discussions, he revealed he worked with the CIA. I couldn't hide my excitement and bombarded him with questions, including how the CIA recruited. I was sure they didn't put an advertisement in the paper or put a job application through Career.com. He sidestepped the question and instead, listed characteristics necessary for a good agent. He confirmed in a subtle way that I fit the criteria, but that was as far as he went.

Half-way through the semester, my instructor took me to meet the CIA director. Together they decided to test my aptitude and psychological stability. I passed with flying colors, and they offered me a position within the CIA. I accepted their offer, but of course, I couldn't divulge any of this to my family or friends. I continued with my career path, going for a degree in business administration while I trained for the covert business. There was field training in research and investigative techniques, but my favorite was the weapons, and I excelled in hand to hand. The business administration degree still bored me, but it was manageable because of my "real job."

A month after I graduated, the CIA set up a small but legitimate company with four employees. It is a perfect front for our real business. My boss and I are the only two connections to the CIA, a necessary precaution in order to keep our covert activities, well, "covert." We have a few legitimate clients, but most of the time, I research data my boss brings in from companies suspected of illicit activity including personnel and their clients.

My first case was a simple test case investigating a money-laundering scheme. It was a smalltime operation, and the parties involved planned to break into the big game. I kind of felt sorry for them when they were busted. I figured out their plan and how it worked, devised a strategy to uncover the laundering and had them indicted within the week. I passed, and my career took off.

Counting the training that took place during college, I've been with the CIA for seven years and loved every minute. I travel overseas to potentially dangerous confrontations but usually with backup in case a situation gets out of control. One time while on a mission in Switzerland, I was shot. Fortunately, I had followed protocol and had my safety vest on.

My cover story for traveling to the country was a ski trip, which allowed me to explain my injury as a ski accident. Lying to my family, especially Mom, doesn't agree with my upbringing, but I understand the reason, and if I deviate from our directives my career would be over. I love what I do, so I follow the rules.

Recently, my director asked me if I was ready to participate in more complicated and dangerous cases. Of course, my answer was a definite yes. Research interests me, but I'm bored unless there is action involved. This recent so-called automobile accident I had, must have something to do with one of those riskier situations, but I can't remember what it is.

I feel a presence next to me.

"Hello, Gabriel. I almost decided you and my dad are figments of my imagination, but here you are again."

"Yes, here I am. I'm pleased to find you stable. You have more clarity, and the reason you are in danger isn't a mystery. It won't be long now until you recall everything. My responsibility is to help you as you escape your way out of a dangerous predicament."

"Oh, and out of curiosity, how am I doing?"

"Overall, I'm pleased. You are more than capable, and your choice of career suits you. I also know you have great faith, and you rely on the Father for encouragement and insight. He guides you more than you realize, and in this case, He frustrates the perpetrators and saves your life. Your current case has the potential to save thousands of lives if completed successfully."

"That's nice to know, although I don't have the stamina to save anyone right now. And to be perfectly honest, Gabriel, I don't care. My mind is in overtime, and I want to sleep."

"Yes, go ahead and sleep, but don't let go of your life while you sleep."

"Is that supposed to be—uh—what was—uh—don't remember..."

"Yes, dear Monique, that is a warning. I hope you remember my words."

Chapter Eighteen

Torrie was on her second pot of coffee when the phone rang again. She looked at her watch; one o'clock. Her caller ID told her it was Connor. Initially, she chose to ignore him but then considered his hysterics of the last call and changed her mind.

"Hello, Connor. Yes, I'm still alive, and no, I won't go into the office right now. What other questions do you have?"

"Besides my question of what the hell has gotten into you, only one – maybe two. Do you even care about the presentation tomorrow? And if you do, would you like to meet with the team again? They want to go over the changes they made and firm up the presentation before tomorrow."

Ugh—just what Torrie didn't want, to be reminded of her duties or what was at stake. She had no desire to be responsible for the client, her mom, Monique, or anyone else.

"I will not dignify your first question with an answer, but to your second question, one more meeting to finalize everything and make sure all of the "i's" are dotted and the "t's" are crossed is in order. Is the team ready to stay later this evening? I'll be in the office at five-thirty, and we'll be finished by seven-thirty."

"I already prepared everyone for the possibility of a late meeting. I also assured the gang it wouldn't be too late because you wanted everyone to be fresh and alert in the morning."

"Thank you. Then I'll see you at five-thirty."

Torrie looked at her watch again. One-thirty. She had four hours before her meeting. One look in the mirror and she decided a trip to the spa for damage control was in her future. She quickly made an appointment and requested a makeover with her hair and face and threw in a massage for good measure. They did great work for people on tight time schedules. She picked out her outfit and gathered what she needed so she could go straight to the office from the spa.

A horrible thought interrupted her preparations. *Monique. How selfish can one person be?* She dialed the number of the hospital with a mental note to put it into her speed dial.

"ICU. How may I help you?"

"This is Torrie, Monique's sister. I didn't want to call Mom in case she was in the middle of something or even resting. How is Monique today, and have there been any developments in her condition or treatments?"

"In fact, your mother went down to the cafeteria with the reverend a few minutes ago for a late lunch. Monique is comfortable. She went for a CT scan, which confirmed the blood clot has dissolved, plus there is a reduction in the fluid around her brain. The doctor is hopeful that a shunt won't be necessary after all. He'll recheck it tomorrow."

"That's great news. Thank you so much. Please tell my mom I contacted you, and I'm fine, just in a late meeting. I have a big client conference in the morning, so I won't be going to the hospital until after that—unless, of course, I'm needed."

"I'll leave a note for your mom. Good luck with your client."

"Thank you."

The positive, friendly attitude of the hospital staff never ceased to amaze Torrie. She had tried to get her mother to transfer Monique to a more prominent hospital in the next town, but her mom would have none of that. Now she realized it was a better plan to keep her in Mercy Memorial Hospital.

Chapter Nineteen

After Torrie hung up from Connor, he spent the next two hours going through the notes from conversations with his handlers. Connor was not a brainiac, so contrary to explicit instructions, he circumvented his handicap by using a type of shorthand to remind himself of relevant information. No one could decipher his shorthand; at least he thought so before Monique came into the picture. She found out he was involved, somehow, and got into the safe in his office and took pictures of his notes with her little camera or whatever they use nowadays. Maybe not a camera at all, but her phone. He had to find the name of anyone who might be able to assist him. He found initials GBW with a scribbled shorthand message as a clue of who this person was and his function. To his exasperation, Connor didn't remember what the scribble meant. He leaned back in his chair, closed his eyes, and let his mind drift.

This mental exercise assisted his recall, especially when he overthought...

Knock—Knock—Knock ...

Dazed, Connor sat straight up. He was disoriented for a moment and couldn't remember where he was until he saw the time. Great! He had fallen asleep for over an hour, and he only had twenty-five minutes until the meeting. Good news, though, he remembered the name, Geoffrey Burnett Wilson, the person trained to take care of business. There was that knock again ...

"Come in. The door is open."

Connor quickly pulled out some papers, made sure they were faced the right way, and picked up a sheet to mimic deep concentration.

"Hi, the team is ready to congregate in the conference room. I took the liberty and ordered coffee and snacks. Is Torrie on her way?"

Connor wondered if Reed had plans to take his place as Torrie's assistant. He already had the confidence of the team, and the initiatives he took were beyond his position. This time Connor appreciated the foresight.

"Yes, Torrie will be here soon, so let the team congregate. I will wait for her to confirm whether she'll conduct the meeting or if she wants me to."

"Ok, see you in about fifteen minutes, then." Reed closed the door, and Connor locked it behind him. He was anxious to make the call to Geoffrey Burnett Wilson and get things in motion. Torrie was sure to be a few minutes late. He went to his safe, pulled out his list of phone numbers, took his burn phone and dialed Geoffrey using the unlisted number for emergencies.

"This better be important because no one is supposed to know this number, much less call it."

Not a good start to this conversation. Connor had second thoughts but quickly suppressed them. After all, it was necessary.

"This is—uh—the delivery man. I wonder if you could assist with —uh—the disposal of a contaminated package."

"Ah—of course. We took bets on who you would contact for assistance. I guess I am the lucky winner. Again. I am happy to do it, and I will have a better plan this time. Of course, the price has to be right."

"No surprise there. How much?"

"I want half of your portion…"

"Half! Are you out of your mind? I'll give you one fourth."

"I'm the one who can get close and the one who will risk exposure. All you have to do is sit back and wait. I won't settle for anything less than half."

"If you would have done it right the first time, we wouldn't be having this conversation!"

Connor didn't have time to quibble. Gregory was stubborn enough about money and wouldn't budge. Besides, he had to get out of this jam, and half his earnings were worth it. There would still be enough to retire in an out of the way place where no one could find him. If he invested wisely and discreetly, he would be good for the rest of his life.

"Ok, you get half. Just do it. Let me know when it's finished, and I don't want to know how you do it!"

Connor detected he had raised his voice and hoped no one could hear outside his office door. Someone knocked on his door, and then Torrie called his name. Great. He lowered his voice.

"Do you understand?"

"Of course."

Geoffrey disconnected, and Connor quickly put the notes and the phone back into his safe and locked it. He hurried to the door and opened to a furious Torrie.

"What are you so angry about?"

"You ignored my first knock, and then I hear your loud conversation with someone on the phone about taking care of it. Who was it, and does this have anything to do with Global Resources?"

"I can't believe you eavesdropped on my private conversation. Why would you do that?"

Connor was shaken by the fact that she heard part of his conversation. He was glad she thought it had to do with work and nothing more. If he could put her on the defensive, maybe she'd let it go.

"I did not eavesdrop. I heard you yell, and if this is anything to do with the client, I don't consider it a private conversation."

"You're right, of course. If it were about the client, but it wasn't. It was my wife. We—uh—her car needs to be inspected. She asked when I planned to take care of it. I overreacted and told her to take care of it herself. I'll apologize later, but right now, the team is ready."

Torrie wasn't satisfied with Connor's answer. She couldn't put her finger on it, but he appeared almost guilty of something. They did, however, have this meeting to handle. When it was over, they would have a discussion to resolve whatever needed to be fixed.

"Okay Connor, we will table this discussion for now, but we are not finished by any stretch of the imagination."

Torrie turned away from Connor and headed toward the conference room.

Connor reluctantly followed Torrie. The best he could hope for Is that Torrie would forget about this conversation by the time the meeting ended. He knew he could hope all day, but in the end, Torrie would get her way and finish what she started.

Chapter Twenty

Eve was busy at work when Mike sat down at his desk directly in front of her. He dropped his notebook and cleared his throat to get her attention.

"Okay, Mike, enough of the dramatics already. If you want my attention, just ask. Let me guess, something doesn't make sense and you would like to bounce it off me."

"You're right. I can never pull anything over on you. Something isn't right about Monique. She works at a business that doesn't seem to have enough clients to keep the doors open. I can't get any background information. When I attempted a computer search, I got 'restricted.' Why would a search for background information be blocked? Unless, of course it's for government or military purposes. Her family and even the secretary and receptionist claim she's a glorified bookkeeper with an impressive title. It makes no sense at all."

"Why look into Monique's background? She's the victim. Though it is ironic, you should mention her background. I've completed most of her journals. They go back to her college days, and most of the entries speak about how bored she was with her degree choice. There was an entry that mentioned she enrolled in a class on Criminal Investigation. That ended her college journaling. Except I noticed she tore out some pages."

"Really? Any mention of her instructor? Maybe we can contact him and get some information. Hmmm, you said that was the last entry about her college days. Did she journal after she graduated?"

"There are some entries in a new journal. Nothing significant. Monique wrote some poetry, which is actually quite good. A few entries mentioned her uneasiness with Torrie and someone Torrie is seeing. Then suddenly nothing. There's no mention of the instructor's name, but that's easy enough to look up. I'll call the college and ask for her transcript."

"Better get a warrant. Those educator types are pretty guarded when it comes to the police looking for information on former students."

"Not a problem. After all, we are on an almost-homicide case."

Mike remained seated after Eve left to get her warrant. He reflected on the information from the scene of the accident. There were no skid marks, so Monique didn't try to stop or avert her plunge into Gipper's Gully. The night of the crash was cloudy but no rain, so the streets weren't wet. Maybe she fell asleep at the wheel like the report indicated. Mike reviewed the pictures that were taken the night of the accident. The officers took photographs of Monique before she was removed from the car. She was slumped over to the side, almost like she couldn't sit up straight. His eyes rested on her seatbelt. Why did she strap her belt over her right arm instead of under it? A noteworthy observation. Why did the officers miss that detail? He was almost sure the accident was staged after he found the evidence at her apartment, but these crime scene photos convinced him a hundred percent. He pulled out the evidence bag with the cufflink. Mike had yet to discover anyone in her life with a first or last name with a "C." Forensics hadn't sent their report, so he didn't know if they had viable fingerprints or not.

Mike took a legal pad so he could make a list to organize everything swirling around in his head.

1. injuries not consistent with a car crash
2. apartment, neat, but evidence of a struggle
3. object matched the site of the injury
4. is cufflink significant
5. no one knew much about Monique
6. something not right about her work
7. had few friends or no friends.
8. background too clean
9. restricted, security clearance required

Mike didn't like the summary he created. There wasn't much of anything, and he felt like he was at a dead end. He leaned back in his chair with his hands behind his head thinking about the next step. Maybe Eve could get Information from the school about the Instructor. The criminal justice class was an unlikely choice for a business major and if she really did take that class, there must have been a good reason.

Not wanting to remain idle, Mike listed the witnesses he should talk to. There weren't many witnesses to Interview, but there was one or two. No one had gone to the hospital to talk with the mother or sister yet. Maybe one or the other could clear up some of the mystery around Monique. Now was as good a time as any, and maybe he could speak with the doctor who pointed them towards this crime.

Chapter Twenty-One

"Thank you for lunch, Steve. I ate more than I have in a while. I think mostly because Monique is improving."

"Anytime. I know the cafeteria food isn't the most elegant, but it is edible. Do you want me to sit with you? Torrie's not been around lately."

"I'm sure she's busy with work, but I'm concerned that she hasn't called to check in. Maybe she left a message with the nurse while we were downstairs. Meanwhile, please don't feel like you must keep me company. Other patients in this hospital would welcome your encouragement. I don't want to become a project."

Steve was shocked by her last statement.

"I never intended to make you a project. Please forgive me. I like to spend time with you, but you reminded me that I do have someone to check on. You have my number and know where my office is if you need anything."

"I sure do and thank you again."

Constance watched Steve walk toward the elevators. She appreciated his support and prayers. Life had been more comfortable since he had taken an interest in Monique. He might be someone worth pursuing as—*my gosh, Constance! Where did that thought come from?* She hadn't been interested in anyone since Greg, so why now? Monique's accident, or whatever happened, magnified her loneliness. If she still had Greg, they would share this burden. Torrie helped, but her capacity to be supportive in adverse situations was limited. She used her work to cope with stressful events.

"Excuse me—nurse. My name is Constance Yorkshire. I'm Monique's mother. Are there any messages for me?"

Constance noticed that there was yet another nurse she hadn't seen before. This nurse was a male.

"Uh, yes, Ms. Yorkshire. I just came on duty and was on my way to check on Monique. Let me see if anyone wrote a note in her chart or somewhere."

Constance waited while he searched the area for any messages. Odd, this wasn't usually the time of day for a shift change. But of course, he could have been called in because they were short-staffed, or another nurse left early for some reason.

"Here, this is from Nurse Chapel. It looks like a Torrie called. Here's the note."

"Thank you, nurse—what is your name? You don't have a name tag."

"Really? Gosh, I forgot to put it on. I hope it's in my coat pocket. I'm Nurse Shaffer; Carl Shaffer. I will get in big-time trouble if I don't have a name tag."

Constance took the note from Carl, quickly read it, and breathed a sigh of relief at Torrie's message about her meeting with an important client. She'd planned to update Torrie about Monique's progress, but Nurse Chapel would have done that when she called.

Carl watched Constance walk toward Monique's room. He hoped his actions and lack of name tag didn't prompt Constance to question his presence. The already out-of-control situation didn't need to be further complicated by unfavorable attention. He'd better get that name tag if he intended to blend in. His plan was to stay out of everyone's way and work mindless duties until the right opportunity came. In another lifetime, he had been a trauma nurse, and his experience made it easy for him to insinuate himself into the ICU.

The first time he attempted to silence Monique, he'd been able to sneak into Monique's room to administer the potassium. His mistake was not dressing the part, so when the door opened, he had to grab the needle and escape to the bathroom before the vial emptied. When he was sure no one would notice him, he slipped away. This time he decided to infiltrate the ICU to give him easy access and more time.

"Oh, hello. I didn't know we were getting a new person today. I am Candy Chapel, and you are?"

"Hi, I'm Carl. I'm the temporary filling in for someone who couldn't make it. I came early to get acquainted with the routine and the patients before my shift. I hope that's not a problem."

Candy was surprised and a little uneasy. Something about Carl wasn't right. She was about to continue with her questions but was forced to hurry away to check out an alarm.

Constance heard the alarm and peeked out the door. Thank goodness it wasn't Monique this time. She glanced again at Carl, who remained at the station but looked out of place. Hopefully, he wouldn't be Monique's nurse for tonight. Constance sat down in the recliner to spend the rest of the evening with her daughter.

"Hello, Monique. I just had lunch—well, since it's about five, it may be considered an early supper. Anyway, the reverend took me to the cafeteria. He is such a nice man. I wish you were awake to meet him. You would like him as much as I do. Torrie is never happy to see him and is constantly rude. I can't figure out why. Maybe if she gets un-busy at work, I can have a heart to heart talk with her."

"Excuse me, Ms. Yorkshire? I am here to check Monique's vitals. Do you mind? I'm her nurse this evening."

Constance fear was realized. This Carl person was the night nurse, and she wasn't happy.

"Go right ahead, nurse. I'll sit over here out of the way."

"Thank you."

Chapter Twenty-Two

Detective McPherson arrived at the hospital in short order, shut off his engine, and checked his notes. Monique was in ICU on the fourth floor in room twenty-four. Her mom or sister, either one or both, should be with her. He hated hospitals! Mike took a deep breath and extracted himself from his unmarked car. The antiseptic smell hit him full force the minute he entered. He found the elevator and rode it to the fourth floor, got off, and looked for the ICU. An ICU without a locked door? He wondered about the lack of security. Most hospitals kept their ICU patients locked down. Mercy Memorial was a small hospital, so perhaps their regulations were different. He made his way to the nurse's station.

"Hello—uh—hello?"

Carl had completed his pretend duty with Monique's vitals, which allowed him to inspect the room and plan his attack. He was back at the nurse's station and turned to answer the detective's query. His eyes followed the massive torso and settled on the badge. Time stopped, his heart skipped a beat and his palms began to sweat. How did the police find out? *Easy, don't panic. They couldn't know what he planned.* Carl took a second to compose himself before he responded.

"Yes?"

"I'm here to speak with Monique Yorkshire's mother. Is she here by any chance?"

"Yes—sure—she is in room twenty-four. I just left there. Do you know the family?"

Mike took a long look at Carl before he responded. This young man got nervous when he saw the badge. Maybe it was just the badge that made him nervous. Maybe not.

"No, I don't know the family. I'm here on police business and I can find my way to the room."

Carl couldn't believe there was a detective on the floor. Neither could he fathom his amateurish reaction. He'd done this type of thing a gazillion times and knew how to fit in and act natural as he planned and carried out an execution. Why was this time so difficult? Maybe he should back out and walk away before he was in any deeper. Then he thought about the money. The money was worth the risk. *Geoffrey, uh Carl, get a grip!*

"Excuse me, Ms. Yorkshire? I'm detective McPherson, one of the detectives on Monique's case. May I speak with you for a few minutes?"

As soon as Constance heard the detective's voice, she looked up from the magazine she was pretending to read. Her first thought was *oh, my, but he's big! I'm glad he's one of the good guys.*

"Sure detective. But let's talk in the room across the hall. It's usually reserved for family members when the doctors or the nurses have bad news about their loved ones. I'd rather not speak in Monique's room if you don't mind."

"Of course. I understand that coma patients may be more aware of their surroundings than we know."

Once they were settled, Mike took out his little notebook.

"Before we begin, I want to say I'm sorry about what happened to your daughter, and that it took so long to establish that a crime happened. I'm anxious to talk to the doctor who discovered the discrepancies and thank him if he's around."

"Dr. Nevarez is unique, and I'm sure he'll talk to you, though not this evening. He came earlier and told me the tests he ordered show Monique is better. I understand he's gone for the day, so unless it's urgent to speak to him now, he'll be back tomorrow."

"I won't disturb him after hours. When you see him again, please give him my card and ask him to give me a call. Maybe I can set up an appointment for a visit."

"Of course. Now, detective, what questions do you have for me."

"My first and most obvious one is if you know of any reason someone would want to harm your daughter? An estranged lover, boyfriend, maybe someone who didn't like what she did as their bookkeeper?"

Constance paused a moment before she responded.

"Detective, you have to understand that both my daughters are extremely independent young women and inclined to keep their personal affairs to themselves. After their father died—my husband—I think they made a pact with each other that the less I knew of their lives, the better. The short answer is, I know nothing. From the little I know about Monique's life, she doesn't have any boyfriends or lovers, as you put it. If she has any friends, it's a mystery to me, and I know even less about her job. When I ask about her job, the answer's the same. It's boring and there's nothing to report. She likes to travel and has been out of the country many times but always travels alone. It's possible she meets someone wherever she goes, but that too is kept from me."

"Interesting —you said she thought her job was boring. I wonder why she stays. Has her boss been in to check on her?"

"To tell you the truth, in answer to your first question, I was surprised Monique majored in Business Management. My daughter is brilliant, 4.0 average through high school and college, plus she isn't one to sit around with busy work. Adventure and excitement are more her style. I suppose that's the reason she travels. It somehow satisfies her sense of adventure. I didn't try to discourage her choice of careers because it's safe and there is less of a chance for trouble. Although I wonder if any profession is safe. Someone attempted to kill her after all. To your second question, I haven't seen or heard directly from her boss. He keeps updated and communicates through the secretary. I think her name is Stephanie. She's been here a few times, mainly to let me know that Monique will continue to get a paycheck and not to worry about finances. Her boss is extremely generous. Monique is the only employee who did the work for his clients. I don't know how he is managing without her unless he's doing the work himself."

"Do you remember some of the places she went when she traveled? Was there anything strange about her when she got back?"

"She's been to Australia, Berlin, Argentina, Greece, and one time she went to Switzerland. The places she chooses are not the typical tourist countries, but then she was always interested in the not-so-typical. A couple of times, she didn't contact me for a week or two after she got back. I remember she came back from Switzerland with broken ribs from a skiing accident. She was pretty bruised up in addition to the broken ribs, so it took a few weeks for her to get better."

"What about her college days? Maybe something from that period is coming back to haunt her."

"Um, college. Not much. Monique moved out and lived on campus even though it was a local college. She carried a heavy load and went to summer school to graduate early. Most of her time was either in school or studying. She graduated with honors and was valedictorian. Her speech was lovely, all about the love of family and country with the hope this country she loved would always remain a protector of the innocent. After the ceremony, Torrie and I didn't see her right away. When we finally found her, she was walking away from a gentleman. I assumed she knew him, but when I asked her who he was, she denied it."

Mike assimilated the information in his memory before he responded.

"What I hear you say is Monique, though beautiful, is a loner, doesn't date, doesn't have many or any friends and travels alone. How can someone like that get someone angry enough to kill?"

"I'm sure I don't know, and glad you're the detective."

"I think that's all for now. Wait, have you ever been to Monique's apartment? I found an odd trophy shaped like an egg and wasn't sure what it was."

"You mean she still has that thing? She helped sponsor an Easter egg hunt for underprivileged children, and the association gave her that award. I remember how hard we all laughed when she showed us. I guess she thought it was special enough to keep. So, the answer about the trophy is, I knew about the egg. As far as visiting her in the apartment, no, she's never home enough to invite me over. I saw her apartment when she moved in, and I have a key to water her plants when she's away."

"Thank you for your time, Ms. Yorkshire. Here is a card with my contact information for you. If you think of anything, no matter how small, please don't hesitate to call me, day or night."

"I will, but don't hold up your investigation for me to come up with anything else. Goodnight, Detective."

Mike left Constance in the room but decided to walk by the nurses' station on his way out. He wanted another look at this nervous nurse. To his dismay, there was no one there. He guessed that was normal. After all, it was ICU, and the patients on this wing had to be more closely monitored than the regular patients. Instead of waiting around for the nurse to return, Mike chose to get back to the precinct for a report from Eve. He hoped she had more information than he got.

Chapter Twenty-Three

"Are you sure this is the original transcript for Monique? Where is the information on the Criminal Investigation class?"

Eve was frustrated. First, it wasn't easy to get a court order to coerce the college to provide the transcript. Then, when she got that, the secretary wouldn't tell her anything until the Dean of Students gave his approval. The secretary wasn't impressed when Eve threatened her with obstruction because she knew the threat was not enforceable. The Dean was the only person who had authority over student transcripts, and he didn't get back to the campus for two hours. When he finally found and presented Monique's transcript, there wasn't any evidence of the Criminal Investigation class.

"I'm not sure where you received your information on the classes Monique took, but it's wrong. This is the original transcript, and as you can see, the class isn't there. Besides, Monique was a business major. Criminal Investigation doesn't have anything to do with business."

"All right, thank you for your time, sir."

Eve turned and walked away. There was something awry about Monique's transcript. Her journal had several entries which mentioned Criminal Investigation. She had another thought and returned to the Dean's office.

"Excuse me, I am sorry to bother you again. May I have the name of the instructor who taught that class? Surely there aren't more than one or two for such a specialized study."

"That's for sure. Let me check my instructor list. Instructors' names are not protected information."

The secretary went into the file room. When she was gone for several minutes, Eve thought perhaps she'd been duped, and the secretary left by another exit.

"Here it is, the instructor was Charles Davis. He only taught one semester. Strange."

"What's strange? Can I see?"

"Yes, but we don't have any details on where he came from or where he went. Not even an address or a date of birth. I wonder how he even got the job. Something else, we take photographs of all

70

instructors and put them in their files. Either we failed to take his picture, or someone removed it because we don't have a picture of him."

"Okay, thank you for your trouble."

Eve was stumped and suspicious that something was amiss. She hoped Mike was back at the precinct when she got there to discuss the inconsistencies and what it might mean.

Mike was indeed at his desk moments before Eve walked into their office. She noticed his expression depicted almost as much puzzlement as she was experiencing.

"Hello, cowboy. What are you deep in thought about?"

"Quit calling me 'cowboy.' I don't even like cows! This case gets stranger by the minute. The only thing the mother knows about her daughter is she works, and she travels. My vibes tell me there is more to Monique than anyone knows, or at least most anyone. I hope you have more answers than I have."

"Well, cow... uh, sorry Mike. I hate to disappoint you, but I have even less. Monique's transcript doesn't show a class in Criminal Investigation, but stranger still, the instructor taught only one semester. His file doesn't provide information on who he was, where he lived, no picture—nothing. Just a name and the title of the class. If you ask me, this has government written all over it."

Mike and Eve became aware of the Chief's presence at the same time. They were taken aback because he rarely came down from his office. If he required something, he'd call or send his flunky, but he never made a personal appearance.

"To what do we owe the pleasure, Chief?"

"I need to see you two in my office. Now!"

Mike and Eve looked at each other. Why did the Chief seek them out personally, and why was he angry? He was almost to the elevators by the time their paralysis ended. They hurried to catch up while their colleagues looked on in pity. Anytime the Chief personally escorted someone to his office, well, it wasn't good news.

They rode the elevator in silence. Mike felt like he was on the last walk of a condemned prisoner. The detectives followed the Chief into his office and, to their surprise, saw two other gentlemen there.

"Have a seat you two. This is special agent Anthony Todd and special agent Stanley Gross. They are with the government—to be more specific, the CIA."

Both agents pulled out their badges to confirm that they were, in fact, who the Chief said they were.

Eve stared at agent Todd with disgust.

"I knew this had something to do with the government. There are just too many questions and no answers. What took you so long to get involved?"

"Detective, we have been involved from the beginning. As is our modus operandi, we work covertly so as not to bring attention to an investigation in process. You two seem determined to turn up something, so our superior decided it is in the organization's best interest to make you aware of us so you can back off. We requested that your Chief take you off the case and leave the rest of the investigation to us. We don't want to muddy the waters further."

The two stared at agent Todd for a minute. They couldn't believe what he said. How could they just back off an investigation?

"Excuse me? No. You can't tell us to just walk away! We have hours invested in this case."

"Eve's right. It isn't fair. We have mounds of information and surely, it's better to work together. Besides, we know the territory, and you guys are from another planet—so to speak."

This time Agent Gross spoke up. He gestured to the Chief as he spoke.

"I'm sure we have the same information you have and more. Your Chief here spoke to our superiors already and understands that protocol must be followed. Monique is an important agent in our organization, and we are doing everything we can to expedite a resolution."

The Chief confirmed the agent's statement.

"I was told by the mayor to turn over everything related to this case to these agents and then walk away. Non-negotiable. I know because I've already tried."

Fifteen minutes later, all evidence was given to the CIA agents and all computer information was purged. Eve, Mike, and the Chief sat still and watched them leave.

The Chief broke through their shock.

"Well, I guess all that's left for you two is to leave. Go have a drink, maybe dinner, then go home and get a good night's sleep. Tomorrow there will be another case for you."

They were dismissed just like that. No more discussion. Just leave and forget about Monique and the person who tried to kill her. Eve and Mike walked away without a word. They were both angry, but worse, they couldn't do anything except take the Chief's advice. They went to Barney's, the destination all off-duty detectives, k go to wind down.

Chapter Twenty-Four

Oh, my goodness! I remember! Someone tried to kill me in my apartment. I remember the struggle. I was getting the better of my assailant, but he found that silly silver egg and hit my head. He must have put me in my car and staged the accident. Gabriel didn't tell me where the accident happened, but I bet everything I have it was Gipper's Gully.

Gabriel said something before I drifted off—it was—a warning. It was 'hang onto my life.'

No. Surely no one is reckless enough to try another attempt while I am in the hospital surrounded by people. Brother, Monique, you work for the CIA. You expose evil people who do evil things. Why wouldn't they make another attempt? There has to be a way to surface from this world. If I stay here, I'm in danger. Where is the instruction booklet when you need it? Logically, I can start to defend myself by not fading or sleeping.

Constance got up to go to the restroom when Carl came into the room. *I wonder why he creeps me out.*

"Is everything all right with Monique? You seem to be checking on her more often than usual."

Uh-oh! He'd been overzealous with his attentiveness, and now Mom was suspicious. Maybe not suspicious exactly, but her hostility was palpable.

"I apologize, Ms. Yorkshire. There isn't anything wrong with your daughter. This is how I learned to work with patients in ICU. If it bothers you, I won't check on her as often while you are in the room."

Goodness, ever since I spoke with the detective, I see a boogie man in every corner.

"Don't worry about it, I am just a little on edge tonight. It's time for a break. I'll be back, then I guess I'd better go home for tonight."

"That is an excellent idea."

This strange nurse acted a tad overexcited. If only Torrie were here to talk her out of her paranoia. Ah, a Snickers and a hot chocolate cures anything, even fear. Steve offered to be available if she needed him, no matter what time of day or night. *Stop it, Constance. No reason to interrupt his night with the hysterics of a frazzled mom.*

No! No! I will not let this exhaustion overtake me. This is different. Usually, I phase out. This feels wrong. Mom! Anyone. Can you hear me? Help! Someone, please, notice me! I don't think I can hang on much longer! Think, Monique. I can't breathe! Where is Gabriel when I need him, or better, where are Michael and his army of angels? I want to give up. But wait – Gabriel said—oh, I can't breathe—he said I will save people. Monique—fight, move those arms, those legs—I raise my hand, but it isn't good enough—not nearly good enough. Work—I will do this! Move. My. Arms. And legs!

The minute Constance returned to the ICU, she knew something was wrong. No one was at the nurses' station. Not unusual—so what? She felt a surge of fear and looked towards Monique's door. It was closed and dark. The only time the nurses closed her door was for a procedure or an emergency. Constance ran to the room in a panic. Oh, help! Monique, her daughter, in a coma for weeks and literally immobile, thrashed desperately. The frightened mother ran out of the room and yelled for help. Where is Carl? She would even welcome him.

"Help!—someone, please! There is something wrong! Monique needs help!!"

"Ms. Yorkshire, what is it?"

"Quick! Something terrible has happened to Monique. She is thrashing, and I don't know what to do and..."

"Ms. Yorkshire, slow down. Let's see what's happened."

The women rushed back to Monique. The patient was clearly in distress. The heart monitor danced irregularly, her lips were blue, and she continued her frantic movements.

"I think someone did something. She doesn't look right and has hardly moved since her accident. Now this, and her lips are blue and—and—doesn't that mean she's not getting any oxygen?"

The nurse's thoughts were going wild. Her favorite shows and books were murder mysteries. The one she just finished had a person die of a lethal injection of potassium. Without hesitation, the nurse grabbed the oxygen mask, hooked it up to the oxygen supply and applied it to Monique. She hurried to the medicine locker to get the drug to counter an overdose of potassium. Monique's movements knocked the oxygen mask off. Constance attempted to rescue her.

"Monique—sweetie—listen, please hear me—the nurse is here to help you, please calm down."

Get away from me! Help! Help! Someone! Get this person away from me! Can anyone hear me?!

A firm, yet kind voice penetrates my terror. Monique, I'm here beside you. Listen to me. The nurse is here to help you. Relax and let her. It's time to rest now."

I relax and realize how tired I am. Gabriel told me to fight and I did. But now I want to just fade away.

Chapter Twenty-Five

"—and—here's to the CIA!"

Mike raised his glass to Eve yet again in a sarcastic toast to the officials who had confiscated their case. When his phone buzzed, he was tempted not to answer it. He had too much to drink and didn't want to face anything else. However, as is always the case, Mike's intuition overrides everything else, and he had a feeling he should answer.

"Detective McPherson."

"Oh, my gosh! I'm so glad you answered. This is Constance Yorkshire, Monique's mom. Someone tried to kill her again, just now!"

Constance's panic-stricken voice sobered the detective.

"Detective Shaw and I will be right there hang tight!"

"What is it, Mike? You're pale as a ghost."

"That was Monique's mom. Someone tried to kill her again. I told Ms. Yorkshire we'd be there, but we've both had too much to drink to drive safely."

"I'll call dispatch to send a patrol car to take us."

"Good idea! Meanwhile, I'll call the Chief. He can get in touch with those clowns who kicked us off the case."

Constance stood by Monique's room to warn anyone away who didn't belong. She only hoped all who rushed in wanted the same thing she did. Despite the horrendously traumatic experience, a glimmer of hope sneaked in. Her daughter had indicated awareness with her movement, plus she had calmed after Constance spoke to her.

Constance felt so alone. Should she call Steve? Perhaps, after all, this seemed kind of urgent to her.

Chapter Twenty-Six

Torrie watched her team leave the conference room after the meeting. She was confident the client would be pleased with their presentation.

"Connor, wait, don't go yet. I think we have some unfinished business to discuss."

"Torrie, all I want is to go home and kiss my daughters and wife and go to bed."

"Home? You never go home this late the night before an important presentation. Besides, unless I'm not aware of everything, I won't keep you long, so please sit down."

Connor reluctantly pulled out a chair and sat down.

"I'm waiting."

"There's too much drama lately. I know I've not been myself, but you know what? Neither have you. I think you're hiding something from me."

"Alright, you win. I have to tell you something, and it isn't easy. You see, uh, it's like this …"

"Oh, for gosh sakes, Connor, just say it!"

"Damn, Torrie! You are the most—okay, the truth is Bonnie confronted me about our affair. She talked divorce at first, but in the end, gave me a second chance with conditions."

"Wow. I imagined a lot of things, but I can honestly say I didn't see that coming."

Torrie slumped into one of the chairs at the conference table.

"What conditions?"

"She moved me into the guest bedroom, and I have to give up the apartment. Oh, and of course, I promised to end our affair. Bonnie doesn't know it's you, and I'll do what I can to keep your name out of it. From now on, though, our relationship must be strictly professional. I doubt breaking up will cause you grief because from all the signs you've given me, you are ready to end this."

"You're right about that. I think we've gone as far as we can. But, you know, I'm not sure that explains the locked doors or your extreme nervousness."

"You are unbelievable! Why can't you just take my explanation and forget it? There are other things in my life besides clients or this business or even you. Believe it or not, Torrie, the world doesn't revolve around you."

"That's not fair! I have never done anything – I've never acted that selfish. I – I don't think so anyway. Have I really been that way?"

Connor shook his head with a sigh.

"No, I'm sorry. You backed me into a corner, and I got angry. You're not so much selfish; it's more like you're a woman with a mission and a one-track mind. You bulldoze your way until you get what you want."

"I see. Not selfish, but a bulldozer. I'm not sure that's any better, but let's just call a truce. I'm too tired to hash it out. Go home to your wife and fix your marriage. As for the other things, I'm here if you need me. Tonight, I plan on going straight to bed."

"Good idea, and I'll be here in time for the meeting. Uh, Torrie, have you checked in with your mom about your sister? Has anyone contacted you?"

"Connor, go home."

Connor went directly to his office. His entire life was unraveling in front of him, and he didn't know how to make it right. Geoffrey hadn't called him yet, and since Torrie stayed to have this conversation, chances are nothing happened. He was so close! One more deposit to make and then payday and a one-way ticket out with his family beside him. Should he take his gun home? Just in case...

Chapter Twenty-Seven

Constance stood outside Monique's door waiting for the crowd in the room to disperse. She broke down and called Steve, so he was on his way. Constance didn't need him, but his presence always helped her feel less alone.

"Ms. Yorkshire, tell me what happened."

"Oh, Dr. Nevarez, someone tried to kill Monique again. No one's told me any details, but earlier I came back from a break, and her door was closed. I rushed in and discovered Monique moving wildly with labored breathing, so I yelled for help. A nurse came in and hit the code button. Things were confusing after the nurse put the oxygen mask on. Monique kept pushing the oxygen off of her face. I tried to hold her arms down but wasn't successful. It seemed forever before the nurse got back and gave her some kind of a shot. Monique finally calmed enough to allow the nurse to get the mask back on. By then, a team of professionals had answered the code blue summons, and I was told to leave. I haven't been allowed back in yet."

Constance's report startled the doctor. He expected Monique to gradually regain consciousness as soon as the blood clot was dissolved and the swelling was gone, but this wasn't what he planned. Dr. Nevarez left Constance outside the room to check on his patient. Oxygen deprivation severe enough might put his patient into a different type of coma, this time with brain damage.

"Fill me in."

"Hi, Doctor. Monique is stable. Her oxygen level isn't optimal, but better. We gave her an injection of calcium gluconate to regulate her heartbeat. As soon as her oxygen level reaches normal and stays steady, I plan to take her off the pure oxygen. She put up quite a fight."

"What prompted you to use calcium gluconate?"

"Sir, it made sense when I considered the entire case."

Dr. Nevarez didn't understand what the nurse meant but didn't have time to pursue it further because Constance came into the room with Steve. Then following close behind were Detectives McPherson and Shaw and three more men.

"What is going on? Who are you people, and what are you doing here? This is an extremely sick young lady, and I won't allow this intrusion."

The menagerie stopped and stared at the doctor. They didn't know how to react. Steve took charge.

"Let's adjourn to the conference room across the hall and make introductions. Monique doesn't need to be subjected to additional excitement."

No one opposed the reverend's suggestion. Dr. Nevarez took one last look at Monique. Satisfied she was stable, at least for the moment, he followed the others to the conference room.

"Okay—now I want to know who all of you are."

"I'm Reverend Steve Robinson, Chaplain of Mercy Memorial Hospital. I believe you know Constance, Monique's mother."

"I'm Chief Monahan, and these are two of my detectives, McPherson and Shaw."

All eyes turned to the CIA agents next. Agent Todd spoke for both of them.

"I'm not going to say anything until we have a consensus by everyone regarding confidentiality. Nothing goes beyond these walls."

The agent's words surprised everyone prompting a brief silence. Soon Dr. Nevarez groaned but nodded his head. The others followed his lead.

"Good then. Thank you. I am agent Anthony Todd, and this is agent George Gross. We work for the government and..."

"Yeah—the CIA, and they stole our case."

"Let's not quibble about jurisdiction. However, Detective McPherson is correct, we are with the CIA. This will come as a shock to everyone, and we don't have time for niceties, but Monique is one of our Agents. After her accident, we found out she discovered something sensitive enough that endangered her life. We couldn't verify right away that the accident was staged. We just established that fact today, but this happened before we could assign a security detail. Now, doctor, can you update us on her status?"

Constance couldn't believe what she had heard. The accident, the long days and nights, the revelation that Monique's crash was no accident after all, the detective's questions, the second attempt, and now she's told that her daughter works for the CIA! Constance felt faint and swayed dangerously.

Steve moved quickly and gently led her to a nearby chair and tenderly put her head down. All eyes watched the drama unfold.

"She's good. It's just that she has been under tremendous pressure, gentlemen, and I dare say your news upset her world again. Please continue."

"If you're sure she's fine—Doctor – please..."

"I don't know her status yet. I heard that if Ms. Yorkshire had arrived five minutes later, Monique would be dead. We haven't had time to assess any damage that her lack of oxygen caused, or if there is any damage to her brain. Now, if you are finished with me, I have other patients to attend to. I trust Agent Todd that you and the police will get your act together and do something to protect my patient."

"Of course, doctor, even as we speak. Thank you for your time."

"Humph. Ms. Yorkshire, I'll get back with you later today."

The doctor stormed out of the conference room.

"Chief, I'm sorry you distrust the CIA, but I assure you, we have everything under control. We were slow with the security, and that is regrettable, but ..."

"Regrettable?"

Constance was livid and responded in a barely controlled, deadly voice.

"Is that all you have to say? Regrettable? No, gentlemen. Regrettable is not what it is. Unthinkable, irresponsible, negligent, and—and just stupid. I am furious with you. If I weren't a lady, I would slap you both for your incompetence. In fact ..."

Steve quietly touched Constance's hand. He realized what she was about to do. Constance glared at him.

The agents were flabbergasted by her outburst.

"And you two detectives! You're investigating a crime. Don't you think my daughter deserves to be safe? Aren't you trained to keep people safe? Now, I'm on my way back to Monique, and all of you had better do your jobs and get this monster, and I want it done yesterday."

Steve walked out with Constance toward Monique's room. He ached to wrap his arms around her to stop her tremors and calm her anger but took the wiser action and quietly prayed for peace. To his dismay, Steve's feelings for Constance had metamorphosed into an uncharted situation. How could he minister to her and keep his heart intact?

"Okay, gentlemen, you heard the lady. Chief, in the best interest for all, Agent Gross and I want to invite you and your detectives to agree to a joint investigation. If you agree, however, this case is not up for discussion with anyone outside this room."

The Chief responded with exaggerated politeness.

"Thank you. We're delighted to assist and honored you agreed to take us into your confidence. However, may I suggest to you that first – after security is in place for Monique, of course – we question the staff about this Carl character and find out what they know."

Through clenched teeth, Anthony spoke to his partner.

"Agent Gross, you notify the head nurse we intend to interview her staff individually. Ask her to set up a place and time for the interviews."

Chapter Twenty-Eight

I open my eyes. My struggle to survive whatever attacked me is vividly implanted in my mind. I moved from the tree to a soft patch of grass near the stream, but I don't know how. The sun shines through the trees, and I feel safe and secure in its warmth. The voice instructed me to quit my struggle and rest. Something blocks the sun for a moment. I look up. Gabriel.

"Monique, you are remarkable. That is my announcement and a word from the Father. The danger isn't completely over, but you are more aware of what is going on. Your rest has done wonders, but you will soon leave this world. You will be a hundred percent restored. You have a bit more time to enjoy the quiet before the storm begins. Don't be concerned about protection. Preparations are already in place. All you have to do is stay here and rest."

I notice Gabriel's gaze goes to the horizon. I turn my eyes as well to see what he's looking at. My memory is fully restored now, and I know the person in the horizon is Connor. He's behind all the violence. My investigation into an arms dealer linked to ISIS led me to him. The arms dealer didn't deal directly with ISIS, and ISIS didn't deal directly with the arms dealer. I searched for the middleman for three months. Connor is the middleman. I carefully collected information, but slowly, so as not to alarm him and cause him to flee.

After I discovered that Torrie worked with him and they were involved, I moved my timeframe up. Against every instinct I had, I charmed myself into Connor's life to get more information too quickly. Several days of surveillance led me to a lounge he frequented when he wasn't with Torrie. I look back at Gabriel to ask him a question, and he is gone. Of course. I need to rest anyway.

Connor cleaned out the safe. He planned to make a quick exit as soon as he got his family. The drive to his house was uneventful.

Geoffrey finally contacted him, minutes from his home. He answered quickly, heart in his throat.

"Hey, it's about time!"

"Relax, will ya'? I did the job.

"Good—so, you made sure she's dead then.

"Well, not exactly—

"What! You mean ..."

"Hold on now. There was too much of a chance of discovery, so I didn't hang around until the end, but there is no way she could have survived. Her mother decided to go home for the night, and I was her nurse, so no one else will pay attention to her until the next shift. I even closed the door."

"What were you thinking! I paid you to finish the job, now you tell me you don't know. I am not paying you anything until I know for sure that she is no longer a threat. Look, you don't know her; she isn't someone you can turn your back on and just assume things will work. Luck keeps getting her out of situations which should have been the end of her. I don't want to hear that this is one of those times!"

"No way, man! You came to me for help, remember? This is your mess, not mine. I did what I said I would. I can't help it if she has some guardian angel to help her out. I took the risk, I exposed myself to who knows how many people who can identify me, and now I'm gone. Make sure you get money into my Swiss bank account. The number, by the way, is in a sealed envelope in our shared depository box. If I don't get it on time, well, let's just say I know where you live."

"If that is a threat ..."

Geoffrey disconnected. Connor knew it was not a threat. This was a character who didn't threaten; he just did it. Hopefully, Monique was finished because if not, Connor would have to take desperate action. Right now, he was almost home and had to pretend things were good.

"Bonnie! Girls! I'm home!"

Connor gasped. Three armed men surrounded his family. He reached for his gun, but one of the gunmen put a warning shot over his head. The girls screamed at the sound.

"Ouch! You didn't have to do that!"

"Oh, I think we did. It's necessary to take drastic action. The boss is behind schedule. He expected his cargo days ago, yet there is no sign you've made the arrangements. He thought a little incentive would be good, so here is the incentive. You get rid of the girl. Oh yes, she is still alive. Get the money to the holders of the cargo and get the cargo to the boss or lose your family."

Connor was terror-struck and wanted to fall to the floor and cry like a baby. His wife and daughters were so scared. The urge to act was tempered by his fear of these guys.

"Look, Bonnie ..."

"Don't you 'Look Bonnie' me! How could you get mixed up in something that put your daughters and me in danger? Look at them. They don't have masks. Do you really think we'll get out of this alive? I hate you!"

"Daddy, are we really going to get killed like on the TV shows?"

Connor cringed at his wife's accusations and his daughter's innocent question. How could he refute what his wife said? His entire family could identify them. After he completed their demands, these monsters were not likely to leave them alive.

"You got yourself a smart family, dirt-bag. All we want is for you to finish the job, take your money and family, leave for a very faraway place, and never look back. Really. Little girl, don't you worry your pretty little head. We aren't bad people, and we won't hurt you as long as your daddy does what he promised."

"Daddy, are you going to do what you promised?"

Now his heart broke. He was determined to get this finished.

"Okay, I have a plan. I am ..."

"No. We don't want to know about the plan. We want you to end this."

"Right. Okay—Honey, you have every right to be angry, but I did it to make us a better life, honest. You have to believe me."

Bonnie just stared at this stranger who was her husband. She was scared and sad because she suspected this wasn't going to end well at all. She couldn't respond without alarming the girls, so she decided to just sit there.

"Well, get with it!"

Connor rushed out the door, thirty minutes after he had arrived. It was ten-thirty, and he knew just where he would go first.

Chapter Twenty-Nine

Torrie went home and did exactly what she said. After a quick bite at her favorite restaurant, she went to her condo then straight to bed without her ritual glass of wine. The one glass of wine with her meal was a perfect sleep aid. By the time she got home, she was relaxed enough to go right to sleep with plenty of time to be well-rested.

What is that? Torrie slowly woke to the constant buzzing noise. *Where was it coming from?* The sound was a repetitive buzz, then there was a break, then it started again. Abruptly, she remembered she had turned her ringer off, and the noise was the vibration of her phone. Someone wanted her attention. *Monique! Something's wrong with Monique!* How could she have forgotten to check on her this evening? As she answered, she looked at the clock. It was Eleven-thirty.

"Hello, Mom? What's wrong?"

"Oh, Torrie, something awful has happened. Monique is okay – now – but – someone tried to kill her again. Right in her room. I left for a few minutes, and there was this new nurse, and I think he did something. It had to have been Him. I didn't see anyone else I didn't know. She almost died, Torrie! Again!"

"Mom, Mother! Please, slow down. Did you say someone tried to kill Monique? You mean there is really someone out there who wants her dead? She's okay now? Are you sure?"

"Sorry, yes, she is, at least she's still alive. I'm not sure how all right because the doctor has to get some results of her tests to see if there is any residual damage from whatever it was they gave her."

"What? Did you say poison! How? Why? What is going on?"

"Can you just come to the hospital? There are things I need to tell you, but not over the phone. I know you have a big day tomorrow and a presentation, but this really is important. I need you to be here."

"Of course, I'll come! My job isn't more important than you or Monique, and Connor can handle this meeting. I'll be there as fast as I can."

Constance ended the conversation with Torrie and looked gratefully at Steve.

"Thank you for the water. My throat was so dry. You should go home now that everything is under control. Torrie will be here probably in about an hour and will stay with me at the hospital for a while. You have other duties besides us."

"Listen to me. I wouldn't still be here if I didn't want to be. I know my duties and schedules better than you do. If I want to stay, I'm going to stay. Even Torrie's evil eye will not cause me to run!"

It was too much for Constance. Torrie's evil eye combined with Steve's indignation caused her to burst out in laughter. She felt a little crazy, but she couldn't stop. The shocked nurses looked at her and wondered what could have caused such frenzy. Steve, on the other hand, recognized it for what it was – a breaking point. He watched her for a few moments to determine the best course of action. Should he let her continue until she was spent or attempt to arrest the onslaught? It only took a few seconds for him to decide to intervene. He took her arm and lead her into the small conference room. He prayed:

Dear Father, thank you for Monique's protection tonight. I know You watched over her and made it so that Constance was able to act to save her life. We acknowledge that she is in Your capable hands and that You will see her through all of this. Lord, in Jesus' name, I pray that a great peace will flood Constance right now. Calm her. Smooth out her emotions and comfort her with the comfort that can only come from You. I pray for continued protection for Monique and that this investigation will conclude soon so that this family can get back to living. In Jesus' name—Amen.

Constance's laughter had turned to tears and finally calmed to sniffles as the reverend prayed. By the time he finished, she was utterly exhausted. She thanked God for this gentle, kind man beside her.

"I'm sorry for my outburst."

"Considering the situation, it was inevitable, my dear friend. Why don't I get you a pillow, and you lie here for a few minutes? At least until Torrie arrives. The security detail for Monique is in place, and I'll sit with her. No, don't argue. You want to be calm and rested before Torrie gets here, or she'll worry about you."

"You'll get no argument from me. I'm ready to lie down. I have nothing left to give. – So, I'm "friend" now and not "Madam", huh?"

Steve blushed a little,

"Yes, I guess when one goes through death and life and life and death again, one tends to view a person in a different light. Please don't be offended."

Constance smiled.

"No, I'm not offended at all. It feels kind of nice to have you call me a friend. I think the same way about you, to tell the truth. Now, that pillow, please?"

Chapter Thirty

Thirty minutes after Torrie received the call, she was dressed and packed with enough things to stay with Mom for a few days. Before she picked up her bag, the doorbell rang. Spooked because it was too late for visitors, Torrie quietly moved to the door and peeked through the peephole.

"Connor?"

He didn't look well at all, so she quickly opened the door.

"Connor! What's wrong? Did Bonnie kick you out of the house—what—what are you doing?"

Torrie's concern turned to fear when she saw a gun pointed at her. This Connor, with his face drenched with sweat and wild bloodshot eyes was deranged.

"Honey don't worry. I won't hurt you. I don't want to hurt you. I just need you to do something for me, that's all. Move, so I can close the door. It's good you don't have an alarm system in your condo, although you may want to consider one when this is over."

He's unhinged! What is this about alarm systems?

"I don't understand. You don't need a gun to ask me to do something for you. What could you possibly want?"

"I want you to help me kill your sister."

Torrie was glad she had made her way to the couch. She collapsed and could only stare at this stranger in front of her.

"I don't understand—kill Monique? Why would I do that? Why would you even think I could consider it? You're crazy! Someone already ..."

Everything that didn't add up with Connor stared her in the face.

"You? You're behind everything that's happened to Monique? But, how can you? And the other attempt just now? Why do you want her dead?"

"I don't have time to give you details. I'm mixed up with some nasty people. Now my family is in danger, and this is the only way to save them. If your sister hadn't put her nose in where it didn't belong, nothing would have happened. The job would be finished, and I'd be gone never to be seen again."

"But Connor, what does Monique have to do with you? You two don't even know each other! I never mentioned you to her or Mom. How could she be a threat to you?"

"Your family is a joke! How can you not know that Monique works for the CIA? Not only that, she stole information from me which will bring down a small but destructive army. I stopped her temporarily, but it's still out there somewhere. As long as she is alive, this army is in danger. So, I have to take care of it."

"CIA? Army? Monique? My little sister?"

"Come on! I don't have time to tell you everything—I don't need to tell you everything."

"None of this makes sense. Surely there's another way to get you out of whatever it is you're mixed up in! Please, calm down. Let's think …"

"Stop! Just Stop! Get up now!" Connor didn't want to talk anymore.

"Get to the car Torrie. I don't have time for this!"

His family really didn't deserve to be hurt. Bonnie was content with little things. The high life in the suburbs was his idea, not hers. She didn't shy away from the extravagance, but she would have been just as happy with a less glamorous life.

"All right. Hang on. Connor, you haven't thought this through. What happens to me—if I do help you, are you going to kill me next? I don't know much about what is going on, but you did just confess, sort of, that you were the one who tried to kill Monique the first time, and maybe this time. What will happen if you succeed? I'll know that too."

"I don't know. I haven't gotten that far, but I will come up with something. Right now, let's go!"

Torrie had no recourse but to follow instructions. Absentmindedly, she picked up her bags and opened the door with Connor close by, gun in hand. She locked up her condo.

"Now what? Whose car do we take?"

"Your car, and you drive. Don't make any stupid decisions. Just act normal, or I'll pull the trigger. Not to kill you because I need you, but I can certainly hurt you."

Torrie believed him. She had planned to do something to get the attention of the police but realized that it would be futile. How could he possibly see a positive end? They couldn't just walk into the hospital and casually shoot Monique. There would be guards by now. Connor wouldn't be able to easily justify his presence because she had never even mentioned his name. Then what? Shoot it out with everyone? Connor was irrational and in a no-win situation, which made him dangerous. She was panicky. Maybe she should pray for help. No. It had never done her any good in the past; why would this time be different?

Connor watched every move Torrie made. His thoughts were just as intense as hers. The difference, however, is that his intent wasn't to remedy his dilemma, only to save his family and himself. The money wasn't even relevant anymore.

Flashing lights in the review mirror captured their attention.

"Connor, I swear I did nothing to …"

"Just pull over. Maybe they are on their way to an emergency and will drive right past."

Torrie did as Connor instructed, but the police car didn't pass them by. Instead they pulled in behind her. She quickly got her driver's license out of her wallet. She didn't want anything ugly to happen because this strange Connor wouldn't hesitate to take on the entire police department.

"Good evening, ma'am, sir. May I have your driver's license and insurance information, please?"

"Sure. Right here. I'm sorry, but I can't imagine why you pulled me over. I was right at the speed limit and didn't run any stop signs or anything."

"Be right back, ma'am."

"You're doing good; just remember what's at stake here. You don't want to see innocent people get hurt."

Torrie anxiously waited for the officer to return.

"Here you go, Ms. Yorkshire. Everything is in order. I want to point out that your left taillight needs to be replaced right away. It's a hazard to drive with one taillight. We wouldn't want you to be involved in an accident."

"Why, thank you, officer. I didn't realize it. In fact, I just had it replaced yesterday. The technician must not have installed it correctly. I'm on my way to the hospital to see my sister. Someone tried to kill her, so I'm in a hurry, but I don't want to break any speed limits. My mom is frantic."

Torrie wasn't sure what prompted her to say all of that. It wasn't like her to engage in needless conversation. She felt Connor tense.

"Are you Monique's sister? One of the detectives mentioned a little bit about the case, but it's kind of a hush-hush thing. Why don't you let us lead you to the hospital? We'll use our flashing lights and get you there faster."

"Why, thank you, officer! How wonderful!"

As soon as the officer walked away, Connor pulled on Torrie's arm.

"Why did you do that! What are you up to, Torrie? I don't want to hurt you. I really do kind of love you ..."

"Connor cut the crap. You never loved anyone but yourself. I've got to drive now. The officer just pulled out."

"Forget it. Okay, here's the plan – we walk in with my arm around you. The gun will be close and just so you know, the safety is off, and any sudden movement will cause it to discharge. We've been engaged since Monique's accident, but you didn't want to say anything until things got better. We've considered all that has happened and decided to tell everyone now because you want my help."

"That's just lame and unbelievable."

"Then, wise mouth, what do you suggest?"

"You want me to help you come up with a story? You're not only unimaginative, but you're also crazy! By the way, how did you get your job? You never once came up with an idea on your own, and you skipped the entry-level positions."

"Stop the backtalk! How's this? We tell your mom we couldn't wait any longer, and who knows when Monique will become conscious again."

Torrie thought it was just as lame, but she didn't protest. Something had to happen to show everyone the danger Connor presented. She looked at him sideways. He was anything but composed. Perhaps his erratic behavior would call attention to himself. She had to play it cool, or he might hurt someone.

"Okay, we can go with that. We're here."

"Wait! Let me open the door."

Torrie sighed but did what she was told.

"Come on, dear, let's hurry inside. Thank you, officers! You made our trip much faster."

93

"You're quite welcome. Torrie, take care of yourself. Say hi to Detective McPherson."

The two walked into the hospital just as Connor planned. The late hour precluded any crowds. Torrie was glad about that. Too soon, they were in the ICU. She noticed Nurse Chapel was on duty and wondered why. Usually, she worked the day shift.

"Torrie! I am so glad you are here—uh, excuse me. I don't think I know you?"

"Of course, you don't. Poor Torrie has been so upset about her sister. She hasn't taken time to introduce me to her family. I'm her fiancé, Connor Wray."

"Torrie? Fiancé?"

Candy couldn't believe what she heard.

"Candy, it's still okay to call you Candy?"

"Of course."

"Connor proposed to me about two months ago, right before Monique's accident. I didn't think it was a good idea to tell Mom because she didn't even know I was dating. Uh, where is she, by the way? In Monique's room?"

"No, actually she's in the room across the hall. The chaplain is with your sister until you're ready to relieve him. He wants you to check with him first before you disturb your mom."

"Sure. Come on, Connor, let's go meet the reverend."

Torrie and Connor made their way to Monique's room. The door was closed, and the curtains were pulled. There were two officers blocking the entrance.

"Hello, officers. Can we go in?"

"Officers, it's okay to let Torrie in. She's Monique's sister. Torrie, are you sure you want Connor to go into her room? A strange person may startle her."

"I thought she was in a coma. Why would I startle her?"

Torrie was alarmed by this new development. She had to think fast …

"You have to forgive Connor. He isn't medically inclined. Sweetie, just because someone is in a coma doesn't mean they can't hear. Hearing a stranger's voice could cause Monique to become agitated.

"Candy, I'll keep him quiet and not let him talk so she can hear. I'd like him by my side."

Torrie was surprised she could say that with a straight face. She only hoped it convinced Candy.

"I'm not crazy about the idea, but if you keep quiet, you can go in with Torrie."

The officers moved aside, and Torrie opened the door. The first thing she did was rush up to the reverend and put her arms around him...

"Steve! It's so nice to see you, and I am sooo glad you were here for Mom. I know you are going to be shocked, but this is my fiancé, Connor. I wanted to wait until Monique was out of her coma to tell everyone, but it has gone on too long. This is just too stressful, and I want him to be with me."

Steve was confused with Torrie's greeting. Why did she act like he was her long-lost friend? He almost thought – well, he didn't know what. And to find out she was engaged? She needed him by her side. He didn't like this at all but thought it best to play along.

"Torrie, it's nice to see you, too. I'm always happy to assist your family. Why don't we go somewhere else to talk? I don't want Monique upset with a stranger's presence."

Connor was a little perturbed with everyone's hesitation and inference that he was a stranger and would upset Monique. It was just a little bit beyond ridiculous, but for once, he was smart enough to let it go. There was more at stake than insults to him.

They left Monique's room and went into the empty waiting area where they could talk freely. Most everyone was still at home in bed. Those who stayed all night tended to congregate in the smaller, more comfortable area.

"Now, please tell me what happened. Mom didn't make a lot of sense. —something about poison and—I don't understand. Why in the world would someone want to kill Monique? What did she ever do? And Mom. How is she? I really want to see her."

"She's had one shock after another in the last twenty-four hours, and I left her to rest in one of the conference rooms. Frankly, the announcement of your engagement will be quite a blow for her. I don't understand how you can be so thoughtless at a time like this."

Steve braced himself for the explosion that was sure to happen. His statement was harsh, and Torrie's history proved she did not shy from hostile reactions.

"Oh, I know it sounds selfish, but honestly, I can't wait any longer to tell her. I need Connor with me right now to help me through this ordeal."

Connor squeezed Torrie's arm to let her know she was about to step too far out of character.

Steve was stunned. Now he was sure something was wrong, and he suspected it had something to do with this—uh—Connor person.

"Okay, I'll take you to your mom so you can talk with her, then I'll go back to Monique."

They approached the room quietly. Steve opened the door.

"Hello, Constance, I hope you rested. Torrie is here. She has a— a friend. I'll be in Monique's room if you need me."

"Friend? Torrie? You brought a friend?"

Torrie hurried to her mom and gave her a hug. She knew this announcement was not going to be easy, but to protect her family, she had to make this believable.

"Hi, Mom. I am so sorry I didn't call tonight, and I left you alone in all of this! Steve is such a dear to come and rescue you. I want to introduce you to Connor."

Constance was confused. Torrie didn't have friends. Acquaintances, and co-workers, yes, but certainly no one she wanted to introduce to her family.

"Hello, Connor. Torrie, I don't understand."

"I know. It's out of character, and I'm sure you think I chose a poor time to make an announcement. But lately, there hasn't been a good time. Connor and I decided to date several months ago. Right before Monique's accident, he asked me to marry him. I – well – I accepted, but then Monique had her accident before I could tell you. I hoped to wait until she was better, but it's—I—darn it, I don't want to wait any longer. This is too important to me."

Chapter Thirty-One

Steve left the three to their conversation and sought out one of the detectives or agents, anyone. He knew they were with the witnesses but didn't know where.

"Excuse me, good evening Nurse Chapel?"

"Hello, Steve. This is an odd hour for you to be here."

"Yes, I—Ms. Yorkshire called me. Where are the detectives? I think I have some important information to relay."

"Detective McPherson is in that room just to your right, and Detective Shaw is down that way on the left, and the agents are both in the same room two doors down from her."

"Thank you. I met Detective McPherson once, so I think I'll talk to him."

Steve timidly knocked on the door. He was hesitant to interrupt an interrogation, but then it wasn't really an interrogation. The detective was just asking questions. Surely the repercussions wouldn't be severe.

"Reverend?"

"Please, pardon my interruption, but I think we have a situation—or perhaps a complication to this ongoing drama. If I may have a few minutes of your time when you are finished?"

The detective's instincts told him he should talk with the reverend right then. The chaplain didn't strike him as someone who would be concerned about a trivial matter.

"You can come in now; I just finished with this person."

"Okay, you may go. If I have any further questions, I'll be in touch. Thank you."

McPherson's eyes followed the witness until he left the room.

"Have a seat Reverend. Now, what situation do we have?"

"Something weird, or rather out of the ordinary, and with everything that's happened, I don't want to discount it."

"Sure, I understand. Let's hear it."

"Torrie, Monique's sister, just arrived. She greeted me like we were the best of friends. If that wasn't peculiar enough, she had this guy beside her, and she introduced him as her fiancé."

"Okay. So far, I fail to see the reason for your unease."

"I'm sorry, of course you don't. I can explain. Torrie hasn't liked me from day one. She leaves the minute she sees me, makes hateful remarks, never calls me anything, much less by my given name. In other words, we are not friends, best or otherwise.

"If that wasn't enough to alarm me, she introduced her fiancé and said he made her feel more secure. I'm not sure how much you've been around Constance, but consider this; Monique works for the CIA, Torrie is an executive with a highly visible marketing firm, and Constance raised both girls by herself for the last thirteen years. Why would this hostile, self-sufficient woman suddenly become my best friend and claim to need a male figure to make her feel safe? It doesn't fit."

Mike considered this new information.

"Where are they now? Have they gone into Monique's room?"

"I left them with Constance in the conference room. I'm not sure what happened after Torrie talked to her mom, but I felt like I needed to talk with you more than I needed to stay with them."

"From what you just told me, I'd be alarmed too. Let's go see if we can catch up with the couple. I need to check this guy out. What did you say his name is?"

"I didn't, but it's Connor. Sorry, I didn't get the last name."

McPherson stopped in his tracks. Connor— "C" —cufflink—

I wake up because I feel a chill, and periodically drops of rain splash my face. The wind picks up, and the clouds completely obscure the sun. I sit up quickly and stand—Yes! I can stand now. Though I'm cold, I feel much better and stronger. There's Connor, a few feet away. His malevolent smile sends chills of a different sort up my spine.

I remember the first time I met him, I thought he was kind of sweet. Not the type to be mixed up in ISIS. What I see now is evil incarnate!

I was already at the lounge nursing a drink when Connor came in for the evening. I dressed conservatively sexy, not sleazy. My plan was to portray a lonely woman out to attract a friend, not a lover.

A couple of minutes after he ordered his first drink, I got up and "accidentally" stumbled into him. Wine spilled on his jacket. His anger lasted only until he witnessed my most appealing, helpless, apologetic look. He softened, became attentive and told me it was fine the suit needed to be dry cleaned anyway. He said I looked distraught and asked if there was anything he could do to help. I teared up and sat down on the stool right beside him and sighed dramatically.

He told the bartender to bring us two more drinks and led me to a booth at the back of the room. We talked for hours. I didn't have to pretend to like him because Connor is quite likable and charming. I spilled my guts with the details of my pretend situation. He was adequately attentive without the seduction. After that, we continued to meet a couple of times a week. I was glad when he was with me because that meant he wasn't with Torrie. Torrie isn't naïve, but she is vulnerable when it comes to men.

It took some finagling, but I finally got him to take me to his office one night. I looked around the room and saw his safe behind the desk, where I assumed, he kept his secrets. I made plans to go back there another night when we didn't meet. It had to be a time I knew Torrie would not be there because if she saw me, she would question the reason I was at her place of employment.

The night I went back to his office, Connor and Torrie had plans to go to a play.

I planned to arrive right before the play began to give me plenty of time to snoop. Torrie doesn't like to be late for anything, so I was confident they would be long gone. The guards remembered me from before and I had no problem convincing them I left my sweater. They were fine with me going unattended to get It.

I was ready to attack the safe when I heard Connor outside the door. He mumbled something, and Torrie loudly protested they were late. I barely made it into the adjoining office when he came into his office, muttering something about security people. He stayed a few minutes too long for my comfort. I heard him approach the door to the room I was in. Right before I was exposed, I heard Torrie complain about the late hour and a missed first act. Connor hesitated a moment, but Torrie was relentless, so he left.

I waited a few more minutes and breathed a prayer of thanksgiving before I ventured back to Connor's office. His code to the safe was easily cracked, and the information inside well worth the risk.

By the time I left, it was too late to swing by the office. My rule is that nothing about my job is ever found in my apartment. I have an unregistered safe deposit box for sensitive items. It was the safest place for the evidence.

When Connor showed up on my doorstep, I realized that my impression of his lack of intuition was inaccurate.

Chapter Thirty-Two

Constance listened to Torrie, stunned to hear talk about this stranger and how they met. She looked at Connor. He might be nice looking, but she didn't like him. He looked more nervous than someone meeting his future mother-in-law should. Why would Torrie introduce this – this stranger as her fiancé?

Suddenly, Constance felt defeated. She realized she didn't know either one of her daughters. Monique worked for the CIA. Torrie dated someone long enough to fall in love and get engaged. She wondered where she'd been for the last few years.

"Torrie, I'm shocked. You have no right to bring a stranger into this situation. This is too much, and I'm not comfortable with your decision to allow anyone into our personal affairs. – Connor, please don't be offended, but I want you to leave. Torrie doesn't need you, and you are not welcome in our life right now."

Torrie knew her mother enough to know she meant every word and wouldn't back down. How could she diffuse the situation? He was about to pull the gun out of his pocket!

"Connor, honey, please don't be insulted. It was a mistake to introduce you to everyone. Mom is beside herself and doesn't mean to be rude.

"Mom, I don't like your attitude to someone I love. Connor and I will leave now. I'll send Steve to you and say goodbye to Monique. Connor won't do anything to agitate her, I promise. Connor, let's go."

Torrie pulled Connor out the door. She was livid to think that he would hurt her mother. Steve just had to come through for her. He wasn't dumb, and she must have baffled him by her actions. Maybe he would figure out something. If she ever wanted to believe God would take care of things, now was it.

"What happened in there? I can't believe your mom gave me such grief, and then demanded that I leave. Let's get that reverend guy out of Monique's room. This has got to be finished. Right now. I'm ready to just shoot her. I don't think I can hold out hope that anyone will accept me as an innocent person."

Torrie slowly walked towards Monique's room with Connor

close beside her, frantic to come up with a plan. She wasn't afraid for herself, but an innocent bystander might get hurt. When Steve was safely out of the room, she planned to disarm Connor before he hurt Monique.

The guards were still outside the door. They didn't move right away.

"I'm Torrie, Monique's sister, remember? Where is Nurse Chapel? She'll confirm we're authorized to go in."

"Our orders are to keep everyone out until tomorrow." "But the reverend is in there now, and he isn't even related! I only want to tell Monique goodbye. Look, I'll tell the reverend he needs to leave for a minute to attend to my mom. She isn't doing so well right now, and Steve should be with her, not Monique."

Torrie held her breath. She was afraid the guards would still refuse her admittance. If they did, the repercussions could be deadly. She looked around again. Where was everyone? It was as if someone cleared the floor. Could it be? Maybe she wasn't alone in this. She looked at Connor to see how he was. What did she ever see in him? His looks were about all he had.

"I guess that will be okay. I'll get the reverend out first, then you can go in."

The guard opened the door and beckoned to Steve. "Sir, Miss Monique's sister wants to tell her goodbye. She and the guy have to leave."

Steve breathed a quick prayer for courage. The detective laid out a plan which could work, but only if Connor didn't get suspicious. He left the room and gave Torrie a hug with an extra squeeze on her shoulders to convey the message she wasn't alone in this.

"Hello Torrie, how is your mom?"

"I am concerned about her. I think she's finally cracked. She's hateful, and it's not like Mom to be that way with people. Can you go sit with her again? Maybe pray with her?"

Torrie understood Steve's message, which told her they knew. She didn't know how they knew or what the plan was, but at least they knew.

"Connor let's go in now. Remember, don't say anything because I don't want Monique to become agitated."

Steve watched as the two walked into Monique's room. He

couldn't be sure she got the message, but all he could do right then was to go to Constance. The detective told him they had it covered, and the agents said they had it covered. He just hoped they didn't get into a territorial fight and distract themselves from the job at hand, which was to protect Monique. And Torrie, for that matter. She was in as much, or more, danger than Monique. Steve suspected Connor was using her as a shield.

"Close the door – now."

Torrie's heart began to beat faster, one of the precursors to a panic attack. She knew the signs because she succumbed periodically to panic, but this was not one of those times. She had to focus on a plan to keep Connor distracted. She was certain he hadn't thought about a way to cover her and attack Monique at the same time.

Chapter Twenty-Three

"Connor, I'm not sure how you are here in this world and at the same time are in the real world. Are you even real?"

"I'm as real as you are. Why can't you just die?"

"I'm sorry for you, Connor. You don't know all of the help I have."

"Don't be sorry for me! There isn't anyone here to stop me."

I watch his every move and monitor his body language. He's dangerous in this world. Mostly I fear him and what can happen in the real world. Is he bold enough to make another attempt on my life in a secure hospital with people all around?

I see him leap, and I dodge out of his way.

"Dammit, I won't let you be the reason for my family to be hurt!"

He spirals around, and this time I'm not ready. His fist meets my face, and hard.

Connor realized his mistake as soon as Steve left. He couldn't be assured that Torrie would remain quiet and passive. As soon as he eliminated Monique, she would put up a fight and yell.

"Call your mom and tell her to come here. Tell her—tell her Monique might be trying to say something."

"I can't do that. You don't know my mom; she'll ask a nurse and the reverend to come with her. You won't be able to control that many people. Please, just give up. I'm sure the CIA will be able to save your family and make a deal with you. If you continue like this, you and your family will be killed. You don't want that for your daughters."

"You don't understand these people. Why would the CIA be concerned for my welfare, or my family, for that matter? Now, call your mom! Tell her not to bother the nurses. You just want to make sure you didn't hear something important."

"Okay. I will. Calm down. ..."

"Quit telling me to calm down; just make the call."

Torrie hurriedly pulled her phone out of her purse and punched the speed dial.

"See? I'm calling."

"Mom, hello. No, we haven't left the hospital yet. Can you please come to Monique's room? I think maybe she's trying to communicate with us. No, please, I don't want you to bother the nurses. It might just be a figment of my imagination. I haven't been around her, and it might be nothing. Please, just come."

Torrie didn't know if she convinced her mother to come. She hoped Steve had warned everyone already, but her mother sounded too calm to know something terrible was about to happen. Torrie felt isolated.

Constance disconnected the call and looked at Steve and the detectives.

"She wants me to go to Monique's room alone. What should I do, Detective McPherson?"

"We know Connor has a gun, and he's desperate. The agents requested blueprints of the building to locate any vents large enough to send in a sniper. If we can do that, he is pretty much out of luck."

Steve thought about the ramifications if Constance didn't go.

"Detective, if Constance doesn't go, Connor will realize we've figured out his plan. Maybe he knows now. We can assume his actions won't be rational, and I suspect there's more at stake than just his life. If he has a family and they are in danger, he will do anything to keep them safe. He may decide to shoot his way out. Is it possible for the agents to negotiate with him, show him a better alternative?"

Detective McPherson left the room without a word. He had to know how much the CIA knew about this Connor. Whatever Connor was, he was not a professional and didn't have a clue what he was doing, which made the situation extremely volatile.

Eve was used to explaining the actions of her partner.

"Don't mind him, guys. He just realized the CIA agents withheld important information, which makes our job more complicated, and he is on his way to fix it. He'll be back."

Torrie doubted her mother would come. If she read the reverend correctly, Connor's intent was no longer a secret.

"Connor, you know that everyone knows what's going on by now and that you're behind all of this trauma with Monique. My mom isn't going to come. The best way out of this is to negotiate with the agents. It's better for you and for your family. These guys you're mixed up with are not going to spare you or them."

"Shut up, Torrie! Just shut up!"

Connor was confused, desperate, and angry enough to strangle Torrie. All he wanted to do was go back in time to before all of this happened. What if he got rid of Torrie first? He didn't need her anymore. What was one more body? Before Connor changed his mind, he leaped towards Torrie.

Now I'm angry. This jerk will not be the end of me. I kick his legs out from under him and wrestle him to the floor. He throws me onto my back, and I see he intends to stomp on me! I push myself off the ground, swing around, and swiftly punch his stomach. He groans but will recover. Time stops when a horrible thought enters my mind. If Connor is this determined to harm me in this world, what awful plan does he have in the real world? Maybe he's in my hospital room to kill me! A thought slams into my consciousness and terrorizes my soul. Suppose he hurts Mom or Torrie? I dodge another fist and acknowledge I must call for help!

"God. Father God. Help me save my family. I need to wake up, how do I do that?"

My outcry immobilizes Connor. Good. I'm frantic to wake up. I force myself to breathe to stop the thoughts that race through my mind. Connor looks transparent and fades away before my eyes. I sense I'm not alone. Now it's time to go back to the real world to save my family; I attempt to plunge myself out of here. With God's help, I will rescue them. I will open my eyes and do what needs to be done

Chapter Thirty-Four

Torrie didn't have time to prepare for Connor's attack. He knocked her flat on her back. She momentarily blacked out. At the same time, Connor was aware of unusual activity from Monique's hospital bed. He turned and couldn't believe what he saw. Monique rose out of her bed, ready for a fight! But how can that be? He had the presence of mind to remember his gun in the pocket of his coat.

"Stop! Monique, I swear, I'm not afraid to pull the trigger and end you and Torrie."

"Connor, no. Stop! Do you really want to take a life?"

Connor didn't respond. Instead, he took aim, ready to pull the trigger. At that moment, he heard a scream and felt a body hit him hard. The gun discharged.

The detectives and the agents heard the shot and rushed to Monique with McPherson in the lead. Amazed at the sight he beheld, he roared with laughter. Connor was on the floor, immobilized by the two sisters. There wasn't evidence of blood, so he assumed the shot missed the target. They would find it later. Others crowded in to witness what had caused such amusement.

"Here, ladies. Let me take it from here. Shaw! Shaw, do you have your handcuffs? I must have left mine in the patrol car. Well, well, taken down by sisters. One for the books."

Connor knew he was caught, and there was nothing more to be gained by resisting.

"Look, detective, you got me. I'll tell you everything I know, but please, save my family! They're innocent. I'm begging you; my family knows nothing about any of this, and I don't want them to die!"

Agents Todd and Gross heard Connor's plea. They knew he had a family and suspected the terrorists would eventually use them for leverage but chose to leave the family exposed in hopes they could draw out the top dog of these fanatics. Connor was the lowest scum and a means to the end.

Agent Todd asserted his presumed authority.

"On your feet, everyone. Clear out! Detective, take Connor to the conference room."

McPherson looked beyond the gathered bystanders and saw the doctor approach in a dignified doctor move, presumably to check on his patient. He also saw Constance and the reverend come out of the waiting room, hurrying to catch up to the doctor. The detective cleared the spectators and escorted Connor out before the three got there.

The doctor arrived first.

"What has happened to my patient? Get out of the way."

"I'm sure, doctor, you will be pleased. Look for yourself."

What doctor Nevarez witnessed was nothing short of a miracle. Monique stood straight and tall in her hospital gown, arms around her sister. He couldn't believe she was out of her coma. Moreover, he was astounded she was strong enough to stand. How could that be? Weeks of inactivity should have rendered her very weak.

Monique was relieved to see a doctor arrive and took charge of the confusion.

"Please, everyone, move. Give Torrie some room and let the doctor look at her. She hit her head when Connor jumped her and knocked her flat. I think she lost consciousness."

"Torrie! Torrie. What happened? Are you hurt? We heard the shot. I was so—so—Oh, my God! Thank you, Lord! Monique, is that really you? Torrie is that Monique?"

Constance ran to her daughters and took both into her arms. She didn't know whether to laugh or cry, so she did both at the same time. She enveloped her daughters into her hungry arms and held on tight.

Dr. Nevarez took over. Monique must get back in bed until he could determine what had happened. He was also anxious to get Torrie to the Emergency Room to get her head injury evaluated. Gently the doctor coaxed Torrie away from Monique and Constance.

"Nurse Chapel. Candy. I need someone to put Torrie into a wheelchair and get her to the emergency room. I'll be there shortly.

Monique, back in bed. I will order a few tests to confirm you don't have hidden trauma."

The detective remained during the ruckus to make sure the crime scene wasn't disturbed. After the doctor ordered Monique back to bed, he interceded.

"Excuse me, Doctor, this room is a crime scene. If Monique is to get in bed, it will have to be in another room."

"Oh. Sure, of course. Reverend, can you help out and find a nurse? We need a different room for Monique."

Steve did as the doctor asked, then hurried back to the commotion. The safest place to hang out was back in the conference room. He took command and made the decision to herd everyone there.

"Those not involved in hospital routine or police work, please come with me."

Besides the conference room table, there were also comfortable chairs throughout. Constance and Monique sat close to each other. Everyone else scattered to various spots.

"Well, ladies. I dare say we have witnessed a miracle of the utmost proportion! Monique, welcome back. Your mother and sister were concerned it took so long for you to come back to us. The good Lord helped you back at the most opportune time. I'm quite impressed with you."

Monique was confused because this person talked to her like he was a friend. She looked to her mom for an explanation.

"Monique, honey, let me introduce you to this quite extraordinary gentleman. This is Reverend Steve Robinson. He showed up when I was at my lowest, and he has been a such a help."

Monique closely watched Constance's face as she spoke There was an absolute radiance which hadn't been there for years. She glanced in Steve's direction and confirmed his regard for her mom. The tenderness he displayed went far beyond clergy concern. What happened in this world while she was away? She had come back to an entirely different biosphere.

"Then, Reverend, I am eternally grateful for your intervention. Now, I am going to ask you for some help. I need to find the two agents and a cell phone. My boss would like to know that I have come back. Is that something you can do?"

"Sure, right away. But first, may I say a quick prayer?" Monique agreed and bowed her head, still wrapped in her mother's arms.

"Dear Father, our Protector and Savior, thank you for your protection of this family. Thank You, for Monique's miracle and her strength to come to her sister's aid. Thank You, for rescuing Torrie and please protect her from any major trauma because of the bump on her head. And Lord, thank You for this entire family. My life is enriched because of them. I pray for

Connor and his family. Please protect the innocents with Your power. I pray that Connor has enough information so that the agents can bring down these dangerous people. Thank You again and again for Your protection tonight. In Jesus' precious name we pray—amen."

Now, let me go find the agents and a phone for you, Monique.

Chapter Thirty-Five

Both detectives, the police chief, and the two agents surrounded Connor and waited for him to give them information.

"Here are the notes I have. They're not in any order because I tried to make them look like doodles. That's all I can help with. I never saw anyone. I don't even know their real names. I only handled the money. Now, please do something to save my family!"

Agent Todd continued with his superior attitude.

"Hey, don't worry; we've got a plan. Detectives, will you please escort this piece of shit to the patrol car. We'll be down in a few minutes. I plan to keep a security detail on Monique. Just because we have Connor doesn't mean someone else won't try to kill her. We can't allow that to happen."

The Chief saw the indignation in his detectives' faces and intercepted their retorts.

"We'll be happy to escort Connor out if that's what you really want. But don't you think that the people he's mixed up with know by now we have him in custody? I bet they even have a back-up plan. The minute Connor is out in the open, they will attack. Probably taking Connor to jail through the front door isn't the way to go."

Agent Todd didn't like this police person or his suggestions about how to handle Connor, though he had to admit the Chief was right. He didn't care what happened to this sleazebag, but there were national security issues and Connor's family to think about.

"Thank you, Chief. Stanley, find a place to stash Connor for now. Let's update the media with the news a murder took place in this hospital. If the terrorists think Monique is dead, we can hope they release his family on their own. But they are bad people, so we can't rely on their goodwill. We'll dispatch a rescue team to the house.

Connor, tell us again how many you saw, and describe where they stood in respect to your wife and daughters."

"There are uh—four, no, three men, and they have heavy-duty automatic assault rifles. Two men stood on either end of the couch where my wife and daughters sat. The third guy seemed to be in charge. At least he was the only one who talked. He paced the floor, and then went to the family room window to look outside. They weren't amateurs. Oh, and I might mention that they are going to get rid of the guy who tried to get Monique earlier this evening. They don't mess around with screw-ups."

"So why are you still around? You certainly screwed up. There must be some reason they want you alive."

Connor had wondered the same, but figured it came down to one reason only. His checking account had the last installment for payment of the guns. If something happened to him, there would be unfortunate repercussions.

Chapter Thirty-Six

Constance watched her daughter, still in the hospital gown, as she talked to her boss on the phone. She only heard Monique's side of the conversation but was almost sure she could fill in the words from the other end of the phone.

"Robert, stop the drama already. You know I'm the best person for the job—yes, yes, I know I'm supposed to be dead, and I still can be. These jokers don't know what I look like. Besides, I can use a disguise. -- What the doctor thinks is not relevant; he doesn't know what my job is. I've completed my assignments when I was in worse shape than this. – Thank you, Robert! Now get over here so we can plan. The best plan is for you and me to go to Connor's house alone."

"Steve, I think my daughter convinced her boss she's fit enough to go back to work so she can rescue that family."

"Is that wise? I'd better get the doctor. Surely, she can't be serious. After weeks of inactivity, how can she even think she's strong enough to jump into a dangerous situation?"

"No, please don't run to the doctor. It will only create a scene, and in the end, Monique will do what she's trained to do. Don't you see the miracle here? She came out of her coma completely healed. No weakness, no memory loss, no fuzzy thoughts. How did that happen? Maybe she is the only person who can accomplish this mission."

Steve couldn't imagine the courage it took for Constance not to attempt to talk Monique out of her foolish plan. Well, in his eyes, it was foolish.

Monique took the phone back to her mother. She grasped for the accurate words to let her mom know her plan to return to work.

"Mom, that was my boss. His name is Robert. Please, don't go ballistic when I tell you what we're going to do. My boss is on his way to help plan a rescue attempt for Connor's family. This is something I have to do, so please understand. Right now, I want some clothes from somewhere. I also want to talk to the detectives, the two agents, and Connor. I have to get as much information as I can and hope it's enough to uncover the head of this terrorist group. Please don't be upset."

Constance looked at her daughter through tears. She was scared for Monique, but incredibly proud to be her mother.

"Sweetie, I found out in a few short weeks that your accident wasn't an accident, but rather an attempt on your life. Then another effort was made. Then I discover you really work for the CIA and yet another attempt on your life. Torrie was held hostage at gunpoint. You jumped out of your hospital bed after weeks in a coma and rescued your sister. I suspect there is nothing I can do to keep you safe, but it appears you have the skills to be able to save a lot of people. What can I do to change the course you are on? Go, do your duty, and please be safe while you do it."

Constance wiped away her tears and continued.

"Now, let's get down to practical stuff. You said you needed clothes and obviously, you do. If you try to rescue people in that hospital gown, you'll end up in the crazy farm! Torrie has a change of clothes with her. You may have lost some weight, but you two are still almost the same size, and I'm sure she will be happy to let you wear whatever she has. I want to check on your sister anyway and see how she is. I can find out where her overnight bag is and bring you back something to wear."

Constance gave Monique a quick kiss on her cheek and left to find Torrie.

"Well, Monique, it looks like you and your mom have things under control, so I best go home and try to get some rest. Welcome back. You have been sorely missed."

"I owe you a great big thank you. You took care of Mom, and that means the world to me. Go home and rest fast."

Steve left without a goodbye to Constance. This day was filled with more than one person should have to endure. He thought it best to give Constance some space. Now that Monique was awake, his time to minister as a chaplain was about to end. Was it time for him to move on? Yet, this family meant too much for him to do that.

Maybe he should move on, but not out. Steve decided that this Idea was certainly one to communicate to Constance about in the near future.

Chapter Thirty-Seven

Constance was passing the large waiting room when she heard a news break interrupting regular programming, in the early morning hours.

The police have not provided any updates at this time, but the Chief of Police promised more details at the seven o'clock hour this morning. Repeat, there has been a shooting at Mercy Memorial Hospital around two or three this morning. One person was injured, another one was pronounced dead at the scene. A suspect is in custody. Names are being withheld pending notification of next of kin. We will bring you the live update from the Chief at seven this morning.

Constance shivered when she heard the report, even though she knew it was fake. She turned back towards the nurses' station. The ICU was the center of chaos. Police officers attempted to send reporters away, nurses pushed spectators back to where they belonged while other nurses worked to care for the patients. Ridiculous. There were sick people to care for, and these vultures wouldn't leave.

"Officer—officer!"

Constance approached an officer who was fighting to keep the reporters on the elevators, an exercise in futility.

He looked up at her, poised to contest until he recognized her.

"Yes, ma'am. What can I do for you? By the way, I am sorry about your daughter."

"Thank you; you're sweet. But this chaos isn't. Why don't you have officer's downstairs at the entrance to block the reporters before they get in? There are too many places for one to sneak through to the ICU.

"Yes, ma'am, I agree. I radioed the Chief, and he has men in place now. My problem, though, is to get these guys back downstairs diplomatically."

"I can help you there."

Constance had seen Candy walk past the nurses' station into what had been Monique's room.

"Candy, excuse me. May I please ask you for a favor?"

"Why certainly, anything. And Ms. Yorkshire, I'm grateful Monique came back to us!"

"Thank you. It all happened so fast. I'm still reeling. But right now, we have a problem that has to be solved. See that officer by the elevators? He can't get any of the reporters to leave the ICU. It might have something to do with diplomacy. I think he could use your assistance."

Candy looked at the pandemonium around the elevators and smiled.

"I know exactly what to do."

She grabbed a chair and sat it down in the middle of the activity, climbed up and used a voice that belied her size.

"Everyone listen-up! I need your attention now so, quit talking!"

The shocked reporters stopped talking after Candy's announcement. She lowered her voice to give the rest of her instructions.

"I need everyone who does not belong to a patient or part of the ICU staff to leave now. I understand the Chief of police will provide an update later this morning. He is sure to have more information than you can get from ICU. We have patients to care for. Now, scoot. Everyone."

Constance watched the entire scene with amusement. The crowd stood stunned for several seconds until one reporter motioned to his cameraman. They got on one of the open elevators. He held the door, and soon other reporters got in line for one of the two elevators. The process took about ten minutes for everyone who did not belong in the ICU to vacate.

Constance smiled as Candy came back to her.

"I suspected you knew how to get these predators out of here. Thank you. Now I'm off to find Torrie and see how she is."

The emergency room was eerily quiet. Usually, people were lined up to check in, while others waited in every available chair. Perhaps it was the time of night when there was a lull in the action. Maybe emergencies took a break right before sunrise.

"Can I help you?"

Constance jumped.

"Uh, yes, actually, where can I find my daughter, Torrie Yorkshire? I think Dr. Nevarez ordered some tests to check out injuries she may have gotten when she fell."

"Sure, she is in room 12B. I believe the doctor is with her now or still, or again, I'm not sure which."

Constance thanked the young man and went in pursuit of room 12B. She felt like she had walked for miles before she found the room. There were no doors, just curtains, and the curtains around Torrie's bed were closed.

"Excuse me—knock, knock—it's Mom. May I come in?" Dr. Nevarez was the one to respond. He opened the curtain and ushered her into the tiny room.

"Good morning. I'm happy to report that all the tests show there is nothing more traumatic than a knot on your daughter's head and a mild concussion, probably a headache. Nothing that can't be cured with rest.

"Torrie, I order you home to rest. I know you have an important meeting of some kind, and I'm sure it's a life or death matter, but I'm your doctor, and you will not step inside your place of employment today. Not only that, but I also want you to see me Monday morning before I release you to work."

"I'm not happy with this because I do have an important meeting. However, since you elegantly insist, I will stay away from work. Instead of my home, though, I'd rather stay with Mom. I don't want to be alone. Mom, can you handle a roommate? I have enough clothes to spend the weekend."

"Of course. It'll be a treat to have you spend the weekend. Now, about those clothes you brought. Monique wants to borrow one of your outfits. She's part of the team who plans to rescue Connor's family."

Constance braced herself for the reaction she expected, and the two did not disappoint.

"I have not released Monique to leave the hospital"--

"What did Monique think she could do" --

"I must make sure she is completely well" --

"Mom, why didn't you protest and refuse to help her" --

"Hey! Stop it, you two—listen to me. We are on the same page, but this isn't just about us anymore. There is another family in danger and Monique's boss is on his way to work with her to rescue them. I also overheard conversations talking about Connor and his involvement in an arms' deal with ISIS. If the threat is real

117

the possibility of more injuries is in store for us. Do you think for a minute Monique will stay in bed while innocent people are at risk?"

Constance's words sobered doctor and patient.

"Dr. Nevarez, I hate to admit it, but Mom knows what she's talking about. Once Monique's mind is set, we best not argue the point. My suitcase is in the car. I'll get it and take it to her."

"Doctor, thank you for taking such good care of both of my daughters. Torrie, I'll walk with you to the car in case you have a dizzy spell or faint or something."

Chapter Thirty-Eight

Monique and another gentleman were in the conference room when Torrie and Constance returned.

"Good morning. You must be Robert, Monique's boss. I'm mom, my name is Constance. I appreciate the assistance you provided while Monique was in her coma. But I'm not happy about how things turned out. This got way out of hand!"

"Mom..."

"No, wait. Your mother has a right to say what she said. Ms. Yorkshire, you are right. To get security on Monique at the beginning would have been a better choice in certain situations. I made a choice to leave security out of it because I wanted the bad guys to make a move. The agency watched closely, and we were ready to step in. We wanted the entire cell, not just one patsy."

"I don't understand how you could put my daughter in harm's way like that. And it didn't seem like you were ready to step in fast enough. No. Wait. I don't want to hear anymore – Monique, here are your clothes, and here is a hat. Torrie and I will go home now. She plans to spend the weekend with me. I want you to listen to me! I just got you back, and you had better not do anything to change that."

Monique paused in her preparations. She couldn't imagine what her mother had suffered while she was in a coma.

"Mom, I'm so thankful for you. I know I've not told you enough times how much I love you. You are, and I know Torrie will agree, the greatest mom! Now, go home and relax. I'll update you as I can, and don't open your door to anyone until you see who it is. Call 911 if you don't know them.

Monique watched as her mom and Torrie left the hospital.

"You have a brave mother. And sister, for that matter. Now, get dressed.

I'll request some officers to be with Connor. We'll go out through the laundry area in the basement. I came in that way, and I parked my car as close as I could, by the entrance."

Thirty minutes later, Robert and Monique were on the highway to Connor's house. The agents entertained the idea of a helicopter to save time but the downside of that was the noise factor. Since the objective was to surprise the kidnappers, they disregarded the aircraft. Robert instructed Connor to call his house and tell the kidnapers he had completed the assignment. The announcement was an attempt to delay any reckless moves by the terrorists before the family's rescue. The minute Connor's family was safe, the CIA planned to monitor the phone call to the arms dealer. In that manner, the agents planned to gather details of the money-for- weapons exchange. With that foreknowledge, they hoped to capture a significant victory.

Robert glanced in Monique's direction.

"Cat got your tongue?"

"I'm not a talker, and you know it. If you want to know how I am, just ask."

"I'll bite. Monique, how are you?"

"I've spent the last weeks in a strange world. Now I'm back into reality. How would you feel? Things feel kind of surreal, but I'm fit to do my job."

"I never doubted it. I'm glad your sister had that black outfit. It's perfect, although by the time we get there it'll be dawn. The house schematics showed two stories. The best option is to climb to the second floor and surprise them. I had almost decided to use Connor to get into the house."

"That would prove to be a disaster! Robert, the emotional wreck he is, the bad guys would know there was something wrong. Didn't the satellite pictures show a trellis in the back yard? I think it goes up to the middle bedroom. Even if the window is locked, I'm sure you have something to get us in. Plus, it's 5:15 now, and sunrise this morning is 7:12. Traffic is light, so we'll easily make the fifty miles before sunrise."

The two were quiet the rest of the way to prepare themselves mentally for the mission. The closer they got, the more Monique's adrenalin soared.

Her mother and the reverend made a sweet couple. They were in love for sure. Mom had kept her heart and mind in the past for so long. Monique was pleased the chaplain had finally figured how to move her into now.

Her next thought was of Torrie. She'd been older when their dad died and took it much harder. Monique missed her dad, but

Torrie had always been his favorite.

"What!"

Robert's exclamation brought Monique back to the present. Cars surrounded the Wray's house. Three or four vehicles, lights flashing blue and red, belonged to local law enforcement. There were at least three everyday black SUVs, the type provided to federal government officials.

"Oh, no! We're too late!"

Monique craned her neck to take in the entire scene.

"No. No, I don't think so. Look over there. I see two girls and an adult, probably the mother. Now I see three men in handcuffs."

Robert was not happy with what he saw.

"What the hell?"

Monique attempted to reel in his emotions so he wouldn't do something he would regret.

"Well, let's go see what's happened."

The two got out of their car and walked towards the closest official.

"This is a crime scene, go home. There is nothing to see here."

Robert noticed the officer's voice attracted the attention of someone dressed in black with an assault rifle in his hand. He pulled his credentials to eliminate the hazard of mistaken identity.

"We're CIA, here to rescue this family. Someone got here ahead of us, and I want to know who. No one was supposed to know anything about this."

"Sorry, sir, you'll have to take it up with that FBI gentleman over there."

"Monique, do you know anything about the FBI's involvement? How the hell did they get the intel!"

"Come on, Robert. Don't be a dweeb. The family is safe, and that's what we wanted. And remember, I've been out of commission for weeks. How could I know more than you? Let's go talk to the gentleman and find out what happened. I, for one, am curious to find out who told them."

Monique left Robert while he muttered about how unfair life was. She approached the FBI agent and pulled out her credentials.

"Good morning sir. I'm Monique with the CIA. We have Connor in custody. He reported the hostage situation with his family and we're here to rescue them. It appears you got here first. It isn't that I'm not grateful for the assist, but my boss wants to know how the hell you got the intel on this?"

The FBI agent was caught off guard with Monique. She looked like a beautiful, sweet young lady, but her mannerism, although polite, was confident, almost aloof.

"Alright, then, my name is Reed. The FBI monitored chatter about a new ISIS group and an arms exchange that led us to Connor. I have a background in marketing, and since Connor was a team leader, they sent me undercover as a marketing flunky to get close to him. I was able to find important information by being around."

"You mean you spied on Connor? My gosh! I don't believe this. When, I mean, how did you—wait, it doesn't matter now. Just give us a report. And do you have a plan?"

Reed looked intently at Monique. He tried to decide if her question was genuine or facetious.

"Of course, we have a plan. And even though we don't have to give you any information, I can tell you that we are going to take these men to the local FBI office. They might just be hired muscle, but any bit of information can help. I got here just in time to disable the lead guy with one shot. The other two quickly surrendered their guns. It was all over in a minute."

Monique wasn't sure if this FBI agent was insensitive or what. *Over in a minute? Really?*

"Maybe for you. My partner and I will move Connor to the FBI office with the gunmen. Everyone should be put into separate rooms. Then how about we sit down and exchange information? You agree, Robert?"

Robert, who knew better than to disagree with Monique, had heard the last of the exchange between the two. He didn't understand how she could be cordial to him, but if he did not want to be subjected to the wrath of Monique, he had to agree.

"Agreed, now let's get out of here and get back to the city. We have a scene to clean up."

Chapter Thirty-Nine

Torrie woke with a start confused, then remembered she was at her mom's house spending the weekend. Memories kept coming. This is Friday. She wasn't at the meeting, and neither was Connor. The boss doesn't know anything. The light streamed in through the window, so Torrie knew it was late. She jumped up, put on her robe, and hurried to the kitchen where she knew her mom would be. There she was, sitting peacefully at the kitchen table with a cup of coffee.

"Mom! Why didn't you wake me? I needed to call the office, and there is this meeting I am missing or missed—that is if I even have a job. This is one of the biggest clients we have ever had, and if they are lost—well, then my career is over!"

"Please calm down. You left your phone out, so I looked up your office number and called in for you. I'm afraid I told them generally what happened and explained you won't be back for a few days. Your boss understands and said your team was prepped and had it all together. He was confident the presentation would go well. By the way, he gave you a nice compliment. He said it was a genius plan to allow your team to be part of the presentation. I'm surprised at that, myself. You have never trusted anything of importance to anyone."

"I know. I've amazed myself more than once these last few days. Thank you, Mom. You've always known how to take care of us."

Torrie went for a cup of coffee and joined Constance.

"Talk about surprises, are you and the reverend seeing each other on a social basis now?"

"As a matter of fact, Steve and I had a conversation about our relationship just this morning."

"And what did you decide?"

"We decided we have feelings for each other, although it's possible our feelings are strictly because of everything that's happened. In the end, we decided to pursue social interaction ..."

"Oh, my gosh, Mom! Social interaction? Really? I say just do it, date, have fun, laugh, talk."

Constance thought about how her statement sounded and chuckled.

"If I had said that to Steve, he would have laughed and told me it struck his funny bone! He is fun, and I have a good time with him. I can't believe I'm thinking about dating at my age. Oh, by the way, I invited him to dinner on Sunday after church. It would be nice if you and Monique can join us.

"Sure, we all have to eat, and I will still be here."

"You don't hide your feelings about him, but do you think you can try to be less obnoxious?"

"Yeah, you're right. I'm not sure what that is all about. But you will be pleased to know I've changed my mind about, uh, about Steve. Are we going to go to church with him?"

Constance was stunned, almost speechless.

"Not this time, maybe another time, unless you want to go."

"No, not really, just wondered. Time for me to take a shower. After that, I don't know, maybe catch up with you."

Constance wondered about this new Torrie. The bump on her head perhaps knocked something loose, or the trauma of the evening, or rather this morning gave her a new perspective on life. She liked this new Torrie and hoped it lasted. Meanwhile, she had to catch up on her laundry.

Chapter Forty

Robert and Monique made it back to the hospital faster than they had anticipated. Neither one commented on their thoughts about the FBI rescue because of their different views of the situation. Besides, Monique had gotten used to a quiet world while she was in her coma. She couldn't believe how real it had seemed to her, so real that this world felt like the fantasy. But not a fantasy of her own creation. There were more fun scenarios she could make up.

They arrived in the room where Connor and his guards temporarily resided.

"Okay, guys, let's move out. We need..."

"My family! Is my family safe? Did you—were you able to save them?"

"Of course, we saved them, and the three gunmen are on their way to the local FBI office. The same place you're headed."

Robert looked at the two officers.

"I want both of you to walk on either side of Connor. I will walk in front, and Monique will walk behind. Keep vigilant and move as quickly as you can. The car is bulletproof, so once we get in, we'll be relatively safe."

The five left the conference room and those who guarded Connor continuously looked for suspicious activity. The ICU was quiet with everyone occupied per their job descriptions. Robert made sure no one got on the service elevator with the small parade.

At the basement level was the laundry equipment which made the atmosphere muggy. Robert instructed the guards to take a quick look around and make sure there wasn't anyone who looked suspicious. Three minutes later, the two reported an all-clear and took up their positions. Robert and Monique both knew the most vulnerable time was on the way to the car. It was right outside the door but still a few feet away. A good sniper could take someone out in those few feet.

"Stop here until I open the door to the car. As soon as I do, you move. Monique, you have point from now until we get Connor into the car."

Robert opened the door and scanned the perimeter to spot places a sniper might be positioned. Unfortunately, he didn't have x-ray vision. A shooter could have staked out in any one of the multiple vacant buildings.

He took a deep breath and one step, then two, and another.

"So far, so good …"

He spoke too soon. A shot fired, and Robert dropped. Monique moved in his direction as soon as he fell, but remembered her responsibility to protect Connor, the bad guy. She beckoned to one of the officers.

"Take him back to the elevators and stand ready to take him up. And you, get over here by the door. I want you to cover me while I get Robert."

The officers split up as instructed. Monique went to the edge of the exit, her 9mm Lugar ready to fire.

"I'll fire randomly and dash to the car. You stay here, take a position, and continue to fire until I'm safe. Ready …"

She fired her rounds and rushed out. The officer fired accordingly, but what troubled her were the shots coming from an undisclosed location. It could only be the sniper. Fortunately, she had made it safely behind the car door which protected her from a bullet. *The sniper must not be up high, or I would be down.* After the last shot, it was quiet. Maybe the shooter fled since he couldn't get to his target. She made it to Robert and pulled him to a sitting position behind the car door. He regained consciousness with a moan.

"Robert?"

He groaned. At least he was alive.

"Robert, listen to me. Help me take your jacket off. I want to find where all this blood is coming from."

Monique talked as she deftly took off his jacket and shirt to survey the bullet entry point.

"Connor? Where's the prisoner?"

Robert barely got the words out between moans.

"An officer is taking Connor back to the conference room, and I told the other one to wait on the sidelines to help us get back in. You took a bullet in your shoulder, and you've lost quite a lot of blood already. I want to use your shirt to plug the wound."

"Ouch! You hurt me!"

"You sound like you've never been shot before—We have to get in, can you walk?"

"In a minute. I need to catch my breath."

"We can't wait long. You're losing too much blood and need to get to the emergency room right away. Plus, I want to check on Connor because I'm sure he was the intended target."

"Then why didn't he wait for Connor to come out?"

"Point taken. Okay, good as it's gonna' get."

"Let's go. Officer, we're coming in!"

The officer shot at random points until the two agents made it back. No more shots from the sniper confirmed he had left the premises. They went to the elevators and pushed the button. Monique gasped at what she saw and hit the emergency stop button. She looked at Robert in disbelief. Connor sprawled out on the elevator floor, looking at them through lifeless eyes. His neck appeared to be broken.

"The sniper was a decoy. I thought we had all the officers screened. How did this happen?"

Robert panted to the terrified officer.

"What do you know about this? He was your partner! How could you let this happen?"

"Sir—I—uh—he—he ..."

"Robert! Cut him some slack! He's as clueless as we are, and he isn't the bad guy. If he were, we'd be dead. Now calm down. You'll speed up the blood loss."

She looked at the shaken young man.

"What's your name?"

"Shanks, Officer Shanks. My partner called in sick this morning and Officer Bryant is this other guy. I didn't know him, but he has been on the force for several years. I can't believe he did this."

Monique reviewed the situation and barked out instructions.

"Send someone to your partner's place. I bet he won't be alive. First, though, call the Chief and request Detectives McPherson and Shaw to get down here as fast as they can. Don't leave this place until they get here—and don't let anyone get close. We'll take the stairs—uh, I'll take the stairs and shut down the elevators from up there."

Robert looked pale and sweaty. Monique recognized shock.

"Robert, stay with Officer Shanks, and be nice!"

She arrived at the ICU wing and heard the siren's approach.

"Nurse, did you see an officer come up with the prisoner?"

"I didn't see the prisoner, but I saw an officer head towards the conference room."

"Where did he go after that?"

"He's still there as far I know. I didn't see anyone leave."

Monique thanked the nurse and rushed into the conference room. Sure enough, there was the other officer—Officer Bryant laid out flat, and it appeared his neck was also broken. Bodies piled up faster than Monique could process. She had to get Robert to the ER, and she wanted to get to the FBI headquarters soon.

"Hey, you!"

Monique motioned for a maintenance person.

"Stay here in front of this door. Don't go in and keep everyone else out. Don't leave until the detective gets here, understand?"

"Sure, Okay."

On her way back to the elevators, she noticed an unattended wheelchair and confiscated it to make it easier to get Robert to the ER. Monique took the elevator back down to the laundry department. Robert and Officer Shanks still guarded the second elevator where Connor's body was found.

"Hey, you two. Officer Bryant wasn't a traitor. He's in the conference room dead. Looks like his neck was broken too."

She looked at Robert, slumped over and only semi-conscious.

"I can't wait for the detectives. I have to get Robert to the ER. He's lost too much blood."

Monique moved the wheelchair close to her boss.

"Robert, you have to help me get you up! Stay with me now, come on."

McPherson and Shaw arrived just as Monique had Robert in the wheelchair.

"Thank you for coming. We have quite a mess here. Connor is over there in the elevator, and the second officer assigned to protect him is upstairs in the ICU conference room, also dead."

Detective McPherson was grim as he acknowledged what he heard and reciprocated with bad news of his own.

"It gets worse. Shank's partner was found in his apartment shot once through the head. The window where he fell was broken, so I think it was a sniper who took him out. The creeps got rid of him as soon as they didn't need him anymore."

Monique was not happy with the news.

"I was afraid of that. This is ugly. I'll leave these two crime scenes to you. Robert took a bullet in his shoulder and has lost too much blood. Then I'm going to go to the FBI headquarters to find out what they know."

McPherson usually didn't care to take orders from CIA or FBI agents, but Monique was different. She treated the detectives as comrades, not subordinates.

"We got it covered! Eve, go to the conference room and wait for the CSI agents. I'll call and ask for two investigative teams."

Monique didn't waste any more time at the scene. She could tell Robert was in a lot of pain because he didn't protest the wheelchair. After he was safely in the hands of the trauma team, she was on her way to the FBI office. Two news vans pulled into the parking lot. She decided to call her mom and Torrie on her way so they wouldn't find out about the attack from the news.

Chapter Forty-One

"No, you don't have to give me details, just go and be safe."

Constance breathed a sigh of relief. Torrie was still in her room, so she didn't hear the news report. One of the victims had to be Connor. Regardless of how she felt about him, she was sure to be upset.

Back in the living room, Constance realized it was too late to save Torrie from the shock. Her daughter stood in front of the TV; her face frozen in horror as she listened to the update.

"Mom—did you see this? This is—where is Monique?"

"Honey, Monique just called, and she's safe. The agent who was shot was her boss. He's alive but lost a lot of blood."

Just then, the telephone rang, and Constance hurried to answer it. She wasn't keen on leaving the room while Torrie was processing the report. It wouldn't take her too long to realize Connor was one of the victims. Constance concluded her phone conversation and went back to Torrie.

"But Mom, there are three bodies! Oh, my gosh, you don't think—could one of them be—Mom—Connor? Is Connor one of the victims?

"I'm so sorry, honey. Yes, Connor was one of them."

Constance went to her daughter and sat with her on the sofa.

"That was Steve on the phone. He's on his way over."

Torrie didn't think Steve could be much of a comfort to her, but her mother would benefit from his visit. She'd just stay in her room, and out of the way.

Chapter Forty-Two

Monique had just cleared the security gate at the FBI office. A guard took extra precautions because of the heightened security, undoubtedly because someone tried to get to the three gunmen. The guard directed her to a parking spot, and before she got further than the door, another guard stopped her. Once again, she pulled out her credentials and explained why she was there.

"Ask that guy over there. He'll confirm I'm legitimate."

"Hey, Benny! She's good. She's with me. Just give her the visitor badge. We have to get to a meeting."

Reed collected Monique, and they made their way down the winding halls to a conference room with heavy double doors.

"Guys look who I found. I rescued agent Monique from the hands of our security staff. Monique, meet my boss, Jack Richards and my partner, Jennie Rogers. And here, this is the second team on the case, Barbara Anderson and Craig Stevens. Help yourself to some food and drink.

Monique acknowledged the introductions and gratefully got some coffee. She didn't think it was wise to eat anything yet since she hadn't eaten since the accident.

Reed began getting everyone's attention.

"Let's get started. This situation is out of control, and the body count continues."

He looked directly at Monique.

I understand part of the reason for your attack was the information you got from Connor?"

She thought it strange that Reed took charge even though he introduced someone else as his boss.

"Yes. I took pictures of everything in Connor's safe, which included all of his hand-written notes and doodles. I stored the camera in an unregistered safe deposit box until I could get with my boss to decipher the information. Unfortunately, the accident delayed our investigation. No one knew I had the material except Connor and whoever he worked for. I stopped by the bank to pick it up on my way here. Can we load this chip into a computer and project it so everyone can see the slides?"

Reed delegated the task.

"Jennie, you're the computer expert. Get the slides ready so we can look at them. While she does that, Craig, tell Monique about what happened while transporting the terrorists here."

"Sure. Be happy to. Shortly after you left, Barbara and I loaded the guys and headed to the FBI office, which is about a two-hour drive. Halfway back, I became suspicious of a car that had been following us, and it suddenly came at us faster. I told Barbara to get ready for trouble and looked for a turnoff or a place to hide. We went around a curve which blocked our view of them, and visa-versa. There was a dirt road that went into some trees, so I took it, and made a U-turn to get ready for a fast escape.

"We saw the car speed by, and I hoped they wouldn't see us. No such luck. The car screeched to a stop and turned around to come back to us. I nosed up, and as soon as the driver slowed down to make the turn, I stomped on the gas aiming for the side of the car. We collided before he could react, and the car rolled into and over the guardrail, down the hill and into a tree about fifteen feet down. I tried to get to them to check for survivors, but the car exploded before I got there. I'm sure no one lived. We didn't see anyone leave the car before the fireworks. Barbara called for a clean-up crew. As soon as they sift through the wreckage, we can get confirmation on possible survivors. We didn't waste any time getting here. The guys are in separate rooms right now. We saw the report about the shootings at the hospital and heard about your boss, Monique. I'm sorry."

"Thank you, he lost a lot of blood, but I'm not sure how bad his injuries are. – That's quite a story."

Reed agreed and directed the agents back to Jennie and the slides.

"Thank you for your report, Carl. And now it looks like Jennie has the computer ready. Don't start just yet though. I want to bring Monique up to date on our investigation. When we were at Connor's house, she asked how we happened to be involved."

"That would be great. I am interested to know."

"It looks like we picked up on this possible threat at about the same time. I'm just surprised we didn't trip over each other sooner than we did. We were able to confirm the existence of a new ISIS cell with homegrown terrorists. Though the "army", as they call themselves are homegrown, their leadership team appears to be wholly corporate and out of the states. The target is sure to be a populated area in the United States, but we haven't been able to confirm anything more specific. The weapons exchange was planned for next week, but I don't think that is going to happen now, since we've gotten involved."

Monique listened attentively to Reed's narrative.

"Do you have files on the information you pulled from the internet? I'm somewhat of an analyst myself, and I would like to look at it."

"Of course. We're happy to have another set of eyes. I'll get the data for you when we've finished with your slides. Can you please comment on the slides as Jennie takes us through them?"

"Sure, as long as you realize there are scribbles that I may need help with."

"Of course, that's a given. Jennie, let's go."

Jennie flashed the first slide and Monique began her monolog.

"I took this first slide, which is the outside of the safe, and the next one of everything inside before anything was disturbed for documentation purposes. The first item you see out of the safe is the Smith and Wesson 22 revolver Connor used at the hospital. This is a small notebook. Even though it looked like just scribbles, I took a picture of each page to analyze."

Monique talked about the pages and the data on the pages as Jennie moved from image to image.

"These look like initials of people or contacts and if I took a guess at the words beside the initials, I would say they are descriptive words explaining how they kill, or how they have killed.

RGH – Cut
TST – Hammer
GBW – MD
FGH – Bang
SHB – Rope

"I don't know how we are going to be able to identify the people, but if we can, I'm sure the person who attempted the attacks on my life will be recorded here.

"The next page looks like notes taken during a conversation.

4-inst
50-gn

4-m

4x100K

Hq-PF-BZ-AF

"The 4x100K obviously refers to money, most likely the negotiated price of the guns. Based on that, the 4-inst has to represent installments. They paid in four installments. If we follow the same thought process, we can assume that 50-gn is the number of weapons. Do you suppose that 4-m could indicate the four installments were paid a month apart?"

Monique looked around the room and saw the agents nod in agreement.

"The last line is kind of a puzzle. Hq could mean headquarters and the initials are locations, but how can headquarters be in three locations?"

Jack had come to the same conclusions that Monique had. The shorthand wasn't complicated.

"My question is which headquarters? The arms people or the leaders of the army, or both? The PF has to be Paris, France, and AF is likely Afghanistan. But BZ?"

Jennie intently inspected each image and voiced her conclusions.

"The only thing that comes to my mind is Brazil. Logically then, Brazil is where the weapons are, Afghanistan is the location of the army at this time, and Pairs, France is the location of the leader of the group, which brings us to the next page.

Jennie continued.

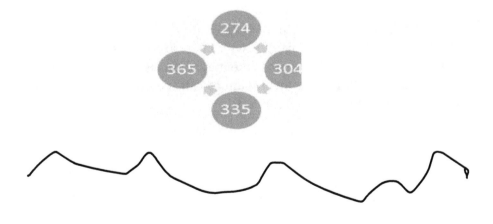

"Jack, can you load the numbers in your program and maybe get some suggestions? Not sure about the line's underneath. They could really just be doodles, but then again, the lines could mean something."

Monique took over from Jennie on the next image.

"I suspect these numbers reference something about shipping or perhaps a to-and-from destination schedule.

GS1LA -20.2976 – XML -GLN - SSCCLO -40.2958 - 25 – GIAI 05423-020274-02200

"This last picture is the phone Connor kept in the safe. My guess is it's a non-registered burner phone. I took a picture of the serial number to see if we can trace any of the calls to a location."

No one spoke a word when Jennie ended the slide show. Each agent was evaluating and drawing their own conclusions. Monique wasn't comfortable with extended silence with a room full of people. She broke the silence.

"Reed, what's next?"

"Thank you, Monique. Let's all take a ten-minute break. When we come back, you can review the documentation we pulled from the internet. How are you holding up? I can't believe that you have been out of your coma for less than a day and look at everything you've been through already."

Reed closely observed Monique. He wanted to make sure her body language matched her words. In his estimation, this woman was unique.

"To tell you the truth, I'm having a hard time with that myself. I think when this is all over, I will take some time to process everything. I feel kind of weird, like maybe this is a dream. If it is, I hope it ends well. Excuse me; I want to call the hospital and check on Robert. See you back here in ten."

Chapter Forty-Three

"Mom, I think the reverend is here!"

Torrie shouted from the bedroom in case her mom didn't hear the doorbell. The chaplain was probably an okay person, but she wasn't ready to fully embrace him. She certainly wasn't anxious to answer the door. Seconds later, the sounds of her mom's greeting came through the walls.

"Thank you so much for coming by. This entire situation gets worse by the minute. Please come in. I made a pot of coffee, and I don't mean to brag, but I'm sure it is better than what you've had at the hospital. Have a seat; I'll bring the pot, and I also have some cookies."

Constance set the tray down when she spotted Torrie in the doorway of the living room.

"Oh, hi, sweetie, come sit down with us and have a snack."

"I think I will. Thank you."

Each adult grabbed a cookie, took their places, and sipped on the coffee.

"Wow, this is the best coffee I think I have ever tasted, at least since I was forced back into bachelorhood."

Torrie enjoyed the refreshments and was thankful Steve didn't ask to pray. She wasn't comfortable when he prayed.

Steve continued with the compliments.

"Yummy, wonderful cookies—I think I'll take another one.

Steve downed the second cookie as fast as he did the first one. After the last swallow, he was ready for serious conversation.

"Have you heard any more about what is going on?"

Constance proceeded with an update.

"I'm sure you heard the news about the shootings and deaths. They haven't released the names of the victims. Thank goodness, Monique called to let me know she was okay. Sadly, Connor was one of the victims. Monique wasn't injured, but her boss was shot in the shoulder. He lost a lot of blood, so she took him to the emergency room right away. Once he was in good hands, she went straight to the FBI headquarters. I haven't heard anything since then."

Steve looked at Torrie.

"I am sorry about Connor. I know what he was and what he did, but regardless, you worked with him for a long time. His death, I'm sure, is not easy on you. Did you know his family?"

"Thank you, rev—uh, Steve. He was my assistant, and I can't believe he blindsided me. He betrayed me in the worst way. When he came to the door—was it only last night? I was caught off guard, and no, I never met his family."

Torrie appreciated the fact that Steve didn't automatically assume they were involved in an affair. She was interested in learning about his perception of the latest.

"I've witnessed miracle after miracle during the short time I've been around your family. Monique said something about strange conversations with strange people while she was in her coma. I would love an opportunity to talk with her about it. And to think, she came out of her coma with no residual after-effects. What a feat!"

Torrie listened with interest and deliberated on what Steve would say if he heard what happened to her. She guessed God could work miracles with her, too, but she hesitated to believe it. She chalked it up to coincidence and stress.

"… and Torrie, you are equally impressive with what you went through and how you handled it. I tell you what, Constance, she came into the room, hugged me, called me Steve, and acted like we were the best of friends. I was stunned but decided something was wrong and played along. As soon as I had a minute, I went to Detective McPherson and let him know about my suspicions. When he heard Connor's name, a light bulb seemed to have switched on, and he explained how he found a cufflink engraved with 'C' in front of Monique's apartment."

"Uh, reverend, can I—I mean, I have, well—Mom, I want to—can I tell you about what happened when Connor came to my door?"

"Of course, sweetheart, Steve and I would love to hear what happened. Before you do, though, I agree with Steve; you are amazing."

"Thanks, I mainly—well, it was scary, and I don't understand how I managed."

Torrie took a deep breath and continued.

"After Mom called, I packed and was about to walk out the door when my doorbell rang. I looked out the window before I opened the door and there was Connor. He looked awful, so I thought something terrible had happened to his family. I didn't see the gun until after I invited him in. He said he wanted me to help him with something. The entire situation felt dreamlike. I asked what kind of help. He didn't raise his voice or even act like it was anything more than asking for a drink of water. He said, 'kill your sister.' When I heard that, I sort of went into auto-drive."

Constance couldn't help but interrupt.

"How horrible for you! I'm surprised you didn't faint."

"I probably would have fallen down; actually, I did fall down, but I was in front of the couch. After the initial shock, I zoned out and just went with instinct. Anyway, we got in the car. My first thought was to do something to flag a police car, but Connor had already thought about that. He told me not to do anything stupid or he would start shooting. The way he looked and acted, I believed him.

"We hadn't driven but a mile or two when we saw flashing lights. I pulled over to let them pass, but the police car pulled in behind us. I was terrified and told Connor I didn't do anything wrong. The police officer took my driver's license and insurance and walked away without a word. He came back and told me my left taillight was out and I should get it fixed right away."

Torrie looked at Steve and her mom.

"That—well—it was strange to be pulled over for a burned-out taillight because I had just replaced it the day before. The really weird thing though is that for some unexplained reason I had the urge to talk to the officer like, well, darn it, Mom, you know I don't small talk, but it was like a floodgate opened. I started to say anything that came to mind, and then I mentioned we were going to the hospital to see you and Monique. Well, he said they knew the story and offered to escort us with lights to get us there faster. All the while, Connor sat there with a gun on me. I think they helped keep me safe. Connor was about to lose it. But—but don't you think it was just a coincidence?"

Steve and Constance sat mesmerized by the events. Steve was first to respond.

"I agree. The police for sure kept you safe."

Constance quickly took over because she wasn't sure what Steve would say, and Torrie was still not comfortable with him.

"You called what happened a coincidence, but you hesitated. What do you think?"

"Oh, I don't know. I think – nothing—and then I think about how Monique woke up and all the other stuff that has happened. To tell you the truth, there's just been too much happen, and I am confused. This bump on my head has me all mixed up. Please excuse me. I'm going back to my bedroom. Mom, the cookies are good."

Then she was gone.

"So, what do you think? She's your daughter. Does she have a relationship with the Lord?"

"She may be my daughter, but that doesn't necessarily mean I know her. I've felt for some time now that she's wrestled internally about something. As far as I know, she has never given her life to the Lord, though we've been in church most of the girl's growing up years. When Torrie left home, she also left the church behind. Monique, on the other hand—I'm not sure when it happened, but she accepted Him with an unmovable faith."

"I kind of got the same impression. Torrie is riding the fence right now not ready to take any action. I see the Holy Spirit at work, though. Given time, it'll happen."

Steve looked at his watch.

"Not to change the subject, but it's time for the news. Can we turn on the TV for an update? Then I'm going to have to leave for now. There are a couple of patients I want to see."

Constance had the news on in a flash and caught a reporter in mid-sentence.

"... confirmed dead. Two of the fallen were police officers killed in the line of duty trying to protect a witness. The third was Connor Wray. It is unclear as to what his part was in the confrontation, but he leaves behind a wife and two daughters. The officers' identities have not been released at this hour."

All of this began when someone attempted to kill one of the patients at Mercy Memorial Hospital. The patient—whose identity has also been withheld, was in a coma at the time. The coma was a result of what was first listed as an accident but was later changed to 'suspicious.' The chief of police made a statement earlier today and provided generalities but has been quiet since then. We will keep you updated as we get word on this unfolding story."

Constance was tired of the news. Monique was safe and nothing else mattered. She suspected they had far more information than the media at this point because, with the CIA and FBI involved, any information would be slow getting to the public.

"So, my dear, on that note, I'll take my leave."

Steve gallantly bowed to Constance and headed for the door.

"I'm glad you came by. Don't forget about Sunday dinner. Torrie and Monique will be here."

"Oh, I won't forget. If your coffee and cookies are any indication of what's to come, my mouth is already watering! By the way, do you want to go to church with me on Sunday? I could come and pick you up about 10:15. Services start at 10:45. We generally are out by noon. I have to respect Sunday lunchtime at all costs."

Constance smiled at Steve's last remark.

"You know, of all people, Torrie asked me if we were invited to go with you Sunday. I told her not this Sunday, but maybe next week. We haven't gone to church for years. This Sunday, I'll listen to a sermon on the radio while I cook to impress!"

Constance walked Steve to the door and watched as he got into his car. He gave a wave as he took off towards the hospital, and then he was gone. She realized she loved this amazing man who had come into her life.

Chapter Forty-Four

The agents were back from their break.

"Jack, did your computer spit out anything useful?"

"It sure did. The numbers are likely Julian calendar dates. 274 for September; 304 for October; 335 for November and 365 for December. We can then assume that the last installment was deposited into Connor's checking account. Just so you know, Monique, we've monitored Connor's checking account and discovered large amounts of money deposited one day, and the next day was transferred to an offshore bank account. Right now, there is $100,000 in his bank account. As soon as possible, we will confiscate it, but first we have to debrief Connor's wife about his secret life."

Reed continued.

"Thanks. Now, consider Connor and what we know so far. He wasn't' the most inventive person on the planet, which means these codes can't be too complicated. Any ideas?"

Barbara began.

"I've studied those lines underneath the Julian dates. I think they look like waves; don't you think? Which could mean some of the other numbers are codes for ships or cargo holds—something like that."

Jennie went back to the slides with lines. Everyone stared at them for a moment.

"By Jove, Barbara, I think you may be onto something."

Reed was excited.

"So, the lines are waves and based on that—Jennie, take us back to the other numbers on the slide."

GS1LA -20.2976 – XML -GLN - SSCCLO -40.2958 - 25 – GIAI 05423-020274-02200

"Okay, based on what we have so far, this information may be tied to the gun shipment which will be coming from—where did we say?"

"Brazil."

"Right, Brazil. Somewhere in these numbers is perhaps the location in Brazil. If those numbers are indeed the Julian calendar, then this is the month for the shipment. Does anyone detect a location?"

Monique spotted the probability nestled between the letters.

"The location is latitude -20.2976 degrees south and longitude -40.2958 degrees west. The letters before and after might have been used to camouflage the numbers. More likely, though, they have to do with the ship's cargo, maybe the specific ship. If I'm correct about the latitude and longitude, the numbers is where the guns cam from. Can someone please look up the location?"

Jack was right there with Monique.

"Got it. It is a place in Brazil, Vitoria Espirito Santo."

Barbara found the location but had a different thought.

"Won't all of this information be unlikely if the last installment for the guns hasn't been paid? Whoever was supposed to take possession of the guns won't want them now that the shipment has been compromised."

Jack monitored the agents during their conversation. The teamwork pleased him.

"Great observation, Barbara. Therefore, we must approach this from the backside instead of the front. Figure out where the final location is meant to be. We know it's in the United States and based on the chatter we've seen and the fact this is a new terrorist group, the target is going to be noticeable and big."

Craig had been quiet until now.

"Jack, I don't think fifty automatic assault rifles fit the scenario you just described."

"And you would be correct. We want to search for any reports of missing C-4 explosives from any base, or even the manufacturer."

Reed was quick to follow Jack's rationale.

"So, you think the terrorists used the guns as a decoy to take our attention off the target. We'd be focused on a plan to track and intercept a load of guns and overlook a small stolen shipment of C-4. It doesn't take much of that stuff to make an impact."

The agents waited as Jack searched his computer for missing explosives.

"Okay—here we go. There was a truck taking a small shipment of C-4 to a construction site. The truck driver made a pit stop. When he got back, his truck was gone. The driver first reported only the truck was taken, but later on he admitted the cargo was explosives."

Monique's mind clicked through possible targets.

"Where was the truck hijacked, and which intended construction site?"

Jack continued getting facts from the article.

"The truck was in Missouri and headed toward Boulder Colorado, where the C-4 was intended to implode an old building in the downtown area."

Jennie asked the obvious question.

"Do you think the target might be close to Boulder?"

Reed interjected.

"Not necessarily, but at least we have a place to start."

Jack took over the team.

"This is how we'll proceed. First, interrogate the three suspects in custody. It's unlikely the autopsies of the two police officers and Connor will reveal anything helpful, so unless ballistics comes up with a nugget, forensic reports are pretty much a dead end. So – Reed, Craig, and Barbara, each of you take a gunman and get what you can. I'll monitor the interrogations and, if necessary, step in to provide some muscle. Jennie, search all sites for anything between Missouri and Colorado as a potential target for the terrorists. Monique, I have the data we've gathered. I want you to go through everything. Maybe you will identify something we haven't. Instinct suggests the attack may be directed to a financial fallout of some sort rather than pure destruction. If we can find a money trail, we may find the source. I want you to use my office, you'll be more comfortable. Ready, team—let's go!"

Jack scooped up his papers and computer and watched everyone file out to their assigned duties. He and Monique started toward his office.

"How is Robert?"

"He lost enough blood that they had to give him some. The bullet caused quite a bit of damage and even chipped his shoulder blade. They had him in surgery to assess and repair the damage. The injuries are painful."

"This has been quite a day for you—so maybe you should go home for the evening and start fresh tomorrow."

143

"I don't have a home right now, though I'm sure my mom expects me to stay with her. Before I call it a day, I want to take a first look at the data. We're short on time right now."

"Fair enough, my office is this way."

Jack made sure Monique was settled in his office before he went to Jennie's workstation.

"Jennie, I want to question the truck driver. Why don't you make arrangements to get him here and then continue with your research for possible targets?"

"Be happy to. I'll let you know when the driver arrives. I'm sure you want to be the one to question him."

"You know me so well! I'll check on the progress of the interrogations."

Jack went into the monitoring room and listened to the suspect Reed was questioning. Reed leaned back in his chair with his feet on the table, relaxed and bored. It was a tactic he used to his advantage. Once the suspect was at ease, Reed attacked with a plan to startle the suspect enough to give up a worthwhile tidbit.

Meanwhile, Monique sat at Jack's desk and sifted through all the data Jack had given her. She felt overwhelmed and forced herself to relax. If she stayed this tense, she would never see anything hidden. Truth be told, Monique was tired, and the best thing for her to do would be to go home and get some rest. Jack was right. She woke up from a coma and jumped right back into the game without a pause. What Jack didn't realize was her desire not to rest or sleep. She feared she wouldn't wake up. Come on, Monique, focus on the task at hand. Hmm, this is interesting.

She understood why Jack thought this had more to do with financial disaster than physical destruction. Some company in Paris, France had loaded an ad, *"Looking for a few top-notch, innovative people willing to take risks and do what is necessary to get the job done"*.

The advertisement was placed on an obscure site few knew about except those who frequented the dark web. Covert agencies left these sites alone and regularly monitored them for something such as this. The ad went on to promise outstanding paychecks for those who succeeded. There was a noteworthy email address listed for interested parties to respond to. The email address had .org which Is typically reserved for government agencies. There was a note in the report that stated an FBI agent had answered with the intent to make contact with the person or persons who placed the add, but the email was rejected from the source.

The next set of data she reviewed was from an expert hacker who infiltrated the email account and monitored responses. There were several. Monique took the time to read each one without analyzing content. She looked deeper on the second read. Interesting. It looked like all the responses were from either Brazil or Afghanistan. The site appeared to have been newly created just for this mission, and only the two countries could have access. But if that were the case, how did Connor become involved?

She continued to read through the information until her head hurt. She looked out in the hallway. Most of the lights were off, which suggested the hour was late.

I wonder if everyone went home. Why didn't anyone say good-bye? Strange. Monique got up from the desk and wandered out into the hallway, stretching as she went. No one was around. Why? Jack wouldn't leave her alone. She strained to hear something, anything—nothing but silence. She felt panic overtake her. Maybe she should call 911 or her mom. A horrible thought hit her—what if this day never happened?

Chapter Forty-Five

"Hello, Monique. I bet you are surprised to see me again."

"No! This isn't real! I woke up. I know I woke up. I talked to everyone. You shouldn't be here. I don't need you to announce anything. You are not real; you are not real; I will open my eyes, and you will be gone!"

"Great mantra, but sorry, it won't work. To set your mind at ease, you did wake up. And to answer the question you most want answered at this time; no, you are not back in a coma. You fell asleep, and I'm merely here to assist. Jack is correct to find the money trail and follow it. The three guys in custody don't have a clue about anything. Your analysis is correct that the website was only available in those two countries."

"You seem to know all about this. Why don't you tell me the end of the story so I can put this chapter behind me? I feel crazy, and my reality is skewed. Gabriel, this isn't fair!"

"I know. You will get your equilibrium back. That's a promise from the Heavenly Father. He'll help you solve this in time to save lives and heartache, but He intends for you to utilize the great analytical mind He gave you. It's late; wake up and go home to your mom's; you need some rest."

"Monique, Monique—wake up."

Jack came into his office and saw Monique asleep among the papers.

"Okay, I'm awake. Thank you. I was in the middle of a strange dream."

"I bet. You talked in your sleep. I couldn't make out much, but I heard something that sounded like Gabriel. Now go home, and that's an order. Be back by seven tomorrow in the conference room. There will be coffee and pastries, some fruit, and bagels. Let me walk out with you now. Tomorrow morning, Reed will meet you to take you through security."

"Thank you, Jack. (Yawn). I'm glad Mom lives close."

The two walked out of the building. Jack made sure Monique made it to her car. He watched her leave and headed home to get a few hours' sleep himself.

Chapter Forty-Six

Constance waited up until Monique got home. Torrie had given up thirty minutes earlier.

"Hello, dear. Come in. I guessed you'd end up here since you don't have an apartment. Your bedroom is available. I laid out some nightclothes I don't use anymore, and the toiletries are on the dresser. You and Torrie will share the bathroom like you did when you were girls."

Monique gave her mom a hug and kiss as she walked in.

"Thanks, Mom, you think of everything. Even when we were still at home, you'd remember things we didn't know we needed. -- This is going to sound childish, but even though I'm tired, I'm afraid if I go to sleep, I won't wake up again."

Constance sympathized with her daughter.

"I can't even imagine what it's like to wake up after being in a coma for a long time, but more than likely, your fear is natural. After this case is over, I think it might be a good idea to see Dr. Nevarez and maybe even get some counseling. Tonight, however, the perfect remedy for what ails you is chocolate milk and Toastettes. It worked when you were in high school. You would come home after a date or a night out with your friends so hyper you couldn't sleep. We talked and snacked until you relaxed enough to go to bed. Sometimes it was a matter of minutes, sometimes it was an hour or two."

Monique agreed.

"I remember, it was better than a sleeping pill. I swore you put magic in that chocolate milk because it always worked. Even though I'm not a schoolgirl anymore, I'm willing to try it. I can't believe you still eat Toastettes. I thought you only bought them for – wait! You got those tonight, didn't you?"

Monique had seen the tell-tale grin on her mother's face. Constance put her arm around Monique, and they walked into the kitchen. Monique got the glasses down while Constance got the Toastettes and chocolate milk.

The pastry was toasted, chocolate added to the drinks, and they both sat down to enjoy the moment.

"How is your boss, and how is it working for the FBI? I've always heard the CIA and FBI are rivals."

"They had to give Robert blood, and he had surgery to repair the damage from the bullet. It could have been a lot worse. As far as working with the FBI, I have no problem. Now, Robert, on the other hand – let's just say in his day they were big-time rivals. Maybe they still are, but I'm glad to have their intel, and right now, the most important goal is to stop a terrorist attack. I've discovered useful information from their data and still have more to review. I hope to find something hidden that they missed, which is what I do best. The cloak and dagger were fine when I was a kid pretending, but I'm more suited for analysis."

"Oh, don't give me that! Now that I know what you really do for a living, all those things that just didn't seem to fit make sense. You've been involved in quite a lot of cloak and dagger. I daresay if the CIA tried to keep you at a desk, you'd go over to the other side."

Monique laughed at her mother's statement. To sit in her mom's kitchen took her back to the days long ago. Somehow this kitchen put life into perspective.

"You still know me even after my absence and secrecy."

"I'll always be your mother, Monique. Time and distance won't change that. Now, do you want to talk to me about what is going on in your mind?"

"No, I don't think so. You really do have magic. I am less anxious. One more swallow of this chocolate milk and I'm ready to get some sleep. That was just what I needed. Goodnight, Mom. I'm sure to be gone before you get up. At least I hope you sleep longer than me. You've had a long night."

"Goodnight sweetheart. Sleep well."

Monique only took a few minutes to slip into the night-shirt her mother left on the bed. She snuggled under the soft sheets with the fluffy comforter
  for warmth and drifted …"

"Hey there, Monique. I'm glad to see that you relaxed enough to sleep."

"Well, well, look who's here again. I'm not going to get much sleep if you hang around all the time. Do you plan to pester me for the rest of

my life? Have you now become my guardian angel as well as an announcer?"

"That's hilarious, child. I don't pester and not for the rest of your life. And I certainly don't want to be your guardian angel. You are too much work."

"Touché! Okay. Why do you continue to visit me in this alter-world, and for how long? What Is your mission and Is It open-ended?

"My mission is not open-ended, only until you save the world—so to speak. You have great intel but discounted the guns a little too fast. They are for a purpose just as the C-4 is. Tomorrow encourage the team to talk about Kansas and research Wichita. Jennie needs you to confirm her thoughts about Kansas".

"Great. Thank you. Now let me get some sleep, will you?"

I look at Gabriel. He's gone. Typical. He came and went on his schedule with no regard for me. But since I'm tired I can—fin—slee—

Chapter Forty-Seven

Monique sat straight up in bed in a panic. What woke her? Did she hear something? It took a few seconds to orient herself. She had left her alternate world and was now in her old room at her mom's. Everything seemed like a dream, even real life. *It's going to take time to be comfortable with this reality, which is the actual reality. Except her other reality was just as real as this one. Is it possible to have two actual realities?*

"Okay, Monique. Get up and get outta here. You could go in circles all day. You don't have time for that."

Things were back to normal. Monique always had conversations with herself. It only took her about fifteen minutes to get dressed and brush her hair and teeth. She quietly exited the house, got into the SUV, and drove the short distance to the FBI headquarters. The news didn't report anything else on the tragedy from yesterday, which was good. Since the shooting and the killing had stopped, yesterday's news would be just that, yesterday's news.

She arrived five minutes later and found a parking space much closer to the entrance than the one she used yesterday. She remembered Jack told her that Reed would meet her at the front door security to usher her into the conference room where coffee and food waited. The coffee was the most important since she didn't take time to make any, before she left.

Reed watched appreciatively as Monique approached the entrance.

"Ah, good morning, Monique! I figured you would be here early. Here's your visitor's badge. Everyone except Jack is here. I guess he figures since he's the boss, he doesn't have to be punctual like everyone else. But believe me when I say that, even though he chooses not to be so punctual, he knows if one of us drags in a few minutes late."

Monique listened to Reed's monolog as they made their way to the conference room. She was grateful Reed talked. His conversation released her of the obligation to say something. Probably Reed talked just for that very reason. He appeared to be intuitive about many things.

The minute she walked into the conference room, the brewing coffee drew her to the refreshment table. She chose a bagel, some plain cream cheese (entirely fat—none of that fat-free stuff), and some strawberries and bananas. She made her way to the table and sat down by Jennie. The team quietly drank their coffee and enjoyed the pastries and fruit. They knew when Jack got there, the work would begin in earnest. He didn't allow idle time.

"Good morning, guys. I see you found the food and coffee. Good.

"Monique, how did you sleep last night? You look much more rested and less pale than you did yesterday."

"I slept fine, thank you. It was short, but I'm rested and ready to go get us some terrorists!"

"What I like to hear. Let's have reports from the research and interrogations. Anything from the gunmen? Reed, you go first."

"Not much, but my guy said something that made me think this is more complicated than just a one-target deal. I wonder if we dismissed the importance of the guns too soon."

Barbara quickly followed with her report.

"Yeah, I got the same impression from my guy. He said he didn't have any information on the guns and wasn't alarmed about the missing last installment."

Carl added his thoughts.

"I agree with Reed and Barbara; these guys are just hired guns. They know nothing, and if they did, they would not cooperate."

"Jennie, have you found out anything in your research?"

"Quite a bit, actually, but nothing to warrant the attraction of terrorists. I'm not finished, though. Maybe another thirty minutes to an hour. Monique, have you seen anything in the data yet?"

"Focus your research on Wichita, Kansas. There seems to be something important there. I wasn't at my best reviewing last night since it was late, so I hope to find something this morning."

"Strange you mention Wichita. That's exactly what I had in mind. What did you find?"

"Not sure yet. I'm anxious to get back to the data. Are we finished here, Jack?"

"Yes. I left everything where you had it. The rest of us will put eyes on anything to do with Wichita. It seems like a stretch. The only noteworthy aspect of Wichita is the Air Force Base. ICBMs were stored at the base until the disarmament treaty. I think they just have planes that refuel aircraft in flight."

Monique was more than ready to get back to her analysis. She wasn't used to teamwork. Most of the time, it was just her, or her and Robert.

Wichita—Wichita—where did I see that? Bingo! It was a news release that was never published. She couldn't figure out whether the story wasn't aired because nothing could be confirmed or some other reason.

This reporter was privy to a conversation in Washington, DC from an unnamed source who wishes to remain anonymous. The gist of the discussion is that the Chairman of the Joint Chiefs of Staff has plans to go to Wichita, Kansas. His purpose is to open a discussion about the possible reenactment of the ICBMs program from the 1970s. The source said that it could be an answer to the threat ISIS poses on United States soil. The source did not provide details or a complete list of attendees. Neither did he confirm the date and time of this "secret" meeting. One can surmise that all the members of the Joint Chiefs of Staff will also be in attendance…

There wasn't much else about the meeting. Monique looked for anything which would tell her why this never made it to the public when Jack walked into the office.

"Interesting observation about Wichita, Kansas. Did you find anything to support your hunch?"

"Absolutely! Read this."

Monique observed Jack as he read the news article. She could tell that he was excited about this revelation but suspected he would keep it hidden from most.

"Curious. Why don't you take this to Jennie and work with her on this angle? Meanwhile, the truck driver just arrived, and I have an interview to conduct. I suspect, like everyone else, he knows more than he reported."

Monique did as she was told, though she wanted to see Jack in action with the truck driver. She could almost bet the driver had vital information, plus she wanted to see Jack get him to talk. She had no doubt he could make anyone confess.

"Hello, Jennie. I found an article of interest which pointed me to Wichita. It was never published, though. Would you like to see it?"

"Sure—meanwhile, look at this."

Jennie and Monique switched places. Jennie moved to the chair to look at the article and Monique sat down in front of the computer. The first thing Monique noticed was that reservations had been made for some unnamed VIPs to fly from an unknown (or unlisted) location to an equally mysterious destination. The report merely stated the locality would be decided and revealed later. She flipped to the next screen.

"An intercepted office memo from an office at McConnell Air Force Base stated all personnel must be made ready next week for meetings to take place. We need to make sure Hangar D is wholly emptied before the meetings."

She looked at the date of the memo. Four days ago. If this was the target, they only had about three to five days before it all came down.

Jennie noticed Monique had read the reports on the computer.

"Well, what do you think?"

"I think we are on the right track. How did you find this memo? Are you a famous hacker that I don't know about?"

Jennie laughed.

"I'll never tell. I snooped around after you mentioned Wichita, Kansas. Thank you for your input. You saved me a lot of time when you gave me a focus."

"Weren't you able to locate additional details? Maybe a specific destination or reservations for their stay. I can't believe that this magnitude of a meeting can be kept secret. Don't you folks have a security detail on anyone who is anyone in Washington DC?"

"You know what they say, 'Great minds think alike' and all. I plan to ask Jack to do his 'boss thing' and speak to the FBI security division in Washington, DC. We may be the same organization, but there is still rivalry between departments. You know, competitions of things that matter like who is more important, who has the most arrests, stuff like that."

The girls had gone as far as they could without additional input. Jeannie was content to sit idle for a minute, but Monique was ready for more.

"Where are the other guys?"

"They all went to their offices to research for possible related articles or information. I think Reed decided to talk with one of the gunmen again, and Jack is in an interview room with the truck

154

driver who hauled the C-4. Why don't we head to the observation room and monitor the interview? I'm sure Jack can get important information."

"You are a girl after my own heart. I've been anxious to get into that room all morning. Lead the way."

The girls entered the observation room and turned on the speakers.

"… Look, Mr. Waggoner, Cecil—may I call you Cecil? Good, Okay, Cecil, I know you have more information than you gave the authorities. You're a smart man. You know when to keep your mouth shut and when to talk. You probably didn't want to talk to anyone local because the information you have would have been way over their heads. Well, you are in a different place now. You can trust us to do the right thing with the information you have."

"I don't got no information. Like I tol' the officers, my job was to take the C-4 to Boulder Colorado so they can blow up some building. I went to take a leak, and when I come back my truck was gone."

"Why didn't you tell the officer's right away that the truck had explosives on board—what else were you carrying?"

"Why do ya think I had something else? I tol' them cops I only had the explosives."

"Look, you drove a big rig and the amount of C-4 you had was tiny. Why did they want a big truck? Your cargo was a lot more than those explosives now wasn't it?"

"Nah. Look, man you brung me all the way from Missouri so you can accuse me of…"

"Cecil, you got me all wrong. I don't want to accuse you. But now that you mention it, if I use my imagination and put you in the company of terrorists who pay you to help them carry out their attacks, that would, of course put you in the same category as they are, plus give you the title of a traitor. We'd be forced to prosecute you as a co-conspirator against your country. That carries some stiff penalties, maybe even death."

"Wait! I ain't no traitor! I love my country. I would nevah b'tray my country."

"Ah, yes, but you also are about to lose your house. Your jobs have been sporadic to say the least since your last accident, and your ex-wife is after you to put you in jail for lack of child support

155

payments. That makes you a perfect patsy to be used if the price is right."

"How did you…"

Jack jumped up and pounded the desk so hard and so fast it took everyone by surprise. Jennie almost screamed out loud and Monique jumped so high she thought she would hit the ceiling.

"It doesn't matter how I know, Mr. Waggoner. I just know. Now, are you ready to share everything, you know? If so, I might let the prosecutor know you cooperated. Perhaps convince him to charge you on something less."

The driver's face got bright red, sweat broke out on his forehead, and he looked like he wanted to cry. Monique kind of felt sorry for him, but not too much. People do desperate things when life begins to cave in on them, and this guy was the perfect stooge for illicit deliveries. But, even in hard times, there are more honorable ways to get out of a difficult situation.

"Please, I don't mean no evil. I'm not a bad person. I don't want ta die or even go ta the jail. It's jus that I got no way out. And I think I might be in trouble with these guys if I say anymore."

Jack brought it back down.

"Now see, Cecil, that is where you have it all wrong. We can put you in protective custody so no one can hurt you. We can even set you up with a new identity if we take these terrorists and traitors to court and you testify. So, what do you say? I have the tape recorder on, and so far, there isn't anything that helps me be able to help you. Don't worry about the order you tell me; just talk until I have all of the information I need."

The girl's watched as Mr. Waggoner's face went through a gamut of emotions. Finally, he resigned himself to the fact that he might as well talk because no one was going to bail him out of this mess. Monique didn't know if Jack could or even would help him out with the prosecutor. She supposed it boiled down to what information he provided and if the attack could be stopped.

"See, i' was like this, I was in a bar one-night jus minding my own business. Not doin' nothing but kind of drinking—you know one drink 'cause I cain't afford no more but I din't want ta leave. This guy—he wore a suit and tie so I knowed he wasn jus want'n to be my friend. He come to me and sat down and offered ta buy me a drink. Course I said okay, so I gulped down the drink I had an waited for a'other one. He starts talk'n bout tough times and how not hav'n money is the pits and how he likes to hep people who got no money. When I asks him how he heped people who needs money, he told me jus doin odd jobs 'at no one es wants ta do. So's I tell him did he have somptin I can do fer him. He tells me as a matter of fact he did. He asks me sum questions and I guess I answered right because he takes my phone number and tells me he would be in touch. He buys me a'other drink and walks out."

"Did this gentleman give you a name? If we had a sketch artist come in, could you give a description?"

"Sure. I can describe him. He tol me hes name is Connor tho. I don't got no last name."

"That's alright, Cecil. We know who Connor is. By the way, just so you know these guys don't mess around. Connor was killed by his boss. You are just lucky they haven't come after you yet."

Cecil was panic-stricken.

"No! Oh, ya gotta protect me. I don want ta git killed. I have more to say."

"Just calm down and continue. This is good information."

"Kay—I go bout my days drivin' sum but not much. I always got my phone with me. I git a call from this Connor, and he asks if I wanna make sum good money. I tells him course I do. He says I can earn $2,000.00 fir jus drivn someone else's truck. He tells me the truck was a'ready loaded. I just had to drive. Then he tells me to make a stop to go to the bathroom at a certain spot an he tol me where and that someone would take the truck whilst I was gone. So, I said Okay. I wasn sposed to look at the cargo but I did. It was on an accident of course. But I looked. There was the explosives as my papers says. I was go'n to Colorado but I really wasn' and there was sumptom more than the explosives. I wasn sposed to call no police neither but cause I knowed what there was I figered I bettr till someun."

"Good for you, Cecil, and brave. You had to have known they would find out if you told."

"Yea—exactly. That wus why I called. But first I din' tell no one bout the explosives. I was afeared to. But then I finally tol a cop. So theys just took my report and sent me away."

"Let me take you back a bit. You said there was something else besides the explosives. What was the cargo?"

"Oh—I don' know fer sure. That's why I didn' tell no one. They was jus boxes. Woodn boxes—long not too wide. Don' know what was in em, but theys looked important. They had stamp-like things all ovr them. Like, sort a anyways—I didn see good but almos like flags of diffrn countries."

Monique was excited.

"Guns! Jennie, they had to have been guns. His description fits perfectly. But nothing makes sense. How did the guns get here and why? The money transfer had not been completed. And where did they go?"

"You're doing great Cecil. Would you like a coke, maybe something to eat? We had you come in awfully early."

"No Coke, but I ken sure use som coffee. Not nun of that sissy coffee jist plain ole strong coffee."

"—I'll be right back."

Chapter Forty-Eight

Jennie and Monique left the observation room and returned to the conference room. The girls were sure Jack was on his way there. They had quite a bit to discuss. Monique wondered if Reed or the others had any additional information to share.

It was as if some announcement was made. Everyone was back in the conference room. Jack walked in just as the last person sat down.

"Well, I've been here too long. You guys know when I am ready for a report. I didn't even have to announce it. So, who goes first?"

As always, Reed started the account.

"I talked with one of the gunmen again. It seems like whatever the target is, there are two phases of the attack. He didn't say so in those exact words, but he said enough for me to infer."

"Thank you, Reed. I agree with you on that, and some of what the driver told me supports your theory. Before I go into details, Monique, Jennie, what did you come up with?"

Monique was ready to defer to Jennie since Jack was her boss. Jennie made a different decision.

"Monique, why don't you make the report?"

"Uh, sure, be happy to. Jennie found a non-published article about the base in Wichita, Kansas. During the cold war, ICBMs were stored at McConnell Air Force Base, but the program was disbanded after the arms reduction act passage between Russia and the United States. The article suggested a possibility of reinstating the Base as a storage facility for the missiles. Jennie and I also learned of a meeting in Wichita, Kansas, at the Air Force Base. We know the chairman of the Joint Chiefs of Staff plans to attend.

Monique made her report, and her facts prompted speculative silence all around. Despite the detailed particulars, the team could not find a clearly defined goal.

Jack prompted further conversation.

"So, where does all of this leave us? Any thoughts playing out in your minds?"

Monique didn't want to overstep her position, but no one else talked. From the time she was a child, she took random information and created a complete scenario. A few more seconds of silence and Monique took the plunge.

"I have a thought. Now mind you, this is only a made-up plot right now, but there is a possibility. We know there are guns and explosives, right? Additional research from Jennie suggests the possibility there are ICBMs in the mixture. Lastly, we have followed random attacks from a group of terrorist-trained-soldiers.

"Go, on."

"My thought is the meeting with the Chief of Staff was completed. The physical meeting in Wichita is a formality and a ruse to inspect the place the missiles are stored. A shipment of ICBMs is scheduled to deliver the day of the meeting; thus, the reason to clear out Hanger D. The delegates will fly commercially instead of using a government jet to keep the meeting secret. The explosives are used to take out the Air Traffic Control Tower at the time the plane called for permission to land. Immediately after the explosion, a team with guns are ready to take over the tower before a warning goes out. Chaos in the Control Tower causes confusion in the skies with the potential for fatal accidents. Another small contingent waits near the base for the bedlam to spread, and extra security measures are initiated. The soldiers pose as extra security and come in to 'assist.' Their purpose is two-fold. First, to make sure the base and Hangar D are secured. The second objective is to take one or two missiles during the confusion.

"The end results of all of the commotion are no meeting takes place, and the delegates may or may not survive the chaos, but these details are not important. The fact that the secret meeting becomes public knowledge and word of the decision to re-establish storage of ICBMs promotes bad publicity in the United States. News of the fiasco spreads to our allies, and the United States will lose face with the other nations. Finally, when the reporters find out and reveal that ISIS has their hands on the missiles, our country will be in turmoil."

The conference room was silent. No one spoke a word. Monique got nervous because she didn't receive a reaction. Finally, Reed broke the silence.

"Geez, Monique! I can honestly say that I, for one, am glad you are on our side and not theirs. That's quite a scene, but not far-

160

fetched. If this is truly feasible, the group is quite a bit larger than we first thought."

Craig had a rebuttal to Reed's observation.

"Not necessarily. Consider the fact that the terrorists have the element of surprise on their side. They only need a few men at the tower because the guns take the place of many. They could shoot everyone before the first alarm was sent. Whatever happens in the air is non-consequential because the true mission is surprise, attack, delay, and confiscate. True genius."

"You realize, of course, all of what I said is pure speculation. It's one option of many which fit all of the pieces."

"No. I think you've found a way to tap into their operation. Any other option would just be a variable of the same thing. The main parts of the mission will be intact. Does anyone have a different theory? I'm all ears."

Jack was sure no one would answer, but he wanted to make sure they all knew he would listen to alternatives.

"Then folks, if you will excuse me, it's time to confer with our team in Washington, DC."

Chapter Forty-Nine

Torrie slowly opened her eyes. She knew it was late morning because she felt rested, and that only happened if she had five to seven hours of sleep. She hadn't fallen asleep until after Monique and her mom had gone to bed, which was late, or rather early since it was after one o'clock in the morning.

Today was Saturday. Nothing special, just a fact, and tomorrow her family planned to have lunch with the Reverend. She had questions that required his expertise, but she wasn't comfortable being vulnerable with him.

Enough rest get up! Maybe she'd go to the gym today and do a stress-free workout. Perhaps not. The doctor wouldn't approve. Maybe her mom wanted to go somewhere with her just to get out. Torrie admitted she was a workaholic and usually proud of it because hard work was one of the reasons for her success. Lately, that didn't seem to be enough. The dilemma is how does one replace an addiction ingrained to the core? Reflection was not comfortable either, so she decided to take a shower.

Constance moved to put on a fresh pot of coffee as soon as she heard Torrie in the bathroom. I wonder what is in store or us today? Monique left early this morning, hopefully with enough rest. She was sure they wouldn't hear from her today since there were no new tragedies reported. Maybe they would find those terrorists so that this season of their lives could go away.

Her mind drifted to Steve and the dinner visit for tomorrow. What a sweetheart, and he was comfortable to be with. She planned the menu, roast chicken with baby potatoes, carrots, onions, and celery. Her famous homemade dinner rolls with real butter, then a green bean casserole and for dessert—what for dessert? Maybe pecan pie! It doesn't have to be just for Thanksgiving and Christmas. Constance compiled a grocery list while Torrie showered and dressed. She also made a timeline on her to-do list. Today, make the dough for the rolls. They had to rise and be kneaded a couple of times. Mix the green bean casserole; bake the pie. Tomorrow morning put the chicken in to cook at ten then the green bean casserole on the second shelf at eleven. The rolls only took about thirty minutes so she would put them in the top oven at twelve. Then set the table and make the drinks while the food completed, and everyone should be able to sit down right when Steve arrived. Constance was glad she had invested in a double oven appliance, one above the stove and one below it. Preparation for dinner guests was much more pleasant.

"Good morning, Torrie! Come join me for coffee. I made a fresh pot. I hope Monique will take the time to come to dinner tomorrow. I can never cook for less than six, or I swear, food doesn't taste as good. How do you feel this morning? Any headache?"

During Constance's recitation, Torrie walked to the cupboard, took down a coffee mug for herself and filled it to the top. She found her mom's cup and filled it up. They drank the coffee black, so it only took her a few seconds to complete the task. She had planted herself in one of the kitchen chairs and had taken a couple of sips before she was expected to comment.

"I feel fine, no residual headache. I think the doctor is too cautious. I should have gone to work yesterday. No—maybe not, but I could have gone in this morning to make sure the presentation went well. I didn't even check in! Maybe I'll call Reed to find out how it went. He won't mind if I call him over the weekend."

Torrie got up from the table to get her cell phone, but Constance stopped her.

"Torrie, please don't get wrapped up in work. I understand you need to make that phone call, but please don't say you'll go to the office today. I thought we'd go to the grocery store and later, maybe a trip to the mall. It's been years since I've bought anything new to wear. Your wardrobe is sure to consist mainly of professional office attire which is a little too stiff for a family dinner."

"Believe it or not, I have no desire to work today. I actually planned to ask you to go to the mall. The only reason I want to call is to check in with my boss. You spoke with him yesterday, remember?"

"He seemed rather nice. Is he?"

"Nice? I could never describe one of my bosses as nice. He's fair and honest and gives credit when credit is due, but he also provides constructive criticism as well. If he were any different, I'd leave. I have a choice of companies to choose from."

Constance knew Torrie's statement wasn't meant to brag, just a fact. They made plans to leave as soon as Torrie made her call. Constance cleaned up the kitchen and went to get ready herself.

Chapter Fifty

Jack left the team in the conference room. He needed time to gather his thoughts and form a game plan. The first step was a phone call to his counterpart in Washington, DC. He expected Bill to be reluctant to converse about a situation of this nature. If Jack presented Monique's theory in detail as factual, perhaps a consultation would be more agreeable.

"Hello, Bill; are we secure?"

"Of course. You only call me when there is a need for discretion and security."

Jack detailed Monique's theory and the events which led them to the conclusions. He finished and waited for a response from Bill. A full minute passed. Jack almost broke the silence to make sure they were still connected, but finally, he heard a whistle…

"Incredible. Do you have anything to back that up?"

"Cut it out Bill; I'm not going to play this game. These terrorists have plans which cross jurisdictions, and I want to propose a joint task force to stop them. I know your agency doesn't want to fall victim to an investigation for misleading the United States into a volatile situation. Tell me, when is your team scheduled to depart, and what is the destination?"

"Okay, you win. We're scheduled to leave for Wichita, Kansas tomorrow morning first thing. The team doesn't know yet so, how in the hell did you come up with all this information? You don't have clearance for any of it!"

"Well, sir, we're just that good. My team and the CIA are working together. The CIA agents had the same intel from a different source, and the local police force stumbled into the mix. We decided it would be best to share information and come up with a theory. You just confirmed most of our conclusions. What I need now is for you to join us or stay out of our way."

Jack knew Bill struggled with his decision. He hoped the safety of the United States would take precedence over agency pride or competition.

"Sigh. You're right about our plans. As far as the terrorists' angle, we were so focused on our mission, we missed the obvious.

165

You're sure about the threat and the way they plan to make the attack?"

"Absolutely sure on the threat; as far as the plan, all I can say is the facts lead to that scenario. We tried to come up with different methods, but nothing fits as well as this one."

Bill thought about steps he should take but needed to know what Jack planned.

"Wichita, Kansas, is the target. I'm in Washington, DC. What is your plan? I know you have one."

Jack was relieved that Bill accepted the plan as gracefully as he did.

"I propose our teams join forces. I suggest you place an agent on the plane with the Joint Chiefs. Don't wait to send a team to Wichita; do it now. Route them directly to the air traffic control tower. Place two or three agents inside the tower disguised as workers with weapons hidden and within reach in case the agents you plant outside don't stop the detonation. An explosion will take out the tower, and it will be useless. I'd like to divert the traffic to another airport, except it will trigger an alarm. We don't want these terrorists to get spooked."

"Okay, so much for my team. What is the plan for your team?"

We will leave in a few minutes to arrive early this evening and go directly to the base. I have six agents counting the CIA agent and myself. Two of us will be in the hangar where the nuclear weapons are. The other four agents will take a position in strategic locations, two inside the base and two on the outside perimeters. Our objective is to intercept the terrorists who offer security backup after the explosion at the tower, take them out and put our guys in their place. If the attack on the tower is prevented, we will scout out the bad guys when they retreat. They must be stopped because if they escape, they'll go underground, and we'll lose them."

Bill had already set the plan in motion.

"While you talked, I dispatched agents to our private jet; they just took off towards the Wichita control tower. I'll instruct my team on the mission after they land. Two agents remained. They'll board the plane as civilians on the flight with the members of the Joint Chiefs of Staff. No one will know they are with the FBI, except the captain. The ideal outcome is to interrupt the attack before the explosives are planted, but we may already be too late."

Jack had that scenario covered as well.

"The explosives, if they are already planted, will be close by the power source to the tower. A possible secondary target is an entrance to the air traffic control employees. An explosion will make an entrance to the tower easier for the guys with the guns. If the bad guys get in, your people are trained well enough to stop them."

"Are you on your way? We don't want to keep these terrorists waiting!"

"We are as good as gone."

Jack walked into the conference room. His team was packed and ready to go. Can he train a team or what!

"It's showtime people. Let's go!"

Chapter Fifty-One

The team gathered their bags and got into the van that took them to the jet. Jack called ahead to make sure it was ready for takeoff the minute they arrived. He'd brief his team on the strategy as soon as they took off.

"Keep alert. If we've learned one thing, these guys are everywhere and unpredictable."

Five minutes into the trip, Monique spotted suspicious activity.

"Rifle! Stop the Van, now!"

To his credit, the driver didn't hesitate to put on his brakes. Shots fired from the van congregated in areas that caused little damage. The driver of the white van was equally fast. He made a quick U-turn, maneuvered directly in front of the FBI's vehicle, and made escape impossible. The agents fell out and positioned themselves behind the side of the van. The doors weren't ideal protection, but they had limited choices. Thank goodness the action was on a road not well-traveled, which meant less chance for civilian injury. Monique scooted back and did what she could to warn travelers away. She waved her MIG 22 assault rifle for emphasis. The other agents prepared themselves for a firefight. The enemy got in the first round and punctured the two front tires. Another volley of bullets smashed into the hood, and smoke billowed from underneath. Jack prepared to discharge his weapon when he spotted what he hoped was merely steam caused by a radiator leak. He fired a round and forced the terrorists to shut the van door, but only for a minute or two. They were sure to regroup and advance from a different direction.

Jack quickly reviewed his agents' positions. Monique was dangerously out of range for protection in her efforts to thwart any other traffic. Barbara held her own behind the back door. She put several rounds on the side and managed to take out two of their tires. So, both vans were useless.

Craig was behind the back door on the passenger's side. Jennie was with the driver. Their shots were directed towards the van's engine. Reed—where was Reed?

"Hey, anyone seen Reed?!"

Jack scanned the perimeter. He glimpsed Reed's jacket in between the trees by the side of the road. Son of a—he was headed around the brush and trees to get on the other side of the van. If he succeeded, Reed would have an opportunity for a sneak attack. It was a great plan, albeit hazardous, but if anyone could accomplish it, Reed was the one.

More shots were fired from the white van. The agents all ducked for cover, except Monique. She maintained her position and continued to block traffic. Monique was well aware of her precarious situation and yearned for police backup to assist with the civilian protection.

Jack looked hard in the trees to locate Reed. He counted the opponents' guns. His agents were severely outnumbered. To gain an advantage, Reed must succeed. Jack was concerned about the safety of his team, particularly Monique. He faintly heard sirens in the background. Excellent; back up was on the way. The local law enforcement could take over for Monique.

Suddenly, Jack heard a round of shots followed by an explosion that lit up the sky and violently deposited car parts everywhere. The FBI agents frantically dove underneath their van to get out of the firestorm. Jack looked at the inferno. Reed must have set off some kind of an explosive device hidden in the truck. No one could have survived the impact. Jack once again checked for his team and immediately saw that Monique was down.

"Monique! Monique ..."

Jack shouted her name and ran hard. A van door landed on top of her. He saw blood but couldn't determine the extent of her injuries until he was closer. Reed was back with the other agents and became aware of Monique's plight at the same time Jack did. He quickly assessed the scene.

"You guys secure the scene! I have to assist Jack with Monique!

There wasn't much of a scene left to secure. As unlikely as it was that anyone survived the inferno, to assume as much could be a deadly mistake. Even someone near death was capable of an attack.

Reed arrived right behind Jack. He had been a medic in the Army and was ready to render aid if needed. From what he could see at this distance, Monique needed more than a band-aid.

"Monique—can you hear me?"

"Move, Jack. Let me check her out."

Reed quickly evaluated the situation. He checked her breath, shallow but steady, pulse weak and thready. What was the source of the blood? He and Jack lifted the door and saw a gash near the artery in her upper right leg. Near thank goodness but didn't sever the artery. Reed removed his shirt and tied a tourniquet to stop, or at least slow down, the blood flow. Next, he checked her eyes. She didn't appear to have gone into a coma, but she was unconscious. He checked her other leg and both arms. Her right arm was bent behind her at an unnatural angle. He was sure it was broken, but it wasn't a compound fracture. He checked her head for any sign of impact. No abrasions near her head, but a gash on her cheek bled. Reed figured it would take about five or six stitches. He took out his handkerchief and told Jack to apply some pressure to her cheek while he continued with his examination.

Meanwhile, police cars and emergency vehicles arrived. Thankfully, someone alerted the paramedics to the injured Monique. Officers surveyed the destruction and watched a fireman douse the flames with water. Monique stirred and moaned as the paramedics approached.

"Ma'am, ma'am, please lie still. We need to check you out."

Reed stepped back.

"Her name is Monique. Is she conscious?"

"Not really. She moaned and opened her eyes, but they were non-seeing. Please get back; I have to start an IV. Her blood pressure is too low. Harry, get the board and the gurney, and hurry! She may not have severed an artery, but she has lost a lot of blood, probably from some internal injuries."

The rest of the team relinquished the scene to the local officers. They took their place a short distance from the activity, anxious to learn the extent of Monique's injuries. It wasn't a secret that the CIA agent recently came out of a coma. This trauma was sure to set her back.

Reed looked angry.

"What was she thinking being so reckless and irresponsible. And not only that, but it also wasn't necessary!"

The paramedics completed their work and prepared Monique for transport. One paramedic jumped into the back with the patient to monitor her vitals and the other into the driver's seat. The stricken team watched the emergency transport take Monique away.

Jack looked at the other agents.

"Okay, team. This is tough. It's never easy when one of our own is injured. We don't have time to stand around and mope. We have to keep going. Barbara, will you notify Monique's family before the news reaches them? They need to be reassured that even though she is injured, she is still alive. They can get up to date information at the hospital. Do we know which hospital?"

Barbara was already planning what she would say to the family.

"Mercy Memorial, the same hospital she was in a few days ago. Does anyone have her mother's address? I'll give them the message and meet you guys back at the private jet."

Jack was having a hard time keeping calm.

"Thank you, Barbara—let me see. I think I put the address—damn! Reed! where is your cell phone? Can you pinpoint her mom's address for Barbara?"

"Sure—what is the last name? Oh, it has to be the same as Torrie's since she isn't married—Yorkshire. Okay, let's see here—I found it. Barbara, the address is 4201 St. Freeman's."

"Thanks, Reed—I'm on my way—see you guys soon."

Barbara stopped and looked at the truck.

"Uh, Jack, we have a slight problem here. Have you noticed that our van isn't going anywhere?"

"Ugh!"

Jack quickly ran to the SUV and pulled out the radio to arrange for transportation.

"Agents requires assistance with transportation—over—(static). "Hello, anyone there? Our transportation has been compromised, requesting assistance, need transportation—over—(static—squeal—static). Okay, plan B—or C—or D, where are we in the alphabet? Any suggestions?"

Jennie was quiet, but she knew how to organize a situation in the most efficient manner.

"Hey, Jack! —Guys—I found two officers to assist us with transportation. Officer Glen in that police SUV over there will take everyone but Barbara to the jet and this nice officer—Beacon, is it? He will take Barbara to Monique's mom to let her know about her daughter. He'll wait there and take Barbara to the jet after that."

Jack was proud of his team and how they used their talents.

"Thank you, officers; you are lifesavers. Okay, team, now let's go!"

Barbara jumped into Officer Beacon's patrol car as quickly as she could. It was a short drive to the Yorkshire's, which didn't give her much time to come up with a delicate way to tell the family about Monique. She did not relish this responsibility, but Jack was inclined to trust her for these types of tasks. The trick was to appear calm and unhurried, then break away to get to the jet as soon as possible. The attack served to delay their mission. She was sure Jack would contact the Washington, DC, team to update them on what had happened. Hopefully, he wouldn't discover a similar situation with that team. They arrived at Ms. Yorkshire's house.

"Officer stay with the car. I'll be out as fast as I can, and we'll need to get to the airfield fast."

Barbara reached the front door and didn't find a doorbell, so she knocked firmly several times. Someone peeked out the side window, so she made sure they would be able to see her and know she wasn't dangerous. The curtain fell back, and the door opened slightly, but the safety lock was in place.

"Hello?"

"I'm sorry to bother you, Ms. Yorkshire. My name is Barbara with the FBI. I work with Monique on a task force. Do you mind if I come in for a moment?"

"Monique. Oh my God, please, no! Of course, come in."

Constance released the safety lock and opened the door wide enough so Barbara could gain entrance into her home. Torrie heard the knock from her bedroom and entered the living room at the same time Barbara came through the door. She heard her mother's agitated response and rushed to her side.

"Mom, what's wrong? What happened? Who are you, and what did you say to my mother?"

Barbara was taken aback by the forcefulness of Torrie's reaction. She sure hoped she never got on her wrong side.

"I just introduced myself. I'm Barbara with the FBI. I work with Monique on this special task force."

"Oh, no. And you are here to give us some bad news. We don't need bad news. Mom look at me. Listen to me. It may be bad news, but Monique is not dead, or Barbra wouldn't have said she works with Monique—she would have said 'worked' or 'was working.'"

Barbara was amazed at Torrie's powers of observation under duress. She probably had the same innate abilities which made Monique so successful in her job.

"Right. Monique is injured but still very much alive. From what I could tell, the injuries are not life threatening. Her right arm is broken. She's lost a lot of blood, probably from a deep cut on her leg, and she definitely needs stitches for a nasty cut on her cheek. It's possible some of the blood loss is due to internal injuries, which will be confirmed at the hospital. Fortunately, she did not suffer head trauma. The ambulance transported her to Mercy Memorial Hospital. I'm sure by the time you get to the emergency room, the doctor will have more information for you."

Now that the news was dispensed, Barbra was in a hurry to leave. She waited a moment or two just to make sure Monique's family was stable enough to get to the hospital.

Constance was aware that both Torrie and Barbara looked at her intently to make sure she didn't collapse. She certainly would not collapse! She was the head of this household and responsible for her family.

"Thank you so much, Barbara. Torrie, get the keys; we need to get to the hospital. Barbara, I'm sure you have a mission to complete so, good-bye! We'll be fine. Thank you for taking the time to come tell us in person."

Constance opened the door for Barbara, reached for her purse, and she and Torrie hurried to the car at the same time Barbara got to the patrol car. Barbara was glad that the Yorkshire women all appeared to be tenacious and competent.

"Officer—let's get outta here!"

Chapter Fifty-Two

"I refuse to be here again! I am not injured, I will get on that jet, and I will be part of the team that takes those terrorist bastards down! Gabriel, where are you, Gabriel?"

"Oh, my goodness, Monique. You are just a tad bit overwrought. I'm here, and I'll explain what happened. Please be calm. You won't be here long, and I don't want you to display such agitation when your mother and sister get here."

"Where is here? And why would they come? Please don't tell me..."

"You're injured but will be fine. This is hard information to provide, but your injuries will prevent your participation in the rest of the mission. Your analysis and deductions aimed your team in the right direction. A lot of civilians survived the attack this morning because of your heroics. It's time to let it go and rest up so you can get completely well."

"I'm so— I can't. Where? No—don't. . ."

Monique was rushed into surgery as soon as the emergency room staff identified all of her injuries.

"Is everybody set? Doctor, let me know as soon as she is safely under."

"She's mumbling something. Monique, please, lie still. You'll be fine. Don't pull on the oxygen mask."

"No, I refuse. . ."

Constance and Torrie hurried into the emergency room at Mercy Memorial. Torrie was the first one to get to the check-in counter.

"Excuse me! Hello? Excuse me; I'm looking for my sister. Her name is Monique Yorkshire? She was brought in by ambulance with injuries from an accident. Can you please tell me where she is?"

"Please, have a seat over there, and I will get someone to meet with you."

Torrie looked at her mom in exasperation. She didn't understand why they couldn't get a straight answer.

"Torrie, honey, come on. The system won't speed up because we are angry and upset. I'm sure a doctor will give us some answers soon."

They barely had time to get seated in the uncomfortable waiting room chairs when the nurse came over with one of the ER doctors.

"This is Dr. Chang. He was the attending doctor when Monique was brought in, and he will be happy to provide you with particulars. Doctor, this is Constance Yorkshire, Monique's mother and Torrie Yorkshire, Monique's sister."

"Hello, ladies. First, I want to assure you that Monique's injuries are extensive but completely treatable. I understand she was injured from a car explosion. One of the van doors landed on top of her. The impact gave her a broken arm, and her leg has a gash where the door sliced her. The force of either the door or the explosion caused her spleen to rupture, and she has a couple of broken ribs. Her lungs were not punctured. We don't expect to find any additional internal injuries.

"Monique is in surgery to remove her spleen, stitch up her leg, set her broken arm, and close the wound on her cheek. She has other minor contusions which will heal over time. The surgeon thinks that her leg injury will heal nicely with little or no permanent damage. Her arm requires two pins, which will leave her arm useless for a few months, but with physical therapy, she should get back a full range of motion. The surgeons aren't rookies. Monique's recovery will be long and tedious, but she'll be fine. Do you have any questions?"

The doctor looked expectantly at the ladies and waited for questions. He was sure they wouldn't have any right now because of the shock factor, plus the plethora of information they received.

Constance was drained and her mind numb. Only the apparent questions registered.

"When did she go into surgery, and when will she be in recovery? Where is the surgery waiting room, and can we sit there?"

"She was taken into surgery about ten minutes ago. We expect, with everything the surgeons will do, she'll be in surgery no less than four hours, maybe longer. You may wait in the surgery waiting room on the second floor. A surgeon will talk to you when she goes to recovery. Any more questions?"

"No, not now, thank you. Except, can you give us directions to the waiting room?"

"Sure. Take a right at the exit sign and take the elevators on the left. As soon as you get off, follow the arrows and there will be a sign that says something like 'Surgery Waiting Room'."

Torrie and Constance trudged to the second floor waiting room to begin their vigil.

Chapter Fifty-Three

"Thank you, Officer Beacon."

Barbara boarded the plane.

"Okay, guys, I'm on board. Jack, give the word to take off now!"

Straightaway, Jack gave the order as everyone buckled up for takeoff. No one spoke until they had made the ascent. They had about a two-hour flight. Jack estimated their arrival for two or three o'clock in the afternoon, too close for comfort. As soon as the jet leveled out, an attendant magically appeared with a tray laden with coffee, water, assorted cheeses and fruits, cups, plates, and utensils. The agents had no real appetite but were wise enough to recognize their bodies would require fuel to get through the next several hours. Jack observed his somber team fill their plates dutifully and obtain the beverages of their choice.

"Barbara, how did the family do when you told them?"

"Of course, they were upset as expected, but Monique's family is strong. Ms. Yorkshire pretty much dismissed me right away so she could leave for the hospital. I didn't take the time to make any inquiries as to what Monique's condition is, but I have the mom's phone number if you want me to check later."

Jack thought about it for a minute before he responded.

"Noooo, I don't think I will ask you to do that. We, all of us, need to stay focused. Right now, we know Monique is in the care of competent doctors, and her injuries are not life-threatening. We can take comfort in that and complete this mission for her. I know the minute she's conscious and discovers we had to continue without her—well, let me just say I wouldn't want to be the person in the room. No more drama allowed, agreed?"

Everyone nodded in agreement, and Jack continued.

"Before we left, I spoke with my counterpart in Washington, DC. He confirmed most of the information we thought we knew; plus, he was quite concerned about our—rather, Monique's hypothesis. It didn't take him long to agree that it fits all the facts, and his team was deployed to Wichita while we spoke. Bill's unit is assigned to rescue the control tower. A second team, which includes him, is scheduled to travel on the same plane with the Joint Chiefs of

Staff. We both felt it was a logical precaution.

"Our part of the plan is to go straight to McConnell for reconnaissance first, then take positions which will put us in line to overtake the guys as they infiltrate the security. I'll go to Hangar D, which in my opinion already has the ICBMs. A team of two will patrol the perimeter of the base. I want the other two on the base looking for anything out of place or suspicious. Each team will have a two-way radio to stay in touch, and we'll check in every ten minutes."

Craig asked the first question.
"What happens if radio contact disrupts surveillance or alerts a bad guy?"

"The safest thing to do is to send a quick Morse Code SOS message if anyone sees danger in a radio contact. Once the danger is over, radio to update me on what happened. Is everyone clear on this? Any other questions? Yes, Jennie?"

"If Bill's team can divert the planned destruction, what does that do to our end of the plan?"

"The best answer I have is—we have no idea. The obvious takeaway is to round up everyone involved, both at the air force base and at the control tower. There are a lot of variables in play here. The worst-case scenario is that nothing happens, and we get no one. Not that I want to see anything happen, but if they get or already have been spooked, they will go underground and disappear—at least for now."

Reed was concerned about what the attack on their team meant. "Do you think the attack on us means they already suspect that we have figured out their plan?"

"Of course, that is always a possibility. More likely, we were targeted as a delay tactic and, if possible, to remove as many investigators as they could. I'll talk with Bill directly and update him on what happened. Any other questions? Good. Take this time to rest as much as possible, we've had a long weekend already."

Jack waited a few minutes just to make sure no one had anything to say and then walked toward the front of the jet. He took the satellite phone out of its holder and placed the call to Bill.

"Jack? Is that you? You had us worried. There are reports on the news about gunfire and an explosion. Was that your team, and what happened?"

"News sure does travel fast. Most of us are good. Monique has serious injuries, but nothing fatal. It's bad enough to put her out of commission, so we are down a team member. Did anything happen to you guys?"

"Not so far. I am about to board the commercial jet now. I've yet to see anyone from the Joint Chiefs of Staff, but we have another twenty minutes before take-off. I'm sorry about Monique. That has to hurt your plans."

"Thanks, Bill. We'll manage. Our concern was that the terrorists suspected we had figured out their plan. I think the fact that your team wasn't attacked means we can assume they only wanted to delay our investigation. The explosion took care of anyone in the van, so I don't look for any more trouble, at least not right away. My guys have two-way radios and will report every ten minutes. If there are terrorists close, we'll send an SOS signal to indicate check-in is not possible. I hope we can get this done without a hitch."

"A little late for that, don't you think? But I agree with you, no more excitement. Jack, gotta run, time to board the plane."

"Good luck. I'll check in when we land."

Chapter Fifty-Four

Goodness, Mom. We've only been here for two hours! It feels like ten. I thought we were supposed to be updated during the surgery."

"They probably haven't had time. I'm sure if there are complications, someone will notify us."

Constance hadn't contacted Steve, for fear of taking advantage of his generosity. He was after all chaplain for the entire hospital population.

"Mom, look. Here comes Steve. Did you decide to call him?"

Torrie noticed a look of relief the minute her mom saw that Steve headed their way.

"No. I guess he gets updates on new admissions or surgeries—Hello, Steve! Good to see you."

Before Constance had time to ponder how she should react, she stood and hugged him.

"How are you two? I just got the word about Monique, though no details. How long have you been here? Why didn't you call me? You know I would have been here."

Constance smiled at his attentiveness. Despite the gravity of the circumstances, her spirit raised a level or two, and hope soared with Steve's presence. The minute he walked into the room, Constance regained her assurance that Monique would come through this just fine.

"Monique has been in surgery for a little over two hours and is only about halfway through. The doctor said her injuries are extensive but completely fixable. They will have to put pins in her arm for the broken bones. There's a horrible gash on her leg, but nothing broken, though it went down to the bone. The doctor will remove her ruptured spleen and clean that mess up, she has some broken ribs, and I think she needs stitches on her cheek and maybe a couple of other places."

"What happened? Was she in a car accident?"

"Oh, no, not that. Monique and the FBI team were on their way to go somewhere to stop something from happening. They were attacked by some bad guys in a van who had guns and explosives.

Someone shot through the van and hit something which caused an explosion. The blast sent car parts flying, and one of the doors landed on top of Monique. We haven't had an update yet, but I'm going with the 'no news is good news' theory."

"My goodness! It just never seems to stop—I dropped in to check on her boss earlier. He is sedated against the pain, so I've not been able to talk to him. He'll be furious when he finds out Monique was injured again. I hope they can keep him out of it a bit longer. You both look frazzled. Why don't you let me bring you something? Be right back."

The ladies watched Steve get up and head toward the cafeteria.

"Mom, I think he likes you just a little bit, and you don't seem to mind his attention too much. And, I guess Sunday is canceled. It isn't a good time to entertain."

Constance figured Torrie was talking just to stay busy and didn't reply.

Five minutes later, Steve was back with coffee and, to the delight of Constance, some pastry.

"What a treat! We haven't eaten anything since breakfast. I forgot to remember to be hungry. Torrie, you choose your pastry. I can't decide which one I like the best."

"Go ahead and eat them both. I really don't want anything except this coffee."

"Honey, please eat something. Maybe just half of something."

"No! I really don't want anything to eat. It isn't unusual for me to skip meals, and I've survived all of these years on my own without someone telling me what to do. Please excuse me; I can't sit still any longer. Call me on my cell if the doctor or anyone comes with an update."

Constance and Steve watched as Torrie practically stomped out of the waiting room.

"Well, so much for a nice mother-daughter weekend."

Steve felt the tension between the two.

"Her stress level is definitely high. I hope our relationship isn't causing her grief because I'm not going away just to make her life easier."

Constance had to smile.

"I'm sure it isn't you. Torrie isn't one to sit still and wait. And even if she were upset about you, I wouldn't let it be the reason for you to walk away.

"I appreciate the snacks, but you don't need to stay here. It's a long wait, and Monique isn't the only one in the hospital. Go take care of your job."

"I know I don't have to, but I have some things to do before I can call it a day. I'll be back as soon as I can. Please call me when you get word on Monique if I haven't made it back."

"Of course, now go."

After a quick hug, Steve hurried away.

Chapter Fifty-Five

Reed looked out the window of the jet. With only twenty minutes to go, the others slept or at least pretended. He'd tried to sleep but gave up after an hour. Instead, his mind went back to Monique. She shouldn't have left herself open to injury. Now, because of her actions, they were one agent down at the most critical time. Of course, he was suspicious of his motives for being angry with her actions. Monique had been a valuable asset during the investigation, but he feared his feelings went beyond gratefulness for her contribution to his team. Reed just hoped the Washington, DC field agents held their own. If the Washington team succeeded in their part of the mission, this team would mainly be a cleanup crew. He looked at his watch and then surveyed the rest of the agents. It was close to arrival time, and as if a dinner bell rang, team members made their way to the food tray. Jack stood in the spot he used when he provided instructions.

"Hey, guys! Hello. Go ahead and get your food. We have about fifteen minutes before we land. But listen to me. There will be three cars for us with directions to McConnell and the coordinates as to where you are to place yourselves. We didn't have time for scouting, so pay attention to the instructions. I will hand you the two-way radios and your weapons on the way off the plane. Please make sure everything is in order and ready for action. I don't want any surprises. After everyone is off the jet, I'll make a quick call to Bill to check the status of his team, give last-minute instructions, and then we'll be ready. If anyone has any questions, now is the time."

The team looked at each other, but their eyes gravitated to Reed with expectation. Reed knew he had unanimously been voted to ask the question on everyone's mind.

"Jack, the main question we have right now is, what have you heard about Monique's condition? Have you checked on her yet?"

"As a matter of fact, I checked, and she is still in surgery. I don't have details except that she is critical but stable. We need to not dwell on what happened and stay focused on our mission. I hope to catch someone who will trade buddies and details for a lighter sentence. All right, the seatbelt light is on, so everyone get settled."

The private jet landed without incident. To the dismay of everyone, the weather was cold, snowy, and windy. A climate of this type could make the covert activity a bit easier, but it made discovery more difficult. Of course, it was that time of year, so everyone was prepared. Jack opened the weapons cabinet as the pilot released the exit and directed the field tech where to position the ramp. The others bundled up in protective clothes and formed a single file line behind Reed. Each one accepted the equipment from Jack. The minute they had their gear in hand, the team descended down the ramp and hurried into the small lobby. The inside temperature was cold but not frigid. The small building protected travelers from the elements. Jack entered the hangar but didn't join the team right then. He made a detour to a small office and pulled out his satellite phone. Before they could make a move, they needed to get status from the DC team.

Bill looked at his phone and knew it was Jack. He spoke without any preamble...

"Have you landed yet, and are you on the base?"

"Well. Hello to you too, Bill. Yes, we just landed. No, we haven't made it to the base. We'll get going as soon as I get a status update from you. Did you request this weather?"

"Funny. Of course, I didn't request this weather. The status is the commercial flight was delayed because of this weather. My pilot didn't foresee a problem when the first team left, so everyone on the private flight is there. I think part of the danger is over as far as the Joint Chiefs of Staff go. But if the control tower is a target, we are still vulnerable if the control tower is compromised. I don't know, Jack, the more we get into this, the more something doesn't feel right. We could have gotten our information all screwed up, and everything we've planned is just a waste of time, energy, and manpower. The hypothesis doesn't seem to fit anymore."

"So, what? Do you want to abort this mission on the chance it's just a figment of our imaginations?"

Jack looked outside at the weather and sighed. Bill put to words the thoughts he'd ignored the entire flight. Yet, at the same time, his team was attacked. Why would someone go through the danger of capture or death if they weren't on the right track?

"I hear you, Bill, but I don't want to abandon what we started. Maybe we do have it all wrong, but then again, what if we're right?"

184

"I know. If there is even a slight chance that anything we guessed, is correct, then it's worth the time. If we didn't follow through and something happened, I'd kick myself because we could have stopped it."

"Let's just go forward and put our people in the places we planned. You have the protection detail for the Joint Chiefs of Staff, so I can only assume the part about the missiles is correct, or they wouldn't have planned for the entire team to fly out of Washington, DC on a horrible night like this. I'm going to go straight to the base commander and speak openly to him. If there aren't any missiles, I'll call everybody back, and we can go home."

"I can live with that. My team is there, after all. Good luck, Jack, and please keep your people out of trouble!"

Jack made his way back to the lobby and his team. He wanted to get this over and go home.

"Let's go!"

Chapter Fifty-Six

All three SUVs traveled in a convoy for the first few miles. When they were about ten miles away from the airbase, two of them broke off in different directions. One was going to approach the base from the north and the other from the south. Jack drove straight to the main entrance and was stopped at the gate for an identity check.

"Good evening, sir, miserable night! May I have some ID, please?"

Jack didn't say a word; he knew the Sergeant wasn't interested in a conversation. His only interest was confirmation. Jack monitored the MP for any reaction to his FBI credentials. Not surprisingly, the guard didn't show any emotion.

"Thank you, sir; who are you here to see?"

"The base commander, but Sergeant, he doesn't expect me. My visit is urgent and top-secret, only for the ears of the commander. Time is of the essence. If you can please get me cleared, I will be grateful."

The MP looked at Jack for a moment, observed his dress, looked surreptitiously into the back seat. None of this went unnoticed by Jack. Thankfully, the assault rifle and the two-way radio were out of sight. Jack could not have talked his way out of that. A few seconds later, the Sergeant went back to the shack, hopefully to announce his visit to the base commander. Jack rolled his window up to keep the frosty temperature outside. The Sergeant's conversation went on for too long. Jack was due to check in with everyone in a few minutes. He unquestionably hadn't put enough thought in about base security. If the missiles were indeed here, it stood to reason security would be high. Anyone who claimed to be some top official would be suspect. He hoped they decided to check on his credentials before they arrested him.

Crackle, static, screech, crackle.

"Team one reporting in. (More static—) Can anyone hear me?"

Jack looked at the gate and saw the MP in deep conversation, so he rescued his radio from the floor.

"Yes, team one, command reads you—although not loud and clear—must be the weather. Are you in place?"

"We were able to breach the entrance without too much trouble. Have you heard from team two yet? The weather is shitty and getting worse. I can hardly see my hand in front of my face. This will not be easy."

Suddenly another voice came over the radio with as much static and noise as team one.

"We—not—yet. Repeat having—something…"

"Team two, please repeat! I only heard a few words—what is going on?"

Nothing but static. Jack attempted several more times to raise team two, but they didn't respond, either because of the interference from the weather or something else. Jack wasn't sure if he should abort and attempt to find Craig and Jennie. Jack had to sign off and hide the radio quickly as the MP approached. He lowered his window and looked expectantly at the gentleman.

"Well, can I go? I have to see the commander immediately."

He used his most authoritative voice to relay the urgency of the situation and emphasize the possible danger. The MP's bored expression communicated clearly that he was not in the least impressed.

"You check out, sir. We haven't located the commander yet. It is after hours, so he isn't in his office. He might have gone home by now, but I'll try all of the spots he frequents before I attempt to reach him at home."

Jack started to protest, but the Sergeant had moved away from the car before he opened his mouth. Now what was he supposed to do? He got back on the radio.

"Team one, can you hear me? Were you able to get anything from team two before they shut down completely?"

"Command, that would be negative. I don't like the sound of their cryptic message. It seemed more than just garbled communication. What do you want us to do?"

"I think you are right. Are you in a position to get back to your vehicle and drive around to the other side? I'm concerned, but right now, I am stuck at the MP shack. I don't have permission to enter the base yet."

"Already back at the truck and just left the base. We'll drive around the perimeter until we find team two, then contact you."

"Approved—be careful!"

187

Jack was impatient, and he was concerned the Sergeant was stalling. He tapped on the steering wheel and thought hard. Suddenly he got out of his vehicle and strolled to the door of the shack. The MPs were startled by his action and went for their rifles. Jack backed off and put his hands up to show he was not armed.

"Hold on, guys, take it easy. I apologize for my abruptness, but I really must talk to someone now. If the commander is not available, who is? I assume you were able to confirm that I'm with the FBI, and I would not be here in this godforsaken piece of the world on a night like this except for something major. Please, find me someone."

"Agent Richards, please get back into the car. We will find someone who can escort you onto the base. You did not bother to notify anyone of your visit, so you will have to be patient."

Jack stared at the guy. He was dumbfounded by the response and just about to let all his indignation loose; he even had his mouth open, but before the first words made it out, his well-trained mind reigned him in. Instead, he meekly said okay and went back to the SUV. Jack closed his eyes for a moment and attempted to breathe out his anxiety.

Ten long minutes later, the first MP was back and motioned Jack to lower his window. "You've been cleared to enter the base. Go straight in and make a left at the first corner. Follow that road to the back where the hangars are until you see Hangar D."

The hangar where the ICBMs are supposed to be.

"Okay, thanks."

The night was awful, thunder, blinding lightning, and in all that mess, snow. How can there be a thunderstorm in a blizzard? Jack slowly drove toward the hangars and looked at the identifying numbers. When he located Hangar D, his heart jumped into his throat. It was lit up like daytime with a flurry of activity. He pulled up in front, braked and put the car in park. Jack marveled at the commotion. Nothing covert about this setting. He got out of his vehicle, anxious to discover just what this was.

Jack stopped in the entrance, stunned. Huge semitrailers were parked in the bay doors, soldiers swarmed all over the place. One team unloaded trucks, several men drove forklifts, and another group directed the drivers to different locations. The cargo was housed in wooden chests about six feet long. The crates didn't contain labels or logos. Jack stood rooted to the floor, gaping at the scene. Soon, an officer spotted him and headed toward the surprised FBI agent.

"Good evening. Hell of a night to invite yourself to a tour of the base. I'm Commander Silverstone. Welcome to our humble base, Mr. Richards. I bet I know why you are here, but please don't let me guess. Explain."

"I'm here because the FBI and the CIA have monitored terrorist activity, and all information pointed to an attack on your base. We also suspect there are ICBMs in Hangar D, the reason terrorists targeted this base. Our mission is to keep these dangerous weapons from bad company."

"Noble duty, but futile. For one, it's illegal for us to even have one missile here much less enough to fill a hangar. And second, the bad guys probably have as many or more than we do. The third reason is kinda funny, really. You have fallen into a Homeland Security trap. For months, the agency spread false rumors about an ICBM shipment to lure terrorists. We never imagined we would capture another agency."

"You mean to tell me this is one big ruse?! And you had no idea other agencies had been investigating? I have had good people seriously injured, and several good officers killed to stop a bogus terrorist attack! I cannot believe you didn't hear about the tragedies!"

Jack ranted on as he paced around the commander. This jerk probably wasn't a real commander but an agent from Homeland Security. He didn't understand the reason, and indeed the plan did not justify the catastrophes. He was livid.

"Whoa there, sir! Don't take this so personal. How could we know about what other agencies are doing?"

"How could you not know! The attacks are all over the news. You had to have suspected something. What is your real name? I'm sure it doesn't have commander anywhere in it!"

"Okay, you caught me. Now simmer down. I work for Homeland Security, and my name is Clint Jordan. Since you and your team came all of this way, I cleared it with my boss to allow you in on the assist."

Jack was too livid to speak. His silence prompted further communication by Clint.

"Also, you might be interested to know that the alleged meeting with the Joint Chiefs of Staff was also bogus. The weather gave us an excuse to stop the flight and the meeting has been indefinitely postponed."

Jack was furious. Absolutely furious enough to spit nails! How could this jackass be such a—a—he couldn't think of a word. After fierce internal raging, Jack took a deep breath, several deep breaths, in fact, and attempted to calm himself. He had to get control of this situation and now. His team was outside in this weather. It was past time to check in with them, plus he also had to notify Bill and his team.

"I don't pretend to like the way this was handled. I won't even pretend I want to assist you. I will give you the benefit of a doubt that you thought this through, and you had a good reason to set up this scam. My team and I won't like it, but we can work with you. I have to salvage our time and expense somehow. But first, it's past time to check in with the guys. I have a question for you. Do I bring them in or tell them to sit tight and wait for further instructions?"

Clint didn't know that his plan had caused all this chaos. If the scheme really did trigger the attacks, he couldn't blame Jack for his anger. The mission was never intended to be complicated, and the threat of injuries was considered negligible. All of the agencies involved needed to have a meeting and find out where the breakdown was. But now wasn't the time to mention it to Jack. Clint needed to maintain his calm and give instructions.

"Ask your team if they are in a position to sit tight safely and stay out of this weather. If they can do that, no need to call them in now."

Jack went back to his car to retrieve his two-way and decided to talk with his agents from the SUV. He could say exactly what he wanted to say without any interference.

"Team one, team two over."

He heard nothing but static and hissing, so he adjusted the frequency and tried again.

"Hello? Can anyone read me? Over."

"—can—not clear—what is …"

Jack adjusted the frequency one more time.

"Can you read me more clearly? Over."

"Yes, much better, Jack. What is going on? It's been thirty minutes since we've heard from you! Are you in trouble? Over…"

"Thank goodness—Reed, were you able to find team two? Are you all together?"

"That's an affirmative. Team two had a flat and slid into a ditch. Right now, we are all in one SUV. We abandoned the other one. I assume it can't be traced back to anyone here or the agency. Again— are you in trouble?"

"It seems, ladies and gentlemen, we have stumbled into a mission initiated by Homeland Security and are kind of in a mess. For now, I just need you guys to trust me and hold your position. Keep warm and out of sight. Do not - I repeat, do not attempt to locate or intercept any bad guys."

Jack's statement was met with complete silence except for the static. He wasn't sure if he had lost them or if they were too stunned to respond. A full minute passed. Still, no one spoke.

"Hello, anyone there? Please respond."

"Uh, yeah—sure—still here. I think we intercepted another message. What we heard doesn't make much sense."

"No, Reed, you heard me, and I know you understood what I said even though you don't understand why. I have to contact Bill and let him know what happened. We still sort of have a mission, and I have to work out the details with Homeland Security and Bill. Stay put and wait for new instructions."

Jack could visualize his team as they looked at each other in disbelief and wondered if he was under duress.

"No. The answer is I'm fine. I don't need to be rescued. This is for real. You have to trust me on this."

"Roger that, Jack. I still think you need to be rescued, or maybe this Homeland Security team needs to be rescued. We'll wait for further instructions—over and out."

Jack had to smile at Reed's statement. Reed was more accurate than he knew. Clint was in danger of his wrath and the fact that Jack was able to restrain himself proved he had become more of a politician than agent. He took out his cell phone to call Bill. The phone had a better connection than the satellite phone.

"Jack! Why the hell did you call me from your cell!"

"Calm down, we're good. Discretion is no longer necessary, and I'll explain after you update me on your progress."

"I'm still not good with this non-secure contact, but I have good news. My agents surprised three suspects outside the tower, captured them without incident, searched them, and discovered explosives. They are on their way to the FBI office in Wichita. The main objective is to keep them secured until we decide the best plan of action. Now, explain to me what's up with you?"

"Finally, something went right. Great job by your team. Now, you'd better sit down for my report. The news from this end is not quite so positive. Actually, I don't have anything positive to report, except no one is injured at this time."

"Why did you say that? Did something happen?"

"No. Well, one of our SUVs had a blowout and ended up in the ditch, so we are down one vehicle. I was grasping for some good news to share. I ran into a snag when I tried to get to the base commander. It seems that we have been victims of a scam created by the Homeland Security people. They have staged all of this to lure a team of terrorists into a trap."

"No way! This is a scam? Do they understand the serious repercussions of what they did? You mean to tell me, there are no ICBMs? So, can I assume there was never a meeting set up with the Joint Chiefs of Staff? The canceled flight was part of the scam? What—How—Why?"

Jack could tell Bill was just as outraged as he was.

"Watch your blood pressure, guy. You don't want to be a casualty of your mission. You caught some terrorists, and I get to gaze into the face of this Homeland Security jerk as I tell him. I'd take a picture but probably need to keep some semblance of propriety."

"I can't believe this. I'm almost too angry to enjoy our success."

"I know. I'll put in your two cents worth to the creator of this fiasco. Congratulations again to you and your team. Stand-down for now but remain alert."

Jack closed his cell phone, looked back at the hangar, and noticed Clint in the doorway with a cigarette. No time like now to break the "good" news. He pushed himself out of the truck and, as an afterthought, grabbed his rifle and made his way back to the activity.

"My team is on standby right now. By the way, the agents we deployed at the traffic control tower have three suspects in custody. They rounded them up and found explosives planted around the tower. The terrorists are on their way to the local FBI office right now."

"What? You heard about an attack at the civilian airport? How did you figure that out?"

"Well, Clint, it wasn't too difficult to make that leap. After all, what better way to hurt the United States than to confiscate illegally stored ICBMs and to take out the entire Joint Chiefs of Staff? Your little scam created all kinds of moving parts across the country. When this is over, we will have a little get together for a game of show and tell."

Jack felt no end of satisfaction as Clint's smug face turned into astonishment. The FBI agent felt like he had just won a championship fight.

"Now, let's hear about your plan and talk about how we should change it."

"Hold on. Don't be a smartass. We don't need you for this mission; we are just showing some courtesy for the trouble you took to get here. I have a unit ready to move out as soon as our scouts give the word. We have surveillance all around the base, on every intersection within a five-mile radius. Everyone reported in about five minutes ago with an all clear. As soon as anyone spots suspicious activity, we'll know and begin deployment. Your people need to get linked into dispatch so they can begin their observations and report anything out of the ordinary. Do you think you can relay that information to them? They don't need to go anywhere, just stay where they are and observe."

"Oh, I imagine we can accomplish that. We have some experience with surveillance."

Clint chose to ignore Jack's sarcasm. He turned and went back into the hangar.

"Hello, team. Do you copy?"

"Loud and clear, boss man. The wind has died down some, so the static is gone for now. What's the update?"

"I have some good news and some bad news. What do you want first?"

"The good news, of course. We always have to have the good news to make the bad news easier to handle."

"Okay, the good news is that Bill's team was able to take three suspects with explosives into custody without a fight. They are on their way to the FBI office here in Wichita."

"Super! Now, that is something we can brag about back home! I suspect the bad news has to do with the plan Homeland Security has. If I know them, they said we could be part of the team as a token of goodwill, am I right?"

"That's a roger, Reed. They will allow you guys to stay where you are and look for anything of a suspicious nature, then report back so they can deploy their units. Set your frequency on station 32.5 to report any unusual activity. We'll play out their little game and then go home."

Chapter Fifty-Seven

Constance looked up at the clock in the waiting room yet again. She felt like she had waited a full forty-five minutes before she looked up and discovered it had only been fifteen. Waiting was the pits. The next time she looked up, she saw Torrie.

"Hi, Mom. Sorry I abandoned you. I had to get out and get some fresh air. Hospitals are not my favorite places."

"Hey sweetie. Do you feel better?

"Yes. I went to a restaurant across the street. Here is a cup of coffee and a sandwich. That pastry wasn't the best thing to eat for someone who hasn't eaten since morning."

"Thank you, dear, I really can use some food, and I'm sure the coffee is much better than hospital cafeteria stuff. I haven't heard anything yet, but they should be out any minute now. I'm glad you're here."

Constance unwrapped the sandwich, took a bite, then a sip of coffee. Yum, it was the best sandwich and cup of coffee she'd had in years. The two sat in silence while Constance ate, and Torrie stared at the wall. About ten minutes later, she saw Steve look into the waiting room. He didn't come in immediately, and Constance knew he debated whether to join them or not. She looked over at Torrie …

"Honey, it's about time for Steve to get off. I'm sure he'll want to check on us. Would you like it better if I go find him and talk to him?"

Torrie was so absorbed in her thoughts about her life that her mom's voice startled her. She turned her head towards Constance and, out of the corner of her eye, spotted Steve hovering in the doorway. She gave a half-smile.

"Mom, please. I don't mind the reverend. I'm not angry now, nor was I angry when I left. I get impatient and hate to wait. Wave him on over."

With relief, Constance stood up and went to Steve. They hugged each other and walked arm in arm to the spot where Torrie waited. No one spoke up right away, so she decided to say something to ease the awkwardness.

"Hello, Reverend. Welcome back. Before you get the wrong idea, I'm glad you and Mom have decided to date. I am a moody person. If you hang around long enough, you will have to get used to it."

Before Steve had a chance to reply, they all looked as a doctor strolled into the room.

"Good evening, I assume you folks are here for Monique Yorkshire?"

"Yes, doctor, I'm her mother Constance, this is her sister Torrie, and I assume you know Steve. How is she?"

The doctor nodded to each person as introductions were made but didn't feel the need for a verbal response.

"First, she made it through surgery better than we had anticipated. I want to ease your mind about that. She's a sick young lady with serious injuries, but there isn't any reason to doubt she'll make a full recovery over time. Just how much time will depend on Monique's resilience. I understand she had just been discharged. Actually, the specifics in her chart are that she discharged herself after waking up from a long-term coma."

"That tells you that if Monique is anything, she is resilient. What all did you do?"

"We set her arm with three pins in various locations to hold the bones together. She'll have a cast on for several weeks to keep it immobilized, then physical therapy. Unless the pins cause problems down the line, we won't put her through the trauma of removing them.

"Her spleen ruptured, so we cleaned her up inside, and I put her on a strong antibiotic to reduce the chance of infection.

"Her leg was delicate. The injury came close to her femoral artery. We had to proceed with caution when we put her flesh back together. I didn't want to accidentally nick the artery myself. The leg is fine, not pretty, but functional. I'm sure if she feels the need to make it look pretty, there are any number of plastic surgeons happy to assist with that.

"She has stitches on her check, we had to stitch a small cut above her eyebrow, and there was quite a long cut along her neck. She's in recovery now and will be there for another two hours. I plan to send her to the ICU for at least tonight. I don't expect her to wake up at all for another thirty minutes, so if you guys want to take a quick break and get some dinner, please do so. Monique is stable; her

196

vitals are strong. She is, of course, heavily sedated, and we'll keep her that way for a day or two. We want to keep her as comfortable as possible. Does anyone have any questions?"

The Yorkshires and Steve listened carefully as the doctor gave her report. They were stunned to hear from the doctor just how badly Monique had been injured and thankful at the same time because they also knew if not for the grace of God, she could have been fatally injured. The doctor waited patiently for them to absorb everything. Monique was her last patient, and she had time before she went home.

Constance couldn't think of anything intelligent to ask but felt it was her duty to respond.

"Uh, I'm not coming up with any questions right now. Thank you so much for taking care of her. Torrie, do you have any questions?"

Torrie looked at her mother, then to the doctor.

"Thank you, doctor. I don't have any questions. If we think of something later, can we get in touch with you?"

"Certainly, the nurse or nurses on duty will know how to reach me. If anything happens during the night, I will, of course, come back. If not, I usually make rounds between seven and nine in the mornings and six and eight every evening. If I don't come, then my partner will step in for me. By the way, my name is Dr. Elizabeth Barton, and my partner is Dr. Clifford Yancey."

Constance took out her little notebook and wrote both doctor's names down. She still couldn't think of anything to ask.

"Thanks again for your care. Have a good evening."

"Your welcome. I'll see you later."

Steve was aware of how exhausted Constance and Torrie were. He decided to accentuate the positive.

"Well, ladies, I think we heard some good news in all of that. Monique will survive, and except for some scars, she won't have any residual damage. I know you won't want to leave the hospital, but …"

"No. Actually, I do want to leave the hospital. Torrie found a restaurant not far away. The coffee is good, and I just want to get out of here and breathe some fresh air. Torrie, would you like to join us?"

Torrie thought about it for a moment. She didn't want to be intrusive, but she also didn't want to be by herself, either. Her mind was full of random disquieting thoughts.

"Yes, as a matter of fact, I do, but I'll take my own car. Steve, if you drive, take a left after you leave the main entrance of the hospital, and the restaurant will be on your right three blocks down. It's called Esther's Place. They'll be open for about two more hours, but we won't be there that long."

"Thank you."

Steve looked sheepishly at Constance.

"I'm happy to drive, but I think you'll be more comfortable in your own car. Mine is strictly a bachelor's car with no luxuries at all."

"Here are the keys, then. Torrie, we'll see you there."

The three left the waiting room without delay. After a long and stressful six hour wait, they were glad to take a break from the hospital.

Chapter Fifty-Eight

Donna heard Monique moan and gave her some more medication. The poor girl had only been in recovery for fifteen minutes and didn't need to surface to the pain just yet.

I am aware of excruciating pain! I can't open my eyes, and I panic. The feel of this place is not the same as it was before. I can't, of course, be in a different world because there isn't any such place. However, I'm equally as sure Gabriel will appear.

"Hey girl. You are right, I'm with you. Right now, you are in the recovery room. The surgery took five hours, but you did fine."

"I don't feel fine. I feel groggy. Gabriel, I am really tired of this cycle. Actually, I'm just tired. The doctors probably gave me some drugs. Did the FBI complete its objective? By the way, I doubt we are on the right track. I can't think now, but I thought of something right before the attack. Now, my head hurts too much to remember."

"You aren't the only one with those thoughts. It played out like a disorganized crime spree. The FBI and the CIA tried to fit it all into order. You had great ideas, and most of them were correct. The reason it felt wrong was another agency involved set up a scam that precipitated the events. Your teammates are in Wichita, but they will be back tonight. It was successful in a roundabout way."

"Not sure what that means. I really don't want to hear anymore. I hurt too much, and I'm too tired. Please, show yourself out. Oh, and Gabriel, one more thing …"

Monique's words faded away. Gabriel smiled and waited for her to resurface. He knew what she wanted to say, but it was important for her to finish the statement.

"Uh—Sorry, one more thing, I don't intend to talk to you anymore or have anything to do with an alternate world. You were swell and all and thank you. But please leave. Now."

"You are quite welcome, and I might add quite correct. There are still things to be discovered before your mission is complete, but this is the end of my mission. You will heal nicely, and your life will settle into a normal kind of routine. At least as much normal as the life you have chosen will allow. Thank you for the privilege of working with you."

Gabriel watched as Monique drifted off to sleep. He had enjoyed this mission, but his part was over now, and it was time to say goodbye to Monique and move on to the next mission.

Chapter Fifty-Nine

Jack stared out at the gloomy night. This was the worst case with which he had ever been involved. People hurt, lives lost, screw-ups. They did have some terrorists in custody, but so far, the captured suspects hadn't given any information. Hell, at this point, Jack didn't even know if they knew anything to provide. If they didn't, was the loss of life worth it? He was never comfortable with the justification of a few deaths to save many more. The members of his team slept, except Reed. He was sure Reed's mind worked even though he shut his eyes for a moment. He expected the young agent to give up pretending to rest to come and have a conversation.

Jack was correct in his thought that Reed was too angry about this entire fiasco to relax, much less sleep. Punching someone out would help, but since he couldn't do that, he decided to talk to Jack, who wasn't even pretending to sleep. Reed pulled himself out of the recliner and made his way to the bench seat opposite his boss.

"I wondered how long it would take you to abandon your pretense. Please have a seat. What seems to be on your mind?"

"Nothing positive, for sure. I don't like the way any of this went down. Did we accomplish anything? Hours of work and investigation, arms deals, money laundering, kidnapped family, dead suspects and police officers, injured agents. The entire escapade resulted from a scam put on by Homeland Security?"

"It does seem kind of a mess. When we get back and get some rest, we'll regroup. I think the scam got out of hand unbeknownst to those jerks. Don't forget, we did intercept a group that tried to take down the tower with explosives. If we hadn't intervened in their mission, we'd see a huge casualty list of civilians. I think there are some unrelated activities at home that we need to look at."

Jack agreed, but his mind skirted to another matter.

"Monique won't be happy she missed being with us. Though she will change her mind when she hears about this misadventure we had. It was anticlimactic the way it went down. The DC guys take credit for the Wichita Airport save, and the Homeland Security Agents claim victory because they arrested two suspects that they claim are terrorists. If you ask me, and you haven't, but I'll tell you anyway, I don't think those guys know anything. Do you suppose all of this went down to keep us from the discovery of their end purpose?"

"Could be. Bottom line, though, Homeland Security set the pieces in place for the Wichita debacle. Unless there is a mole in their ranks, then it was a comedy of errors."

"Yeah, only it wasn't so funny. Jack, we have to forget everything we've discussed and go back to the beginning with fresh eyes. Most of the information we've worked with only serves to throw us off track. Maybe Monique can see a different perspective."

"I don't know. She's suffered extensive physical trauma and may not be able to see any perspective for some time. I agree, she has a great analytical mind, but a person can only suffer so much before it affects objectivity."

Jack waited for Reed to say something else, but when that didn't happen, he ended the conversation.

"We have about two more hours until we land. I want to close my eyes and at least rest. Maybe I'll either pass out or come up with a brilliant thought that will solve this case."

"Good luck with that."

Reed went back to his recliner, and Jack stretched out on the bench. While it was just a bench, it had leather cushions and pillows. The combination made for a comfortable lounging experience. He felt defeated at the moment and wished for that brilliant idea. One thing was for sure, he did not want to hash through these last few hours anymore.

Chapter Sixty

"Gabriel? Is that you? Where are you? I can't see you. Am I blind?"

"What's that, dear? Did you ask for someone? I'm your recovery room nurse. You just got back from a long surgery and are probably in a lot of pain, not to mention confused. You are going to recover, but meanwhile, do you need some pain medication?"

Monique heard the nurse speak, but her mind was slow to make a coherent thought. All she could think about was Gabriel and pain. Nothing made sense, which scared her because that meant she didn't have control over what happened! What did the nurse ask her again?

"What do you want to know? I—I'm not sure—Who are you?"

"Please relax, Ms. Yorkshire. You just woke from surgery, and I know nothing makes sense right now. I've given you something in your IV for the pain. You will be asleep in no time. Your mother and sister came by about fifteen minutes ago while you were still out of it. I'll let them know you woke up but are back out. If you don't mind, I want to suggest they go home now. You will go to ICU from recovery."

The nurse waited for Monique to calm down and her vitals to stabilize before she went to talk to her family. She hoped the reverend could help her convince them the best thing for everyone was for her mother and sister to go home and rest. It had been a long day.

"Mom, look, there is the recovery nurse. Why did she leave Monique? I thought they weren't supposed to leave the patients alone for even a minute."

Torrie, Constance, and Steve stood up as the nurse made her way to them. Constance was certain the nurse would not be out here if it weren't safe to leave Monique. She accepted her presence as positive.

"Hello, nurse, is Monique awake yet?"

"She did wake up but was in a lot of pain, so I gave her some more medication. Otherwise, she is doing well, or you wouldn't see me. The best thing you three can do is to go home and get some rest.

Monique will be in recovery a while longer and then to ICU. We are going to keep her pretty sedated for the next few hours. If anything happens, you will be notified immediately."

No one said anything for a moment. Steve looked at Constance, then at Torrie, then back to Constance. He decided he would not attempt to sway their decision. Torrie observed Steve and could almost hear his thoughts out loud. When she noticed he unconsciously stepped back, she knew he decided not to say anything. She'd made the same decision. Her mother was the one to make the call. Constance, on the other hand, paid no attention to anyone until she made up her mind.

"Thank you, and I like your suggestion. It's been a long day, and I am not liking hospitals right now. If you're sure you will call me if anything should happen, then I think we'll leave for the night."

"You have my word. Now, go home and have a good evening."

With that said, the nurse hurried back to her patient.

"Torrie, if you want to go to your home tonight, I understand. I love having you stay, but please don't feel obligated on my account. And Steve, I'm okay for you to go home, too. In case you have any doubts, I won't be fixing Sunday dinner as planned."

"But Mom …"

"But Constance …"

Both Steve and Torrie spoke at the same time, and both stopped at the same time. Steve couldn't help but chuckle a little.

"Please, you are first."

"What—did that strike your "funny bone" again?"

This was said a bit sarcastically but not with the usual bite. Torrie was almost smiling.

"Darn, now I have a reputation to live down."

"Mom, I really want to stay with you if it won't interfere with anything. I am more relaxed than I have been in years, and I like how it feels."

"Goodness, what could you possibly do to interfere with anything in my life? And, Steve, it might be nice to order pizza, gather at my place, and play trivial pursuit. Torrie, remember when we used to play that game when Dad was still with us? Most of the time, you came out ahead of everyone. I think I have increased my useless knowledge since then and can give you a run for your money."

Torrie was flabbergasted! Her mom had actually suggested a social activity, something she hadn't done since Dad died. One of the reasons Torrie drifted away from family gatherings was boredom. This Steve person seemed to have a positive influence.

"Sure. Steve, I'm game if you are? As Mom said, I'm the undefeated trivial pursuit champion of the family."

"I say let's go for it. I have one visit to make before I leave. Constance, if you want to order the pizza, I can pick it up on my way. I'm happy to pay for it, and it will save delivery charges plus the tip."

"Sounds good. What kind of pizza do you like? We both like the supreme with stuffed crust, and cheesy breadsticks with Alfredo dipping sauce."

"Order exactly that, and I'll bring it to your place."

Chapter Sixty-One

All was quiet at the police station. The detectives had gone home for the weekend except for Detectives McPherson and Shaw. They continued to investigate the "Monique Yorkshire" case as they called it. Neither one thought to forget what they knew, and once something was theirs, they felt responsible for following through until the end. Once more, they reviewed the news reports and events and compared and matched the information they gleaned from their investigation. Since it took the bigger part of the day to put the information in order, the detectives were glad they were low on active cases.

Eve summed up their evening.

"I think these supposed special agents, who probably get three times more money than we do, overlooked a major piece of the puzzle. They were in such a hurry to solve this case; they didn't look beyond the obvious."

Mike leaned back in his chair and stretched. He was ready to call it a night and get something to eat. Lunch was a long time ago.

"I agree, and because of their carelessness, the only thing they accomplished was putting out little fires. Unless they locate the root cause, the fire won't die – so, it's late, and I for one don't want to be here all night. Let's call it a day and start fresh in the morning. We have time to get some greasy burgers and ice-cold beer from Barney's, what about it?"

"Ah, Mike, you know what greasy burgers do to my girlish figure. All I want to do is go home and catch the late news, and I want to watch it from the comfort of my home in my comfy P Js, not some loud bar."

"Spoilsport! I guess I'll drive through McDonald's and grab me something from there and eat it at home. I'm not in the mood to sit in a bar by myself."

"Now that is a healthier choice. Honestly, Mike, the way you eat and as much beer as you confess to drinking, I'm surprised you don't weigh a ton."

Mike laughed at that last comment. Little did Eve know that he was all talk when it came to what he ate and drank. If she followed him around, she would discover he didn't eat junk food or even drink beer by himself. There wasn't even any at home.

"Get outta here. I'm out as soon as I put this stuff in my locked drawer. I don't want anyone in our business."

Eve walked out the door, and Mike locked up their investigative work and followed after his partner.

Chapter Sixty-Two

The weary agents arrived back at the sanctuary of the FBI headquarters. It was late, and they felt like they had been gone for a week when less than twenty-four hours had passed. The team congregated in the conference room for a quick recap. Jack was aware of the exhausted countenance of each of his people, but it was the discouragement and despondency which concerned him most. The agents pointedly observed the seat Monique typically populated and then quickly lowered their eyes. What he said now was critical to motivate them back into the investigation. The truth was, he felt just as dejected as his team. However, the boss has the responsibility to encourage. He tried to look each member in the eye, but no one looked in his direction. Jack decided on his approach.

"Come on special agents. Reed, Jennie, Barbara, and Craig – what do you think this is, a funeral? We had some successes today! Snap out of this mood you guys are in. Monique isn't dead. In fact, she made it through surgery just fine. I spoke with her mom. They think she will only be in ICU for twenty-four hours. This is a strong, dedicated, and driven woman. If we don't want to look like fools in her eyes, we have got to pull it together and figure out the root cause of these attacks! Today was tough. We may not have succeeded in our goal, but again, we are not finished. You are the best of the best, or you would not be on my team!

"The next step is for everyone to go home. It's midnight, which means its Sunday. Because this is Sunday, I want you to take the entire day off to recoup. Don't think about the case even for a second. I want you back here bright and early Monday morning with a blank mind and no preconceived ideas about this case. We'll go over everything as if it's the first time to see it. We will—I repeat—we will figure this out! Now, does anyone have a word, be it a gripe, an observation, or an opinion? This will be the only opportunity to voice any concerns."

Even though Jack knew his team would realize pessimism was counterproductive, he gave them another minute. Jack noticed the change in his team's demeanor and also saw the faint glimmer of a spark. He was glad he'd had the foresight to get a report on Monique before he landed.

"All right, people, dismissed. And remember your instructions!"

He watched as his team quickly dispersed. When the last one left the room, Jack sank into his seat, leaned back into the chair, and plopped his feet on the conference room table. With his eyes closed, he recapped everything that happened from a few short days ago. If he could just relax and let everything play out, that elusive something would finally penetrate his weary mind.

Jack knew someone was in the room, but he didn't open his eyes. He already knew Reed had come back because Reed's presence filled a room. He even knew what Reed would say.

"What happened to those famous words you just spoke? I believe it went something like, 'don't think about the case even for a second.' I think I got it right."

"The boss is exempt from the rules. I make them for everyone else; they don't apply to me. What are you back for? Do you plan to pester me with something?"

"Not really, unless you consider the fact that I came back to escort you out of this room and into your car to make sure you really leave this place for the day, pestering."

"Yeah, that is pretty much pestering. I don't need an escort. I'm a big boy and can take care of myself."

"Jack, you are full of bull. Even now, you're rehashing everything that has to do with this investigation. Soon you'll go to your office and pull out the datasheets you have gone over a hundred times already. Next, you'll get out a brand-new tablet and list bullet points of all facts as they come to mind. Then you will put them in chrono …"

"Okay! Enough already! So, you know how I work. Just leave me be Reed."

"…logical order. Next, you'll consider every conclusion we've already made, because you would have done all of that without the break you so wisely insisted everyone else take."

Jack finally gave a chuckle. Reed was obnoxiously stubborn and one hundred percent correct.

"You win—you win, okay? Let's just leave. Show me to my car and point me in the right direction. I'll see you here Monday, which technically is tomorrow since it is now one o'clock in the morning."

Chapter Sixty-Three

Steve remained sitting at the table watching as Torrie started putting the game away.

"Let me help you put that away, Torrie. I'm happy to."

"No. The rules of the family are that the winner always puts the games away. Since I am the winner of every game, I happily put this game away by myself."

"Come on, Steve, let's go into the living room and finish your coffee and cheesecake. Then you probably need to go home so you can get up and get to church on time."

"Are you sure you don't want to take a last run to the hospital tonight now that Monique has been transferred to ICU?"

"I appreciate your offer, but the nurse said she's stable, sedated, and peacefully asleep. If nothing happens overnight, she'll be in a regular room by mid-morning. There is nothing I can do for her, and I have faith in the nurses, so until she's transferred to a regular room, I'm not in a hurry to get there and wait."

By the time Torrie finished her task, Steve and Constance were whispering on the couch. Steve took the last bites of his cheesecake, gave a great big sigh of contentment, put his plate down, and picked up his cup for a gulp of the great coffee.

"That was the best last-minute put together cheesecake I've ever tasted. Thank you so much. I can't wait for the rain check on Sunday dinner."

Constance laughed.

"You're too easy to please. The cheesecake was a mix, takes no talent at all, and the coffee is a good brand. I could cook up the worst dinner you have ever tasted. How disappointed you would be."

Torrie walked into the room. She heard her mom's laughter and noticed how comfortable they were with each other. Steve observed her hesitation and saw her turn to leave.

"Hey, winner! You finally put up the game? Come join us. I have to leave in a few moments. Regale us on how you happen to be such an expert in trivia!"

Torrie hesitated, but just for a moment, surprised that she had a desire to accept the invitation. Typically, nothing could make her socialize, especially with religious people. To her credit, she chose not to analyze her reaction.

"Okay, I'll join you. You asked how I became the trivia queen? You have to blame it on Dad. He loved insignificant details and never missed an opportunity to spout them off. He would say things so off-the-wall, and I couldn't believe they were real. I used to research some of the information he gave us to check it out. Everything he said I authenticated. It was great!"

"I had forgotten that about Greg. Early on in our life, his knowledge fascinated me. Later, I just got so busy with all that had to be done. I ignored him on the random topics. I quit listening to what I considered useless chatter."

Steve responded in kind.

"There was one phase in the many phases of my long life before I lost my wife to cancer, that I thought I was supposed to be serious and only think serious, profound things. After I became a pastor, I assured myself that every word out of my mouth must be filled with wisdom and discernment. Holy people don't laugh. I shudder to think about my congregation. Don't get me wrong, I come from a long line of family with a sense of humor. I couldn't be completely serious. Still, my distorted idea of spirituality was sure to have bored many folks. Now, I just go with the flow, try to seriously listen to others, but at the same time, try not to always be serious. I rely on the Holy Spirit to guide me and trust that He knows His job. Of course, in my own humanity, I sometimes get it wrong."

Steve grinned self-consciously with his last statement. He imagined that Torrie remembered the times he got it wrong. But when he heard the words Torrie spoke, he realized he didn't know how her thought processes worked at all.

"Yes, I want that! I finally figured it out. Mom, I want that. I want to be able to be me and not analyze everything I say or every move I make; will it offend someone? Will the client want to hear the presentation? Will I come across as a top performer? Can I do a better job? I'm tired of being what I think my boss or my clients or my co-workers want me to be. All these weeks with Monique and Connor and all the facts I thought I knew about them were absolutely and completely not true. Now I've realized I wouldn't know when I saw or heard the truth even if the word "truth" rode up to me on a horse and told me, "Hey, I'm truth."

Torrie looked at her mother and Steve to make sure they didn't think she had completely lost it. She saw the corners of Steve's mouth twitch and realized how hard he was trying to keep his laughter in check.

"It's okay, Steve. You can let your funny bone out for air. Laugh if you want."

"Oh. Thank you, Torrie. I'm not laughing at what you said, well except for the truth riding up to you on a horse statement. That was what tickled me. I understand why you are at the top in your field. You have a way with words, and people listen. I like that. But seriously, what you said makes sense. Through the ages, people decided what was normal and what wasn't and tried to categorize accordingly. I don't know who made the "box," but no one wants to be out of it, and if a person thinks outside the box, they are shunned. It's rare to find a person not molded into some kind of a façade that doesn't exist. We won't be comfortable with who we are created to be until we understand the One who created us wants us to be just that. God doesn't want us to pretend to be anything except human. The Word tells us in Genesis 1:27, we were created in His image, only on a smaller level. All our emotions are the same ones God experiences. We have free will, but we also have a void inside which only our Heavenly Father can fill. The free will is that we can choose to allow Him to fill that spot, or we can try to fill it with other things, and ..."

Steve stopped mid-sentence. He realized he inadvertently sounded like a preacher, which was not his intent. He didn't want to scare Torrie back into her shell before she discovered from whence her restlessness came.

"I'm sorry, guys, and embarrassed. I've not been in a pulpit for a while, and our conversation ties into my sermon for tomorrow."

Again, no one spoke for several minutes. Steve was self-conscious with the silence but kept quiet. He wasn't sure what else to say or how to get himself out of this spot. He breathed a silent prayer.

Torrie rescued him.

"Okay, I get that, but let me ask you a question. I told Mom about some of the things that happened the night Connor showed up at my door with a gun. Things like how I uncharacteristically talked and made conversation, small talk. I never small talk, even on a good

212

day, much less under duress. I was afraid, but still, thoughts on how to act and what to say filled my head. Things I did without a plan. Is that something God would do? Even for me? Because I haven't accepted the Lord as my Savior. I never felt like He was a Savior for me or that I wanted to live my life for Him. Why would He care about a predicament I got myself into?"

Steve sat there, momentarily stunned with Torrie's questions. Her mind was as active as Monique's. Though why should it surprise him when he considered who raised these exceptional young ladies? He chose his words carefully.

"Why wouldn't He care about His creation? His children? He orchestrates this life within the realms of His rules. But He also made the rules, so He can just as easily alter them to fulfill His plan. His plan cannot be frustrated by anyone, even by the dark forces. What mankind forgets is that in the end, God already won the war when Jesus Christ offered Himself up as the ultimate sacrifice. So, the fact that you reacted uncharacteristically wasn't difficult for Him. In fact, let's go deeper. What if all He did was release your self-inflected inhibitions, and you essentially reacted in character with how He created you?"

Constance sat silently and prayed for Steve and his responses as well as Torrie and her struggle. She couldn't think of anything to add or say, but then the questions weren't directed to her. She had taught the girls about the love of Christ, made sure they went to church, and lived as an example to the best of her ability. Everything that happened culminated in this place in time, right now, where God used Steve to bring it all home to Torrie.

"That is deep. I may have to think on that a moment or day or week."

Torrie's emotions and body reminded her of the lateness of the hour. She was exhausted and ready to quit this conversation for now.

"It's time to end this evening. I'm tired. Steve, I want to hear the rest of the sermon you began. Do you mind if I go to your service? I know Mom will go to the hospital, and Of course, if Monique takes a downward turn, I'll go too.

"I am honored to have you ask and, of course. You are always welcome, as are your mom and your sister. You don't have to ask permission."

"Thank you. Please give Mom the address so I can get to the right church. Goodnight."

"Sleep well, sweetheart."

Constance got the church address from Steve. They walked to the door, and Steve gave Constance a quick kiss on the cheek and was gone before she could react.

Meanwhile, Monique woke to pain, confusion, and chaos. From some far away distance, she heard a few moans, some beeps, and an alarm. The alarm irritated her. She recognized the sounds of a hospital.

"Oh, dear, that silly pump, always going off. Ah-ha, there is a reason it went off. It looks like it's time for another bag. I'll go get one."

The nurse was gone before Monique could form a word, much less an entire sentence. Her memory of what had happened was vague. She worked to remember – it was a ride to somewhere. What happened during the trip, and where? Kansas, but—the rifle sticking out. She yelled, then—nothing. Things got fuzzy after that. Whatever had happened, she was injured. She attempted to take inventory of her injuries but was too dazed to try. Must be drugged with some strong medicine. She didn't want to analyze her mess anymore and let the medication do what it was supposed to do— make her mind blank.

Chapter Sixty-Four

Mike went straight home, fixed a sandwich and a poured a glass of milk. He set the alarm for thirty minutes earlier than usual, to be the first one at the office. No one would be there to know except Eve, but she was the only one that mattered. On a typical morning, he'd hit snooze several times, but today, at the first sound of the alarm, he fell out of bed and stumbled to the shower. The water was more cold than hot, so he came fully awake in a hurry. Mike hurried through his morning routine and left with time to stop at Starbuck's.

Mike whistled as he walked into the station with the two venti coffees, straight up. Neither detective indulged in cream, sugar, or other fancy creations. He pulled open the door, greeted the on-duty desk officer, walked to the detective's wing, and stopped in his tracks. Eve stood at the whiteboard writing. How did she do that? He just stood there glued to the floor. Soon Eve felt his presence and yelled.

"Hey, you're late! Come on over with the coffee. I've worked for thirty minutes without the benefit of caffeine, so who knows what is on this board."

"So why didn't you get your own coffee? I was sure I beat you. Do you have a camera in my place to track my movements just so you can be the first one in every morning? Can't you just let me once get here first? Here's your caffeine."

"Stop whining; you sound like a baby. I knew you'd bring coffee, so I came straight to work; further, my magic is private. Just deal with it! Now, look at this board and tell me what you think?"

Mike sat down in his chair, turned it toward the board, took a big swig of his java, and began to read. He noticed pictures of the victims involved with Monique at the top. There was Monique, then underneath, there was Officer Bryant, Connor, and Officer Shank's partner. Over to the side were empty faces and the number of unknown terrorists which the CIA and FBI had taken out although it was only a best guess. No one, at least no one on the outside, knew the exact number.

First Attack

215

- Car accident, two months later doctor reported it as suspicious
- Signs of struggle at victim's apartment
- No evidence of friends or social life of victim
- List of evidence:
- Silver egg matches wound on head
- Cuff Link with "C"
- Tests showed injuries not related to car accident
- Evidence found at the crash site:
- Sheet hidden in weeds
- Victim's right arm under seat belt
- CIA took case away

Second Attack
- Fake nurse at hospital early
- Fake nurse made mom uneasy
- Mom takes break comes back yells for help
- Nurses take care of Monique, tests show abnormal levels of potassium
- Detectives brought back for investigation
- CIA makes an appearance
- Security for Monique
- Staff is questioned

Third Attack
- ...

"That's as far as I got. What do you think about the seatbelt and the sheet? Those two facts would have sent up a red flag for most officers. This is the first time I've looked at the report in detail. These two facts should have caused us to receive the report weeks before the doctor did."

Mike had chewed on that himself.

"I can only think of two reasons. Someone on the inside covered it up, or a rookie was working the scene. Well, three reasons. It could have also been someone in a hurry to get home who got lazy."

Eve furrowed her brow in concentration.

"I can see a rookie might not understand the importance of a sheet on the scene, but a second oversight by disregarding the seatbelt is too much."

Mike scratched his head. "I kind of agree with that. Who was the lead investigator on the scene?"

"Let's see, I think the names of the officers are—yes, here. The lead investigator was Officer Bryant. Wasn't that ..."

"Yes! Exactly. So, we know it wasn't a rookie or someone in a hurry to get home. Bryant intentionally passed over the evidence to make sure we didn't investigate. I'm sure they didn't expect Monique to survive long. If the doctors hadn't decided to do more tests, we wouldn't be here now."

"Do you think the chief should know about this?"

"Probably. If only to document what we found and possibly to open an internal investigation. There may be other bad guys amongst us. I'll let you write up the report. You're better with paperwork."

"If I didn't agree with you, I might call you sexist. 'Leave the paperwork for the girls,' but I know you stink at it."

"You made your point."

The two detectives went to work sifting through the rest of the evidence they managed to recreate after the CIA confiscated it. They also reviewed newspaper reports and television news transcripts and discussed what they had uncovered during the times they were involved.

Several hours later, Eve looked up from a report and announced it was time for lunch. Mike agreed. They took the short jaunt across the street to the sandwich sub shop and ate in silence. Most detectives on the force had an unwritten rule not to take work out of the station except for field work. Mike and Eve were comfortable with silence. Eve finished the last bite of her sandwich.

"Ready to get back to work?"

"Sure, as soon as I refill my drink."

"Well, make it fast. The sooner we get this solved, the sooner we can—I was about to say relax, but then I remembered who we work for."

Eve gave a huge grin, picked up her trash, and they made their way back to the precinct nourished for the long afternoon.

Chapter Sixty-Five

Constance was up and dressed. She had just taken the last bite of breakfast when Torrie strolled into the kitchen to pour herself a cup of coffee. Now that it was morning, Torrie regretted her decision to attend services. What was she thinking? Bailing out on the reverend wasn't an option because her disciplined nature did not allow for canceled commitments.

"Okay, Mom, it's obvious you've something on your mind. I can see it in your face and almost hear you, so say it already. So, let's hear it, I have to get ready to go to church."

"Am I that obvious? I used to be so good at hiding my thoughts."

"Really, Mother dear, we just let you think that and didn't encourage you because we knew it meant we'd be forced to admit to a plan you wouldn't allow."

Torrie's statement caused a giggle to erupt from Constance, a rarity since Greg passed.

"And I thought I was so good! You answered my question. I wanted to ask if you planned to hear Steve preach and then offer to go too if you would feel more comfortable."

"You must really want me to go. To think you would stay away from the hospital. No, I'm a big girl and have done things by myself for many years now. Monique won't do much but sleep, but she needs to see someone she loves when she manages to wake. Go, see Monique. I only have a short time to get ready."

"I am as good as gone, thanks. Will I see you later on today?"

"Yes, this afternoon after lunch."

Constance went out the door, and Torrie got up to shower. Torrie wondered if the ceiling would cave in when she walked into the church.

Chapter Sixty-Six

This time when Monique woke, there was a different nurse at the formerly beeping machine. Must be morning with a change in shifts. Monique wanted a drink of water to quench the dry desert in her throat. To get the nurse's attention, she did a small cough and gasped at the pain which followed.

"Well, well. Good morning. Here let me get you some ice chips. The doctor doesn't want you to have anything by mouth for at least today but said ice chips would be fine. I'm sure you will think it's the best thing invented!"

The nurse was pleasant enough. She didn't say the usual, "how are we feeling today" and other such nonsense. Why did nurses like to put "we" into their sentences? If she had asked, Monique would have crackled out the truth. "I feel like I have to get better to die." But the nurse didn't ask, so she didn't have to talk. She did nod her head when ice was mentioned.

"Let me get your vitals and go see what I can find for you."

The nurse turned on the blood pressure machine and the cuff, which was Monique's constant companion, inflated.

"Open your mouth so I can check your temperature."

There was a beep from the thermometer, and the cuff began to deflate at the same time.

"You have a fever, about a hundred and one, and your blood pressure is slightly elevated. The fever isn't unusual after what you've been through. The elevated blood pressure is a direct result of your pain. See this pump with the button on the end? I want you to push that button every time you feel pain. Don't worry, you can't overmedicate if you push too often. Usually, patients are conservative when they have control over when to give themselves pain medication."

Monique took the pump and pushed the button right away. The narcotic eased through her system. Once again, she closed her eyes and gave in to the darkness. The last thought before she drifted off was how dry her throat was. The idea didn't linger long before the comfort of oblivion took over.

Constance was at the hospital and had been with Monique for several hours. She sat in the lounge chair and watched her daughter sleep. If only she could have both girls at home safe and sound. Monique was anything but restful. At least that's the way it appeared to Constance. The fever broke an hour ago and sweat engulfed Monique's battle-worn body. There was little she could do to comfort her daughter, but Constance tried. She found a washcloth and filled the emesis basin with cold water to wipe her brow, face, and neck.

A nurse came in and interrupted Constance thinking.

"How is our patient doing, Mrs. Yorkshire? Her color looks better to me."

"I haven't noticed her color, but she's restless. She wakes just long enough to push the pain button, then falls asleep again. About thirty minutes later, she gets restless, then moans with pain and pushes the pain button. She has repeated that cycle all day. I tried to get her to take some ice chips but gave up on that. I'm not sure she even knows I'm here. Honestly, it feels eerily like I've traveled back in time to when she was in her coma."

"I'm sure, but the fact that she moves and makes sounds has to be a comfort. And rest assured, Mrs. Yorkshire, Monique knows in some part of her mind that you're right here with her. She'll continue in this state for at least a day or two. When her pain levels out, she will gradually get tired of inactivity and allow herself to wake up and join the living. That is, if I read her correctly."

"You've nailed her. Monique isn't one to stay down long. In fact, the very day she woke up from her coma of over two months, she was back at work. She's my miracle girl. I think both of my daughters are miracle girls. God was good to me, and I'm thankful to have them in my life."

"We heard about this one when she was here the first time. Mercy Memorial has seen many miracles, but Monique's story will live on, even after we are dead and gone. I've got to check my other patients now. Go get you some lunch. The lunch crowd is gone by now."

"Thank you. I think I will in a few minutes."

Alone again with her thoughts, Constance's mind took her to Steve and Torrie. It was three o'clock, late enough that either Steve or Torrie should have checked in by now. She wished Torrie had

220

asked her to go to church with her. Of course, it wouldn't have been easy to be away from Monique this long.

"Hi, Mom! I am so sorry we're late. How is Monique?"

Torrie didn't wait for a reply. She strode over to Monique's side and looked at her sister's face and the vitals that flashed across the screen.

"Her blood pressure is too high. Are they doing something about that?"

"It's high because she's in pain. They have her on a pain pump, which gives her control on when and how much medicine is dispensed. She had a fever, but it broke a while back. I see that it's up slightly, but the doctor said fever is common after extensive surgery. No cause for concern unless it gets to a hundred and two. You remember from yesterday that the doctor has her on a broad-spectrum antibiotic to help keep infection away. I'm glad you're here now. I'm kind of lonely."

With those last four words, Torrie realized how constantly and unobtrusively her mom had always been there for her daughters. All of these years, she and her sister took their mom's dedication for granted. Once a crisis ended, they both went on with their lives without a thought about the sacrifices she made. What did their inattentiveness cost her? When was the last time they thanked her?

"Well, I'm here now, and Steve isn't far behind. He decided to go to a drive-through and bring you some lunch. We went to lunch after church to continue our discussion and figured you hadn't eaten."

Constance waited for more but soon realized nothing was forthcoming. Why did Torrie have to be so closed off when it came to intimate conversations?

"Mom?"

"Yes, sweetheart?"

"I want to tell you how much I love you and how thankful I am that you are my mother. I know I've never said it, but I appreciate all the times I needed you, and you never let me down."

Torrie reached down and gave her mom a great big hug. When she released Constance, tears glistened in both of their eyes.

"Hello there, everyone—uh, I'm sorry to interrupt, should I come back later?"

Steve noticed the look between mother and daughter and couldn't decide whether to leave or stay. He took the high road and just asked.

"No, please stay, Steve. Mom and I took a moment to reminisce. If you don't know by now, I will warn you that this person is sentimental despite her brave façade!"

Steve's naked tenderness for Constance overwhelmed Torrie. She teared up over the love so evident, though neither one acknowledged it.

"Well, did you bring lunch? Don't just stand there like a blubbering idiot; give it to her. Mom, while you eat, we'll share what our day was like. Your questions are loud and clear without a word."

"Gracious, Torrie! Am I always such an open book? I certainly have to work on that."

"No, Constance, my dear, you do not have to work on that. Here is your lunch; grilled chicken and a side salad with your choice of honey mustard, ranch, low-fat ranch, and vinaigrette."

Steve grinned big as he listed off the salad dressings.

"I wasn't sure which one you preferred, so I brought one of each. Though I initially thought you'd be a low-fat ranch kind of a person, you get your choice."

Constance laughed.

"And you would have been wrong—or right ..."

"Well, that cleared up any uncertainty that I might have had. Wrong, and right? I don't understand."

This time Torrie joined in on the merriment. She understood perfectly what her mother meant, but poor Steve. The look on his face was priceless.

"Don't you know anything about women? Haven't you ever heard the statement; it's a woman's prerogative to change her mind."

Steve gave one of his famous chuckles.

"Okay, I surrender. I can't keep up with the minds of the Yorkshire women!"

"And you shouldn't try, or slow insanity may result."

Conversation ceased as Monique's voice resonated. Several seconds passed before Steve, Constance, and Torrie actually absorbed what she said.

222

Steve was the first one to recover from his stupor.

"Well, well, well, and I must say, we couldn't be more pleased to hear your melodious, crackly, cottony voice young lady!"

"Please, I don't feel young, and I could kill for water or ice chips at the very least. Please stop your stares. I'm not in a zoo, and I won't show you any tricks. Maybe you should want me to push the nurse's button?

Torrie and Constance came alive with Monique's statement. Both made a move to get her ice chips since that was what the nurses had talked about.

"Mom, I will get the ice. Just give me some room please."

Constance quickly changed directions and went to the side of Monique's bed to make sure her ears didn't deceive her. Sure enough, there was Monique, alert albeit beat up.

"Monique. You are awake, finally. How do you feel? Are you in too much pain? Have you pushed the pain medicine pump? Do you want something to eat? Steve brought some food. I can share. But then maybe you aren't supposed to eat anything yet. How about a sponge bath? I'm sure that will make you feel better. Should we leave you alone? I don't want you to get weary of our conversation."

Steve gently approached Constance as she rambled. He put his arm around her and quietly spoke.

"I think you need to step back and regroup while Monique digests what you said and maybe even answer one or two of your questions."

Monique's gratitude for Steve's sensitivity to her and her mom was boundless. She loved the fact that Constance had let someone into her life who cared for her. If that was accomplished while she was in a coma, then it was worth it.

"Thank you, Steve. I think we had a runaway brain. Mom, believe me if I were in lots of pain, I would still be out. I'm far from pain-free, but I'm ready to be done with this convalescence."

"Here are your ice chips, and don't think for a minute that just because you are tired of resting, you will be well. Take your time and learn to stop for a minute. You won't get your way with this."

Torrie was stern because she knew Monique wouldn't listen otherwise. Besides, she was upset that her sister was always doing something. She could never take any time off. It was like—she wasn't sure what—but it irritated her.

"Okay, boss. I hear your command, and I will obey you, just please let go of the ice."

Torrie hadn't relinquished the ice chips, and Monique's mouth needed something in it like now.

"Oh, uh, sure. Here, I didn't realize ...."

Torrie, appropriately embarrassed, decided it was time for her to leave and process her emotions that had accumulated since Monique's first accident. She didn't understand her actions or reactions lately.

"I think it's time for me to go. I've had a long day. Feel Better Monique; bye all."

Constance was aware of the girls' interchange and disappointed with the results.

"Let me walk you out, Torrie, I ..."

"No! I mean, please quit. I'm an adult. I can walk myself out. I can even make it home—or to your house or wherever the heck I decide."

Torrie's confusion caused irritability, and she was ashamed of her reaction. Constance's momentary flash of hurt registered and she felt low.

"Mom, I'm sorry. I didn't mean to sound harsh. I think I'm on overload right now. We'll talk later. And Steve, will I see you tonight?"

Constance was stunned by Torrie's outburst and responded to her accusations before Steve could answer.

"Of course, you are an adult, and I apologize for my forgetfulness. Please go home and get some rest. Also, there is a chocolate cake in the refrigerator if you want a snack."

Constance quickly glanced at Steve.

"And yes, you will see Steve tonight."

There was an awkward silence as Torrie gave her mother a quick cheek kiss and walked out the door. Monique observed this scene. Though her pain distracted her, she still absorbed all the little details and nuances and filed them away to process later.

"Okay, someone will have to explain what that was all about. Either everyone has gone nuts, or I have created myself another world, just as bizarre as the last one."

"What world?"

Constance and Steve asked at the same time. Steve backed off and let Constance take the lead.

"You mentioned something about another world while you were in your coma. Would you care to elaborate? I'm… we—we're curious."

"I guess I walked into that one. First, I need some more ice chips before I begin. Steve, you might as well sit down and make yourself comfortable. The story I have to tell will take some time."

Monique took the replenished cup of ice and began the long story of her alternate world.

Chapter Sixty-Seven

Mike and Eve looked up at the same time. They had just finished going over all the evidence for the umpteenth time. It was late evening. The day was twelve hours of hashing and rehashing everything. Eve noticed the glimmer of a profound thought take form in Mike's mind and waited for him to say something.

"Okay, I think that the best we can do is come up with a generalized idea, only because we aren't privy to anything the CIA has, or the FBI for that matter. We know that this latest attack happened when the FBI team was on their way to a plane to fly off somewhere. I think we can safely assume it was something to do with whatever all of this is. All of these incidents or attacks are related. We haven't sifted through enough to get to the top of the chain, but something is going down somewhere, which will be catastrophic in nature. Part of the drama may have been planned as a decoy. The planners plotted to distract the investigators and hide the target. I'm sure at least one or two crimes were directly connected to the final outcome."

Eve waited some more because she knew Mike wasn't through. No great insight on her part because he had just gotten up from his chair and paced as he spoke. He continued to walk around, which meant he was still processing his thoughts.

"The evidence that hasn't been considered is Torrie's company—rather the company for which she works. Why would Connor end up with that company? It wasn't a random act that put him there. I think we need to take all this information and turn it over to the CIA. They need to get a list of clients that Connor and Torrie worked on. There's something there. I'm sure of it! We've gone as far as we can. It's time to turn this over to the big boys and step back.

"How do you propose we share this information with the CIA? We can't just drive up to the door and ring their doorbell and say, 'Oh, hi, we're the police. We have information for the bigwigs working the Monique Yorkshire case that they would never think about.' We would be laughed out of the state, that or locked up or institutionalized!"

Mike laughed long and hard at the thought of the two of them being carted away in straitjackets. He could almost picture the headline:

"Two Police Officers Arrested"
Last night detectives attempted to break into the CIA on pretense of knowing something!"

He noticed that Eve had joined him in his humor even though he never shared a word. The laughter was a good tension reliever. They had been at this entirely too long.

"Eve, you do have a way of cutting to the chase! Of course, we can't go to their 'home'. You forget, we have an inside track to someone who is or should be in the middle of this investigation, and that is Monique, remember? She's close and likes us and doesn't treat us as some kind of flunky. Remember when we assisted with the murders at the hospital? She trusted us to take point on that. Hell, Eve, she even asked for us."

Eve hit herself in the head with the palm of her hand.

"Of course! How can I be so dense? She should be coming around by now. Let's go right away!"

She said all of this as she gathered her coat and gloves and purse.

"Hold on there, not so fast. First, we haven't eaten anything since lunch, and we've worked non-stop. Let's get something to eat and develop a strategy of what we want to say to Monique. We can approach her calmly and—gulp—humbly put our ideas out to her."

Eve stopped where she was. Mike was right. He usually was. She was one to blindly jump into a fire. He tended to be the one to grab hold and save her neck. That's the reason they made a good team.

"Okay, smarty. Where do you want to eat, and if you say Barney's, I just may have to perform one of my secret moves on you."

Mike chuckled. He knew that Eve could be deadly with her black belt move though she didn't usually resort to violence. She would use any means to calm a volatile situation in place of a physical confrontation.

"I'm not afraid of you, although, I don't understand your sudden aversion to Barney's. Let's head to Betsy's Diner. It's quiet, and everyone tends to keep to themselves, plus it's close to the hospital."

"Wow, what a great idea! Occasionally you can come up with a good plan. Let's go. Give me the keys. I'll drive. Don't even try to argue because you'll only lose."

Mike didn't argue with Eve because he knew he wouldn't win. He was ready to get out of this place and get some good old-fashioned food. Betsy's offered exactly that, good old-fashioned food. He meekly followed Eve out of the door.

Chapter Sixty-Eight

Steve and Constance sat in silence, stunned by the story Monique just finished. It gave them chills to think about her adventure mixed with the greatness of God. He healed Monique's mind from the trauma and shock, prepared her for the battle she faced the minute she came out of her coma, and healed her emotional hurt from the death of her father. All those miracles combined with the fact that God removed all physical infirmities common to one after weeks of inactivity. He provided clarity of mind to bring Connor down and save her sister and herself. How can anyone claim there is no God with evidence supporting the opposite?

Steve was the first to find his voice.

"All I can think to say is wow. Really that is literally all I can come up with."

Constance stood and walked over to Monique's bedside.

"Well, sweetie, you look exhausted, and you haven't used your pain medicine once since you woke up hours ago. Steve and I are going to go for now, and you push that button as many times as you need and get some much-needed sleep."

Constance stopped for just a moment to put her hand on Monique's forehead.

"Your fever is back. I'll inform the nurse before we leave. I love you, and remember, you are not invincible."

Constance gathered her things and kissed Monique's cheek. She practically pulled Steve out of the room.

"What? You didn't even let me say good-bye? What did I miss? Why did we leave so abruptly? I know it couldn't have been because Monique was worn out."

Constance found Monique's nurse.

"Hi, we're gone for the night. Monique's fever is back, so you might want to check it."

"Thanks. I'm on my way to take her vitals now."

"Thank you for not interrupting us. I'm sure you didn't come as often as you normally would have. For your information, Monique

229

had four cups of ice chips and didn't take any pain medication until just now."

"That's a long time without pain medicine. She's pooped out, I'm sure. Goodnight, you two. Have a good evening."

"Night. As always, call me if Monique has any trouble."

Constance turned her attention to Steve. He stood close by with a dumbfounded look on his face. Poor Steve, he had never been a parent, so of course, he would be confused with her actions.

"Well, Mr. Reverend, Chaplain Sir. Shall we make our way to—oh, I guess we drove in separate cars. So, plan b, let's go sit in the waiting room so I can explain all about being a parent."

Steve breathed a sigh of relief. At least Constance hadn't completely ignored him.

"I can live with that."

Steve and Constance walked the short distance to the waiting room. It was Sunday evening, so they had as much privacy as they needed. They settled in two chairs across from each other to better communicate.

"Okay, Ms. Yorkshire, please enlighten me of the mysteries of parenthood."

"Gladly. We both agree that Monique's story was phenomenal, but didn't you notice how much energy it took to give us all of those details? And she talked all afternoon without taking any pain medicine. Her face showed enough pain and exhaustion; I couldn't ignore it. You'd have asked questions, and because Monique wants to be accommodating, she would've done her best to answer all of our questions. I didn't want her to be forced to have to admit that she had to rest, and I didn't want you to be embarrassed when she told you she wasn't up to any more talk. That's the reason I made a quick exit."

"Well, thank you for bullying me away. You certainly have some fascinating daughters. Shall we go to your house to see what's up with Torrie?"

"Yes, let's do. I'm anxious to hear what happened this morning."

They left the hospital, Steve walked her to her car, gave her a quick hug, and they parted ways.

Chapter Sixty-Nine

Mike and Eve arrived at the hospital as Constance and Steve left.

"Mike, this way is Information. They should be able to tell us what Monique's room number is."

"Hello. May I help you?"

"Yes, what room is Monique Yorkshire in?"

Eve asked the question.

"Let's see, Y-O-R-K-S-H-I-R-E. Is that how you spell it?"

"Yes, and the first name is spelled M-O-N-I-Q-U-E, Monique Yorkshire.

She is in room 225, but it's late. It's best if you check with the nurse before you go to her room."

"Sure, we'll do it."

The detectives took the elevator to the second floor and as instructed, stopped at the nurses' station.

"Good evening. May I help you with something?"

Eve spoke for the pair.

"Yes, uh, nurse—Camille, is it? I am Detective Shaw, and this is Detective McPherson."

Both detectives reached for their badges and allowed the nurse to inspect them before she continued.

"We'd like a few minutes with Monique Yorkshire."

"I don't think that is advisable. Monique had a long afternoon and has taken pain medicine. She's sure to be out for the night. May I ask why two detectives are here to see an extremely sick patient on a Sunday evening?"

Mike decided to take up the conversation.

"Nurse Camille, thank you for your diligence in caring about your patient's security, especially Monique. She has had too many attempts on her life. We are the detectives that helped with the investigations a few days ago when someone tried to kill her the last time.

"We have information important to the case she is working on with the FBI. It's important that we give it directly to her so she can get it to her team as soon as possible. It could be a break in their

231

complicated investigation. Can you please allow us just a fewest of minutes with her?"

"Yes, I remember you two. Detective Shaw was the one who interviewed me. I'm sure you can be trusted, but she won't be much help to you at least for a day or two. Her injuries are quite extensive."

Eve was dismayed by the nurse's words, but somehow, they had to get this information into the investigators' hands so they could take over and figure out the rest. What she heard did not bode well for a fast transfer of data. Eve looked over at Mike, and by his reaction, she could tell he was thinking fast.

"I understand, and we don't want to do anything to jeopardize her health. Maybe there's something else we can do. I understand her boss – I think his name is—let me think,"

Mike snapped his fingers.

"His name is Robert. We never got the last name, but I know his first name is Robert. Maybe you can tell us where he is."

Mike was proud he remembered a name, even if only a first name, until the nurse asked him how many Roberts, he supposed there were in this one hospital alone.

"I guess Robert is kind of a common name. Now I'm not sure what to do."

Nurse Camille thought for several minutes. She remembered the day of the shooting outside the hospital and the gentleman who was shot in the shoulder.

"Wait right here, guys. I may have a way to find out. I'll be right back."

The detectives watched the nurse hurry over to the nurse's workroom to make a call. She talked for a few minutes, then paused probably because she was put on hold. She started to smile. Someone was giving her information. She disconnected and rejoined Mike and Eve.

"Great news, I think I found your Robert. He is in the North Wing on the third floor. He will be discharged tomorrow, but I understand he's been belligerent and persistent with his request to get down here to talk to Monique. His room number is 363."

The two thanked the nurse profusely and hurried to Robert's room. When they got there, the door was closed. They heard his side of a less than amicable conversation.

"—and further, don't call back until you can tell me something!"

Eve gave a tentative knock on the door. No response, so she tried again.

"Well, come in! Don't keep pecking away at that door!"

The detectives pushed through the door and wondered if they had made a mistake in approaching this crotchety old man. Robert was sitting up in bed in his hospital gown surrounded by newspapers and printout sheets as CNN played in the background. In other words, the hospital room looked more like a war room at the Pentagon.

"Good afternoon, Robert. I'm not sure you remember us. I'm detective Mike McPherson. This is my partner…."

"Yeah, yeah, Eve Shaw. I remember you two. You were the ones someone called to investigate the fake nurse. Do you know the last time I had any news? I don't even know what the hell is going on. I just now found out Monique is back in the hospital, and I can't even go see her! And those damned FBI guys are unavailable. What kind of answer is that? What day is it?"

Mike looked at Eve and secretly willed her to take over. She was better able to soothe others' ruffled feathers, and Robert fit that description. Eve, of course, knew that would be the case, so she had already come up with a plan.

"SIR!" With one word, Eve had the attention of both men.

"This is Sunday, but you already knew that from any one of the many newspapers you have scattered around, not to mention CNN reports the day and time constantly. The FBI guys probably took a day off after the drama, which you also know about because you have the reports and the newspapers. Even though the articles don't give details, you are intelligent and experienced enough to be able to read between the lines. Monique is in the hospital so she can recover from her extensive injuries. No one except immediate family can see her. Even if she could have visitors, the hospital would think twice about allowing someone with your disposition anywhere near her. And no one in their right mind would want to get close to you long enough to catch you up on anything with an attitude like that—so COOL IT!"

Definitely not the soothing attitude Mike had in mind, but her approach stopped Robert's tirade. He kind of sat there with his mouth open and looked stunned.

"Lucky for you, sir, Mike and I are not in our right minds because we are here, and we will update you with what we know. Not only that, but we also have a theory we want to discuss with someone who can either tell us we're barking up the wrong tree or take it and do something about it. So, just calm down, regroup, and ask us what you want to know."

Robert picked up his water cup and took a long slow drink through his straw. When he pulled it away, he breathed slower and looked slightly embarrassed.

"I guess I deserved that. Thank you, Detective Shaw. You have my attention now. By the way, you are right. I know enough to figure out something bad went down, but not enough to confirm how bad or if there is a break which will point someone in the right direction. I found out the FBI team has been to Kansas and back and stopped something, which is when Monique got hurt. I know she's in serious but stable condition but no details as to what exactly serious means. I know tomorrow the FBI plans to start again, and I don't have a clue about their plan. If you have any more information than that, no matter what it is, I want to hear about it."

"Mike, you bring Robert up to date on what we have. I'll go to the coffee shop around the corner and bring back some real coffee. I'm sure, Robert, you haven't had a decent cup since you've been here. When I get back, we'll let you know what we think. Maybe we can get some work done on this case that will finally close it."

While Eve was gone, Mike explained Monique's injuries and the details as to how she had gotten injured. He pointed out that Monique was an actual heroine because she put herself in danger and kept other people away from the attack. He also highlighted the facts that the detectives uncovered during their investigation of the shootings. Mike was ready to begin the most current theory the detectives had, when Eve strolled into the room with a bag of donuts and three giant-still steaming, cups of coffee.

"Now we can get down to business!"

Robert was in much better spirits by then. His eyes lit up when he saw the bag of donuts.

"I'm sure part of the reason for my earlier behavior definitely had to do with the fact that I haven't had a decent cup of coffee or a donut in weeks! Well, it seems like weeks anyway."

Eve unloaded the donuts from the bag into the pink plastic tub located in all hospital rooms across the nation, for reasons no one knows. The three settled in the most comfortable manner they could and enjoyed the snacks for a few minutes before Robert started the conversation.

"Thank you for the update, Mike. I appreciate your insights as you went, even though you don't have the details I would like. I especially appreciate your update on Monique. She is a special young lady. We've worked together since she joined the CIA long before she graduated. Your notes and analysis of the situations piqued my interest. You were about to mention something you think is important to the investigation. I'm all ears."

Mike had just taken a massive bite out of one of the donuts, so Eve quickly interjected.

"Mike and I have gone over every incident that happened, including those we only generally know about. At first glance, they seem like random acts unrelated to each other. The one common denominator in all this is Connor. Everything is centered on something he seems to have set in motion. He may have been the low man and flunky, but he, for sure, was a catalyst for everything. He had the information on the guns, the money, and though in limited amounts, he had the intel. We figure they can't be random acts."

Mike took over.

"And, since they can't be random, Eve and I suspect all of these smaller catastrophes lead up to one major attack. We've captured all the known players, or they've turned up dead. So, we asked ourselves what the missing piece was, and the one question we keep coming back to is, why did Connor end up at McGregor, Bright & Anderson? Torrie said he didn't seem to have the credentials, and he didn't start out at the bottom like everyone else in the company."

Eve took over again.

"Using that logic, then, we think it'd be a good idea to check out the clients that Connor worked with and look at the background of each client for a company with pull enough to get someone hired on the sly. We figure if someone can get into the root of the companies, there is probably a cover-up of some sort. Maybe more than one. Then we can find the true masterminds behind the planned attack or attacks."

The detectives closely watched Robert's face for any signs of disdain, but years of practice taught him how to keep his thoughts from his face. Even his eyes gave nothing away. They were silent for several more minutes and waited for a word.

Robert looked directly at both.

"I think you've worked long and hard on this, and your logic is sound. Tomorrow morning, after I leave here, I plan to go to the FBI and join them in their task force, listen to what new stuff they have, and give them your ideas. In fact, I have an agent on the way with my computer. Before tomorrow, I plan to research as much as I can into Torrie's and Connor's clients."

"But how are you going to do that if you don't have a list of their..."

"Eve, he is CIA, what do you think? They have tools that real people don't even know exist. They can find answers to questions even before the question is asked."

"Oh, I knew that."

Robert was amused.

"You'd be surprised at how much information comes just from using our senses. If we start to rely too much on the machines and technology, we miss the obvious. I'm sure we'll talk to Torrie soon for an extensive list of their clients because my resources may not be complete. Now, if you don't mind, I need to get up and walk around, freshen up and get ready to do some real work in a minute. I'm honored you trusted me with all of this."

"We're just happy to pass it on to someone else. Goodnight, Robert.

Chapter Seventy

Torrie escaped to her mom's, ran through the house to her bedroom, flung herself face down on her pillow, and cried uncontrollably. She hadn't done this immature act since high school when that was pretty much an everyday occurrence.

When she closed the door on Thursday evening, it was like she closed the door on her life as it existed. Too much had happened for her to keep her emotions in check. Her action at the hospital was proof she was losing the battle. Why had all of this happened, and what was she going to do about it? Torrie knew her life was about to make a radical change. A change she couldn't even imagine.

Torrie cried until exhaustion thrust her into a troubled sleep. She woke thirty minutes later, groggily forced herself up, splashed water on her face, slipped into her nightgown, and went back to bed. Her last thought was hoping she wouldn't wake up until the end of time. Mercifully for her, this time, sleep contradicted the emotional turmoil churning inside and was immediate and restful.

Two hours later, Torrie woke up with a clear head and rejuvenated spirit. Her mind lazily chronicled the day's happenings. She wondered how one day could hold so many events, and it wasn't over yet. Mom and the reverend would be home soon. Staying in bed until the end of time was unrealistic, so with energy that surprised her, Torrie got herself up. She had time for a quick shower. Her mom wanted a report of this morning, and Steve refused to share their conversation without Torrie's permission. Monique chose a perfect opportunity to surface because it gave Torrie time to process her emotions and new knowledge. Without that reprieve, sharing all that happened wouldn't have been possible. The last bit of sleep solidified and resolved much of her internal turbulence.

Torrie had just finished brushing her hair when she heard the garage door open. She considered her reflection and pondered all of the internal changes. The mirror didn't reveal anything different about her physical appearance. But wait. Closer inspection divulged something different. She noticed that the tight, stressed countenance she saw daily was replaced by a more relaxed, almost peaceful expression. The transformation was remarkable.

Constance opened the door just as Steve was about to ring the doorbell.

"Come in, Steve. I'll put on some coffee. Torrie is still in her room, but I hear her moving around. She'll be out in a few minutes. Let me take your coat and hang it in the closet."

"Thank you. Can I do anything to help?"

"Just get comfortable. I've got it under control."

Constance expected a long evening, so she had made a full pot of coffee instead of the partial pot she usually made this time of night. While the coffee finished brewing, Constance prepared a tray with coffee cups and dessert plates for the cake.

Steve and Torrie exchanged greetings as Constance came from the kitchen.

"Ah, and here is the hostess of the day with delectable treats! Here, let me take that from you, dear, it looks heavy."

Steve jumped up and gently took the tray from Constance.

"Where are you headed with it?"

"I think on the coffee table, so it's close to all of us. Everyone can help themselves to coffee, cake, or both."

Torrie cut a piece of cake after Steve set down the tray. While she got her coffee, Steve sliced two servings, one for Constance and one for him. Constance made herself comfortable in her chair. She decided to allow Steve to have the couch to himself.

Conversation was brief while they ate and consisted mainly of trivial aspects of the day. Thirty minutes later, the empty plates were back on the tray. They were ready for serious discussion, except no one spoke. After an awkward silence, Torrie decided to say the first words since she was the "star" of the evening.

"Okay, both of you. Quit being so self-conscious. I won't get upset with every little word or action. Steve, would you pray for all of us?"

Steve was surprised at Torrie's unexpected request.

"Certainly …"

Heavenly Father, our almighty, all-powerful Lord, and Savior. Thank You for Your love and Your desire to have a relationship with us. You withheld nothing, even Your Own Son, to make a relationship possible between a Holy and Righteous God and a sinful people. Because of the sacrifice of Jesus Christ, we can find unmerited favor in Your sight. Guide our conversation this evening and give us divine wisdom to seek out the truth. In Jesus's name, we pray—Amen."

Without explanation, Torrie began.

"Okay. Let me start by saying that Steve presented a powerful message. He elaborated on everything we discussed last night. I couldn't get his words out of my head. The statement he made about, 'what if God just released me from my self-inflicted inhibitions'; remember?"

Constance nodded and Torrie continued.

"While Steve preached, I remembered every Sunday school lesson and conversation you had with us when we were children. I thought about Dad and how it was when he was still with us. During lunch, I talked non-stop about everything I heard as a child and couldn't understand. When I finally ran out of words, I asked Steve to make sense of everything because all I knew was jumbled up like puzzle pieces in a box waiting to be put in order.

"The first thing he told me was that I already had the answers. All I had to do was to trust myself and to turn off the chatter that went on in my mind. I don't know how he knew about the chatter, but it's always a constant and takes effort to shut it out. I've learned how to create something understandable out of the chaos in the business world, but not my personal life. The chatter was only manageable when I worked, which is what I did until exhausted. All of my life was filled with perfecting work and getting better. My goal has always been to climb up the corporate ladder as far and as fast as I could. If I didn't work, or I wasn't exhausted, restlessness forced me to work harder to keep from being fidgety. I tricked myself into believing I was accomplished and confident and on my way to make a name for myself.

"Then the tragedy with Monique happened. It forced me to spend more time in my personal life than I wanted. Feelings and emotions, I had forgotten about, surfaced. The chatter became almost unbearable. In all honesty, I was on my way to a full-fledged breakdown. If things hadn't happened the way they did, I think I would have been forced to take a leave of absence from work and do something drastic.

"When Steve told me that I had the answers already, I wanted to slap him across the face. I opened myself up to him and asked – almost begged – for help, and he threw it back on me! I was so angry and said things that were not nice, but I can't remember exactly what. The only thing I remember thinking is that he wasn't going to get away with it."

Constance use her peripheral vision to monitor Steve's reaction to all of Torrie's emotions. He sat there with that silly grin of his she'd come to love. She interrupted Torrie's speech to ask him a question,

"So, what went through your mind while Torrie shouted at you?"

Steve was so intent with Torrie's perception of the meeting that Constance's interruption surprised him for a moment. He quickly looked at Torrie to get her reaction before he responded. She didn't appear to be upset or even irritated and was waiting for him to answer.

"I didn't know what to think. I sat still and listened, which in hindsight was the best thing I could have done. If I had gotten angry or acted offended, Torrie and I would probably still be there. Her hands were waving so much I pictured our plates and glasses being brushed onto the floor. After a few minutes, I was finally able to catch her hand and hold it down so she wouldn't hit the table. Pretty soon, I saw her notice what I had done and—Torrie, why don't you continue from your perspective."

"Steve is right. I'm sure I took him by surprise. I know I hadn't been the nicest person, and I said hateful things, but most of the time I have control of my emotions. Mom, remember when I was ten, Monique and I got into that royal knockdown, pulling-hair temper tantrum?"

Torrie paused a moment to make sure her mom acted like she remembered.

"That is exactly what Steve witnessed – well, the intensity of my anger without hitting him. As I spoke in the restaurant, I brought my hand down with the intent to hit the table, but at the last minute, I just put it on the table. Things are a bit fuzzy as far as what more I said or did, but my anger was interrupted by a peace I wasn't familiar with. The more I talked, the less angry I became, until I noticed Steve's hand on mine. I finally ran out of things to say. Steve

240

quietly said the server had given us our bill, and it was time to leave. He got up, and I just walked out to my car and stood there until Steve came and told me to go on to the hospital. He wanted to pick up something for you to eat because he was sure you hadn't had lunch yet."

Torrie paused long enough to look at her mom and Steve.

"You more or less know what happened after that."

Chapter Seventy-One

Robert jotted down one more fact into his little notebook. The notebook was small enough to fit into a shirt or pants pocket with enough pages to make it useful for bullet notes. He only used words that helped him remember certain details. The words he chose didn't and wouldn't make sense to anyone else in case someone looked at it. Well, no one except maybe Monique. They had worked together long enough that she knew, even when they were miles apart, what he thought about a situation. He, however, could never guess what mysteries lived in Monique's mind. He chalked it up to the fact that she was a woman, and the woman's mind had always been unknown to him. He was glad that this particular woman was on his side and not the enemy's.

As Robert reviewed his notes again, he formulated a plan. It was midnight. Any minute the nurse would barge through the door and demand lights out. Earlier he had tried to convince her to ease up on the strict rules since he was not an official patient anymore. After all, he was going home first thing in the morning. Her response was to let him know the doctor hadn't signed the form, so it wasn't official. She further threatened to put something into his chart so the doctor would decide he shouldn't be discharged. Her reaction surprised him because he had put up such a fuss in the short time that he was conscious. Why would she do something which would keep him here longer? He was sure the entire staff planned to party the minute he left.

Like a model patient, he proceeded to put away his computer and all of the notes, spreadsheets, and reports. His activity did not interrupt his contemplation of the research. He discovered eight potential companies that could be used to front terrorist activities to plan some kind of attack. McGregor, Bright, and Anderson serviced the companies. He noticed three names that came up more often than any other executives and found the one company that tied them all together. Global Resources. No wonder Connor was able to obtain the position he did. It would have been suicide for the CEOs of McGregor, Bright and Anderson to refuse to put Connor in as requested. Several holes needed to be filled, but with the limited resources to which he had immediate access, Robert was not able to uncover additional information tonight. Still, he could formulate a few theories with the facts and his wealth of experience in the covert world of undercover activities. The nature of the companies gave him clues. For instance, one of the companies was almost the largest construction conglomerate in the world. As such, vast quantities of all kinds of explosives would not flag alarm in the general course of business. Another company planned world excursions for the ultra-wealthy. The types of tours in which the company specialized were safaris, mining for fun in dangerous regions, and underwater treasure hunts. This company could officially work with assault and hunting rifles, spears, harpoons, explosives, and other types of weapons in order to plan unique adventures. Robert also discovered one of the companies was an upper-scale security firm used by politicians in other countries. The other companies consisted of one doing research of an unknown nature, a manufacturer of vaccines, and smaller stable businesses to legitimize the organization. Before he could do anymore research, he had to have access to the specialty tools of his trade. The FBI housed massive amounts of intel. Since Monique was out of commission, he planned to take her place and gain access to their information.

Being old school, Robert wasn't excited to work with the FBI on anything. He resented their involvement and didn't hesitate to let it be known. Once the drugs left his body, however, his rational mind took over and he decided cooperation between the agencies made the most sense to resolve this threat. The detectives had arrived at the peak of his anger. He viewed the FBI as the enemy with the advantage. To join the investigation, he suspected groveling would be involved. The detectives handed him his ace into the "game" and eliminated the need to beg his way in.

"Sir, are you still awake? Do I need to order you a tranquilizer to make you stop?"

Yep, there was the nurse right on schedule.

"No ma'am, can't you see, I've closed my computer. I will now put it into my case and fluff my pillows to get comfortable. Could you please bring me some ice cream out of your stash of goodies?"

Robert poured on the charm. He felt positive for a change and wanted a treat. His plan to get what he desired was to be sweet.

"Don't you even try to wow me. It's too little, too late to change my opinion. I wasn't born yesterday, and you aren't a nice person. I'll bring you some pudding, we don't have ice cream."

The nurse turned and walked out the door.

"So much for charm," Robert murmured. "I guess I should feel lucky I get pudding and not Jell-O or broth."

The nurse came back with some pudding and a pill cup.

"Here, take this before I give you the pudding. It'll help you relax and maybe even sleep. I know tomorrow will be an important day for you. Even though I think you are a pain, and I don't trust you, your work is important. I want you to be fresh when you figure things out."

Robert wasn't sure what to say to that little speech, so he sensibly said nothing. He meekly took the pill and swallowed it with the fresh cup of water from the pitcher the floor assistant brought in earlier. Without another word, she took the pill cup back, deposited the pudding and plastic spoon into Robert's hands, and left without so much as a goody-bye. Robert was asleep almost before he finished the last bite of his dessert. The last thing he remembered as he settled onto his pillow was—actually, he didn't remember.

Chapter Seventy-Two

Constance took advantage of the slight break in Torrie's dissertation to excuse herself to go to the bathroom. Steve cut another piece of cake for himself and refilled everyone's coffee cup. Torrie hardly noticed, so focused was she on what she planned to say next. She was amazed at how clear her thoughts were. Typically, after such an emotional outburst, her head ached as horrendously as a bad hangover. Now, her energy level and excitement for life surpassed anything she'd ever experienced.

"Torrie ..." Constance gently prodded Torrie back into the room where she and Steve were.

"You must have been quite confused with all of the emotions you had. I can almost imagine the different expressions you had as you yelled at Steve."

It took a moment for Torrie to pull herself back from where her thoughts had drifted. She wasn't sure what her mother had said, but she knew "what" wasn't necessary. Her mom talked to give her time to refocus and continue.

"Thanks, Mom. There are so many thoughts going through my mind right now.

"Let's see, where was I? Yes, we stopped on the trip to the hospital. I got to the hospital and discovered Monique was conscious and not in another coma. The realization of my emotional instability hit me like a brick. I could barely keep it together, which is the reason I decided to leave you guys to be by myself. The minute I got in, my tears burst through the dam. I didn't stop until I had no more tears left. By that time, I could hardly see through the slits in my eyes or breathe through my nose. I fell asleep for about thirty minutes. I know it was thirty minutes because I looked at the clock after I stopped crying and the next thing I knew, thirty minutes passed. I forced myself out of bed, splashed water on my face, put my gown on, and crawled under the covers. I was ready to stay in bed for the rest of my life. Two hours later, I woke up and felt like I had just taken a nice long vacation. Well, at least what I had always imagined I would feel if I had allowed myself to take a nice long vacation."

Torrie paused again to slice herself another piece of chocolate cake. She looked up at her mom, and her expression asked if she wanted a second piece, also. Constance shook her head and took another sip of her coffee.

If she were impatient to hear the rest of the story, Torrie couldn't tell. After she had finished her cake, she settled back into her chair again, took a deep breath, and looked directly at her mom first and then Steve.

"After I woke, I heard this little voice—well, my mind heard—I thought ..."

Steve decided to help Torrie out.

"Torrie, you heard the voice of the Holy Spirit. Your soul's ears heard His voice, which is a small, still voice."

"Yes!" Torrie sighed. "That description fits perfectly. Anyway, the voice asked permission to come into my life. I always figured God could take whoever He wanted, and one day I imagined He would force me to make Him Lord. But to be asked permission was so alien to me that, at first, I didn't know what to say—or for that matter what to do. Finally, I heard—Steve, you said the Holy Spirit?-- Well, I heard 'I love you, Torrie, and I've waited many years to hear you invite me into your life. Is this the time?' When I heard the words, 'I love you, Torrie,' I felt love, a pure love which I have never felt before and can hardly explain. Before I even knew what to say, I prayed this prayer—and this is verbatim!

'Dear Lord Father, in heaven, I want You to be my Savior and my Father. I want the kind of peace that I've only heard about. Please take control of my life; it's such a mess right now. I pray that You will come into my life and my mind. Please make sense of the chaos that is continuously present. I'm ready for You to tell me what to do for a change. I know it won't be easy for You because, after all, I have been independent for so long. I'm stubborn and rebellious and ...'"

Torrie stopped for a moment, and tears welled up in her eyes.

"Mom, Steve, I heard what sounded just like daddy's voice say these words—'Torrie, you asked Me into your life. I don't see an independent, stubborn, or rebellious child. I see a precious, cherished daughter of Mine. For years, I yearned to take you into my arms and love, protect, and heal you. Let me dry your tears and show you how much I cherish you! Thank you for inviting me into

246

your life. I rejoice over you and the angels in heaven, and I sing a song over you because you are home.'"

By the time Torrie said the last words, tears flowed freely from all three of them. Tears of joy and celebration.

Constance couldn't contain her joy.

"This calls for a group hug, don't you think?"

Torrie, Constance, and Steve talked into the early hours of the morning. Torrie asked questions, and Steve and Constance answered. Finally, Steve begged his leave. After all, he had a real job to go to in the morning, and he knew Constance would be at the hospital bright and early eager to see her other daughter. Steve left the ladies' presence feeling blessed that the Lord had allowed this little family into his life.

Constance and Torrie went into the kitchen and had Toastettes and hot chocolate before they called it a night. No one knew what tomorrow would bring, but these three people at least knew Who was in control of the tomorrows.

Chapter Seventy-Three

Reed, Jennie, Barbara, and Craig had just settled into their chairs with their pastry and coffee when Jack strolled into the conference room.

"Hello, team! You look more rested than I've seen you in days. I, on the other hand, look like shit, but that's because I slept until the last minute and didn't take time to shave. Let's start our day, then I'll clean up. Your instructions are as follows: go to your individual cubicles, which you haven't seen in a few days, take out a clean tablet and write the most bizarre terrorist plot you can think of, and then reconvene here in ninety minutes."

Jack walked out and left no time for questions or discussion. The four looked at each other, then pushed back their chairs and headed toward their cubicles. Jack had made some strange assignments in the past, but this one was stranger than usual. He didn't say what facts to use to create their plot or even if they were supposed to consider the events they had already witnessed. The team was intelligent enough to guess Jack was vague on purpose. He wanted fresh ideas that had nothing to do with their current theories of these last few days.

Jack went straight to his office. One of the perks of being the boss was his own personal dressing room with all the toiletries, plus a change of clothes. Everything he needed to freshen up after a long night at the office. It only took twenty minutes for him to completely renovate himself and sit down at his desk, ready to plot his own terrorist attack. He raised his pen to put the first word down when his cell phone rang. He had half a mind not to answer it until he recognized the emergency code from the front desk.

"This is Jack. What—Who? —say again? —Okay, okay. Tell him to calm down for Pete's sake. I'll be down in a minute!"

Though Jack didn't know for sure who had caused such a stir since the receptionist didn't get a name, he had an inkling who it might be. Sure enough, before he even turned the corner, Robert's voice clearly assaulted his ears. His angry voice irritated Jack immensely because Robert was a disruption and wasn't invited to join this investigation. Monique was easy to work with, but her boss, not so much, and when did he get out of the hospital? Jack should have sent his soothing diplomat Reed to intercept the beast, but too late now. He swallowed his indignation as best he could.

"Why, hello, Robert! How in the world are you? You must have just been released from the hospital because the last I heard – about forty-eight hours ago you were still out of it."

"Is that supposed to mean something? Was that a dig? You don't think I can contribute anything intelligent? I am here to tell you ..."

Jack no sooner said the last word than he realized Robert was bound to misinterpret his intent. Except, because of his feelings about Robert, Jack had to at least consider that somewhere deep down, his intention was accurate as Robert interpreted.

"Calm down, Robert. You know I didn't mean that. I'm sure you have much to contribute, given your many years of experience. Let's have a civil conversation, shall we?"

Robert took a deep breath. He had planned to be calm and politely ask to speak with Jack. But this—this—receptionist started with the questions. When Jack walked over and sanctimoniously made that wiseass statement about being out of it, his good intentions flew out the door. He was sure Jack meant precisely what his words inferred.

"Of course, I can have a civil conversation. I am a civil person. Now, I need to know where you are in this investigation. I also want to review all the raw material and data you and your team and Monique have so I can get up to speed on the progress—I ..."

"Robert, uh, sir, I'm not sure you've been invited to this investigation. Last I heard you didn't want any part of it. The only reason there is a CIA presence is because of Monique and since she is still recovering from injuries ..."

"Why you little—! Yes, she suffered injuries because of your carelessness! If she had not..."

"You have no business bringing those types of accu—"

"Stop! Both of you! Stop this instant!"

Reed came to the rescue. The receptionist realized the two men had escalated out of control and called for reinforcements. Reed witnessed the gathered crowd excited to see the showdown. Diplomacy and gentleness were not the order of the day.

Both men stopped their exchange at Reed's outburst with words frozen on their tongues. Neither one knew how to react to this stern command. Of course, that was the intent. Once they were shocked out of their anger, the two grown men were forced to think like adults. Jack was about to take command since he was the superior, but one look in Reed's eyes changed his mind. Robert, on the other hand, dared utter another word. Reed immediately got into Robert's personal space and growled…

"Not another word."

Robert was convinced and firmly closed his mouth.

"Back to business folks. The show is over. Nothing more to see here.

"You two. Follow me."

He led the men to the public conference room without a backward glance, confident of the combatants' obedience. Robert and Jack meekly followed behind the young man with the realization of just how childishly they had acted.

Reed closed the door and sat down at the head of the table, so no one doubted who was in charge. Robert sat down two chairs from Reed on his right. Jack chose the chair directly across from Robert on Reed's left. Both gentlemen sat quietly and waited for Reed to speak first.

"Good. Now let me guess. Robert, you demanded that we turn over data files and notes on what we have discovered and gathered from witnesses, and Jack, you more or less told Robert that he wasn't invited into the investigation. Next, I'm sure you mentioned a comparison statement between Monique and Robert, who then, in turn, accused you of being responsible for Monique's accident. Does that sound about right?"

"It seems you could have written the script for our little discussion. But then that is why you are on my team. Robert, I apologize for being so childish, but…"

"Stop right there, Jack, not another word."

Reed was firm but didn't see any reason to raise his voice.

"I'm not finished. Robert, I suspect you have some information you feel is important to this investigation, or you wouldn't have come straight from the hospital to see us. To earn that information, you demanded something from us. The wiser approach would have been an offer to share information with us in exchange for an update. I'm not going to stand on formality because, frankly, we are out of

250

time. I personally want to know what you have. You tell us, and then we will consider your request to join our investigation."

Robert didn't like Reed's plan but suspected it was a take it or leave it proposition.

"Okay."

"Great. Now, without too many details, outline what you have for us."

"Okay, last night, the two detectives who began the initial investigation into Monique's accident came to the hospital to speak with Monique. Of course, she hasn't recovered enough to be able to work any on the investigation. The detectives came with vital information important enough to the investigation to give it a high priority. They changed their approach and came to me to pass on the information. They have some interesting insights, and when they left, I did some background research on their ideas to test the validity. There was enough information to consider their theory as sound and feasible."

For the next thirty minutes, Robert provided details of the discussion he had with the detectives and the information he was able to pull with his research. After he finished his presentation, he waited for a response.

Reed reckoned enough time had passed to dispel hostilities. He sat back in his chair and indicated to Jack to take back the lead. Jack was only too happy to comply, satisfied he had the boss role again.

"Thank you, Robert. Between the detectives' diligence and your research, the theory is solid and something I want to present to the rest of my team. Earlier, I had asked my agents to create a theory of their own. I want to compare all theories and move this investigation in the right direction. You can ask any question you want after everyone presents their ideas. When everyone is finished, I'll show you the pertinent information."

"With all due respect, Jack, I'd like to see all of the data on the case. My idea of pertinent could be, and probably is, different than yours is."

Robert hoped he made his request humbly. He did not want to arouse Jack's indignation.

"Okay. I can see that. Sure. We'll let you look at all of the data we have. I think we have a plan now. Let's head upstairs to the conference room. We'll begin the meeting in say fifteen minutes. I should be able to get everyone there by then."

The group broke up. While they didn't walk together, they took off in the same general path, just different elevator stations.

Chapter Seventy-Four

Monique woke up just as her mother made herself comfortable. It'd been a long night of conversations, so Constance slept until eight-thirty and didn't get to the hospital until ten o'clock.

"Hello, Mom. Have you been here long? It seems like you were here right before I went back to sleep, and here you are now. The only reason I know you left is that you have a different outfit on from yesterday."

"Good morning, sweetheart."

Constance got up to give her daughter a kiss.

"Actually Steve, Torrie and I had quite a long night, so I slept in this morning. The nurse has just updated me on your night. I didn't get in your room until about five minutes ago. The nurse said your doctor came in earlier, so she won't be back until later tonight. I'm going to stay here until she comes so I can talk to her."

"Mom, I have like three or four doctors. You are bound to meet them all sometime today. There is the orthopedic doctor, then the orthopedic surgeon, the internal medicine doctor, and the internal medicine surgeon, and the neurologist comes in as well. I think he feels left out. Can you get me some more ice chips? My throat is still scratchy. I wonder when I can have some real food."

Constance picked up the cup and went to get some ice, as Monique requested. Steve walked in at that moment.

"Hello, Ms. Yorkshire, and how are you and your various Yorkshire daughters this morning? I came by earlier, and you weren't here. I jealously decided you slept in this morning. It must be nice to live a comfortable life and not have to go to a real job like some of us."

Steve did his best to sound bitter and pouty but couldn't pull it off. His disposition was too easy-going. Constance gave him a kiss on the cheek and walked out to get the ice chips for Monique without a word.

"If you want to drum up some sympathy, I hate to be the bearer of bad news. You failed miserably. There is no sympathy inside or outside this room."

"I daresay you are correct, young Ms. Yorkshire. You look slightly better this morning. Well, your eyes look a little brighter. Your bruising looks worse, and you're still pale. Stay away from a mirror for a few days unless you want to get depressed. Have they talked to you about physical therapy yet?"

"No, but I'm ready to get out of this bed. I asked for a different room because this TV doesn't work, and I want to get caught up on world events. Life doesn't stop because I get a few scratches. Have you heard anything about Robert?"

Monique's voice was scratchy, and weak. However, Steve was able to catch enough words to get the general essence of her question.

"Sorry, no can tell. You're convalescing. Shoptalk is not on the agenda or in your charts. In fact, it says here in bold black capitals: UNDER NO CIRCUMSTANCES IS MONIQUE TO ENTERTAIN VISITORS THAT HAVE ANYTHING TO DO WITH HER JOB OR THE CASE!'

"I dare not ignore this message, or you will have to support me."

Constance came back into the room during this little speech.

"Don't listen to him, Monique. He made that up. Your chart says no such thing. One of the nurses told me the detectives who started the investigation came to see you last night right after we left. When the nurse told them, you were down for the count, they found your boss and talked to him. He was discharged today, so don't ask if we can get him for you."

"Thanks, Mom, I wish he would've come by. I had a couple of thoughts, and I'm anxious to know what the latest is."

Steve wasn't sure whether to stay or leave. Fortunately, the nurse walked in and made the decision for him.

"Reverend, the patient's family in room B25 wants to see you. The patient isn't doing too well right now."

"Thanks, Fran. I'm on my way."

Steve looked at Constance and Monique.

"I'll say my good-byes for now. Let me know if either one of you needs me."

Monique thanked her mom for the ice and pushed the button for some more pain medicine. She attempted to do it discreetly so Constance wouldn't notice, but of course, it didn't work.

"Would you rather I leave and sit in the waiting room?"

"No, Mom, I like you here if you don't mind. I know you get bored watching me sleep, but I feel less inclined to fight sleep when you're here. I think I have this fear I'll return to my coma."

"You are less boring now than you were when you were in your coma, so I'm happy to watch you sleep. And I come prepared. In this bag I have books, magazines, a notebook, and snacks with two bottles of water. Just lie back and close your eyes. I'll be here all day!"

"Thanks, Mom, you are so …"

Monique was out before she could finish her thought.

Chapter Seventy-Five

The FBI team was back in the conference room, this time with Robert instead of Monique. No one made a comment on Robert's presence because the look on Jack's face told them all they needed to know. The issue of whether or not he would join them had already been confronted, argued, and resolved. The fact that he was here evidenced that he was admitted into the investigation.

"I'm sure everyone has come up with a plot or plan of attack, so who would like to go first? Jennie?"

"Sure, I guess. Well, mine isn't too imaginative, but it's complex. There are three major targets. In my scenario, the terrorists are backed by money, probably heads of businesses with divisions in strategic countries. These companies have at their disposal aircraft, private airfields, as well as ships with their own port of entries. With access to all aspects of travel, army deployment, training, and even attacks can be integrated with normal business patterns without a red flag. While the target or targets could be any number of places, my thought is that the attack would be the entire eight-block section of Wall Street. If the financial capital of the United States is crippled, the ripple effect would be catastrophic. It's probably also one of the most densely populated areas in the smallest section, which means a high body count. Even more so than the 9-11 attack."

There were several minutes of somber silence as each person digested the scene described by Jennie.

"Quite a graphic picture, Jennie. I agree an attack of that nature could definitely be a blow to the United States."

Jack looked around the conference table.

"Craig, why don't you go next."

"Sure, but first, I want you to know that I did not discuss, at any time with anyone in this room, my attack theory."

Craig looked at each person in the room for an acknowledgment before he continued.

"Okay, already, Craig. Just spit it out. We don't have all day here."

Jack wasn't sure why he was so irritated at Craig. Plus, he was curious as to why Craig felt a disclaimer was necessary.

"Similar to Jennie's creation, my thinking is that there are two groups of people or businesses. There is a CEO over the businesses with a lot of money and a cause. The businesses are large enough to financially support a small army, and the type of businesses are sufficient enough to cover suspicious activity. Now, do you understand why my disclaimer?"

"Uncanny. Please continue."

"Each group – possibly we can call them an army – has a separate target, one on the East Coast and the other on the West Coast. The attack on the East Coast targets the Pentagon and begins with a new infantry on a training mission simulating the defense of the Pentagon during a terrorist attack. Real terrorists infiltrate both sides of the mock scuttle. The mock attack becomes real, but it was so subtle that by the time they figure it out, no one can tell the good guys from the bad guys. Simultaneously, on the West Coast, the attack is chemical warfare in the State of Washington and then California. The attack would be launched around one or two research hospital. I didn't work out details, just the premise."

"Barbara? How similar is your scenario?"

"Actually, mine begins with the same strategy. CEOs of large corporations with sympathies towards radical Islam use their wealth, power, and corporations to wage a terrorist attack in the Midwest to the Central United States. The targets are farms, ranches, and any arena substantial enough to endanger the food supply of the United States. A shortage of food caused by the destruction of corn, cotton, cattle, chickens, and pork would create panic and fear. The fear causes the stock market to crash, which would be bad enough to affect all aspects of the United States.

Jack hesitated for a moment before he looked at Reed. He couldn't decide whether to call on him for his hypothesis or just assume the ill-timed confrontation didn't allow him to complete the assignment. Reed came to his defense.

"Robert, why don't you share with us what the detectives presented to you, why, and what your early research revealed."

Jack followed up.

"That's a great idea. Everyone, Robert, has come up with a possible plan with the aid of local detectives who did not have access to any of the information we've had."

"Incredible. All three of you had the same idea but a little different slant. I used my data and the conclusions from the police detectives who investigated the suspicious nature of Monique's accident to create my attack theory. The detectives continued to analyze the case even after we, uh, relinquished them of the responsibility."

Robert snuck a peek at Jack when he made the last statement.

Jack was aware of Robert's glance. He used his self-control and kept his opinions to himself. It would go something like, "Yea, Mr. Diplomacy, you SOB. You stole the case from them, confiscated all of their records and practically kicked them to the curb." With his incredibly strong non-verbal disproval attitude, a verbal attack was not necessary.

Robert continued.

"The detectives' research and analysis concluded that Connor is the common denominator. Even though Connor was not qualified to be an assistant to an extraordinarily successful marketing executive, he got the job as the number two person and worked closely with Monique's sister. His experience was weak, and he had no creative instinct, plus McGregor, Bright, and Anderson chooses to promote from within, so they made an exception employing a newcomer into a prominent position.

"The detectives suggested we look at the clients of the firm, specifically the clients of Torrie and Connor, which I did last night. A pattern developed with three individuals, affiliated with several corporations. I didn't have time or the ability to get into the details of their private or confidential information. With what you guys came up with and what the detectives and I put together, I think the next step is to collect all you can about these three persons and the corporations they represent. Then while you guys are doing that, I will review your data. We should be able to put our heads together and come up with a solid plan of attack with counterattack options to eliminate them, their corporations, and the threat they pose."

Personally, Jack thought Robert had gone too far but didn't specifically say so.

"Thank you, Robert. I'm not sure it will be necessary to destroy the entire companies of these perpetrators. If we do that, there may be major unemployment issues, among other things. Everything else makes sense. The information from Robert has been downloaded by the administrative team while we had this meeting, and you all have access. There are two teams plus me, and we will do this alphabetically. Reed—you and Jennie take the first person in line, Craig—you and Barbara take the next person, and I will research the third person. Robert, the raw data you requested is set up in the small conference room next to my office. Barbara will show you where it is. Lunch will be prepared and served here in this room. When you need refreshments or nourishments, come get it anytime. Just allow forty-five minutes for it to get here. Any questions? Okay, you're dismissed."

Chapter Seventy-Six

Constance looked up from the book she pretended to read. She knew it was an excellent book because she liked the author. To the general population, the plot made for an excitingly intense journey, but for her, not so much. All she had to do was reflect on the reality of her life to be part of a New York's Best Seller Novel. Monique had just given herself some more pain medication, so Constance felt comfortable enough to leave for a few minutes, stretch her legs, and refresh herself. She went to her daughter's side, and looked at her for a few seconds, leaned over, and whispered in her ear.

"I'll be back, my sweet daughter."

She kissed her cheek and went to the door. Someone pushed the door open as she pulled it to leave and forced her to jump out of the way so she wouldn't be crushed between the door and the wall.

"Oh, my, you just about—goodness …. Why didn't you knock?—uh—Oh, hello, Steve. You startled me and almost knocked me down."

Constance was entirely unhinged by that time, so unexpected was this activity.

Steve caught her by the arms to steady her, and because he liked the closeness held on longer than necessary.

"I'm so sorry! I should have knocked, but if you decided to close your eyes, I didn't want to disturb you. It's past lunchtime. Do you care to accompany me to the cafeteria? You need a change of scenery."

"Why young man, do my ears deceive me, or did you ask me out on a date? That's presumptuous of you, don't you think?"

"No, not at all, my dear. I'm much older than I look, and who would miss any opportunity to spend time with a fair maiden as yourself?"

Steve caught up both of Constance's hands and gave each palm a quick kiss.

"You, Mr. Steve Robinson, are one of a kind!"

Constance took Steve's arm, and they strode out of the room side by side.

"This is a pleasant surprise. I was a bit lonely with no one to talk to. It's different watching Monique sleep than it was when she was in a coma. Not that I wish to go there again. But, then, I talked to her out loud constantly to keep her mind stimulated. This time around, the opposite is important, quiet and restful. The days are long, and I'm bored with magazines."

"How much longer do you think Monique will keep herself knocked out with the pain medicine? Her personality doesn't strike me as one who wants to be left out of the action."

"How insightful. I'm thinking that part of the reason she is keeping herself sedated—well, except for the obvious, which is her pain, is that she is disappointed that she can't be part of the plan to stop a major attack. To be sidelined has, I'm sure, caused her to be depressed. I predict, though, that by tonight, she'll cut the medication by half and be ready to face the world again."

"And now, how is your other daughter, Torrie? Her, I don't envy. As self-controlled and structured as she likes to be, I'm sure this is difficult for her. The life she knew has been reshuffled, forcing her to sift through all of the pieces of her world. Did you see her before you left the house?"

Constance had a different perception on Torrie's reaction.

"We talked after you left last night, and I got a sense that she's in a good place. She decided to take a leave of absence or at least a long vacation to re-evaluate every aspect of her life. That's an ambitious undertaking for her, but I think she's excited about it. I'm excited for her and can't wait to see how she evolves."

Steve shook his head in wonderment.

"I know I have said this before, and I've thought it more often than I've said it—I'm amazed by you Yorkshire women and completely in love with the entire family! Of course, the head of the household is the one I have my sights set on."

Steve and Constance arrived at the cafeteria and chose their items. They took a table in the back so they could sit quietly and enjoy each other's company.

Back in Monique's room, the nurse once again answered the beeping of the IV monitor. It seemed like this machine went off every five minutes. She decided to snoop around and find another one that wasn't being used at this time so she could take this one to the technical department to check it out.

"Hello, nurse."

Monique managed to open her eyes and say something while the nurse was still in the room.

"I would very much like to have a Dr. Pepper, like right now; yesterday, if possible."

"Hello there. Welcome back to the land of the living, my dear. Let me check your chart. Dr. Pepper is kind of a strange request, but if you aren't on a special diet with restrictions, one can be arranged. Maybe not now or yesterday but soon. Would you like some crackers as well? I think the doctor is going to allow some real food. Let's see—yes, you can have your soda—and—no, crackers. You can begin solid food tomorrow, not today. Today, soft foods only, which leaves you with a choice of pudding, Jell-O, some broth, or you can have some ice cream. I know. You can have a Dr. Pepper float. No rule says you can't enjoy what you get on a soft-food diet."

The nurse didn't give Monique a chance to agree with the soda, but then she didn't have the energy to protest. In reflection, the float was probably the best choice out of everything the nurse listed. She wondered how long she had to wait. It seemed like months since she last ate anything. Thank goodness they have clocks in hospital rooms now. The clock showed it was three, but morning or afternoon? Her room was dark, with the shades pulled and only the one light the nurse used. The nurse was too energetic for the night shift, so it was probably afternoon. That plus, she was sure her mother wouldn't leave for the day until Monique was awake enough to say good-bye.

To take her mind off the wait time for her treat, Monique decided to take inventory of her injuries. She closed her eyes and focused first on her lower body. Toes – check, wiggled good; right leg – check, moved, not good. She lifted it but experienced searing pain when she touched it. She opened her eyes to physically look at it. What she saw was a heavily bandaged upper leg wrapped in a thick ace bandage. Okay—that must be the leg the door was on. The gash was down to the bone, so this leg is a problem. Monique settled back again.

Left leg – check, a little stiff from lack of activity. Monique wanted to raise her head and searched for the nurse's button, where the bed adjustments were. Her right arm was immobilized, which rendered the right side of her body useless. She searched with her left hand for the remote. Ouch! Okay, not expected. That must be the spot where her surgery was—what was it?—Spleen, that was it. Okay. Not ready for a relay race yet.

She wondered about her face but decided to forgo the shock of the sight in a mirror. The chaplain warned her not to. Monique continued to look for the nurse's button or the remote, whichever she found first. Now that she had it in her mind to sit up, she wanted to sit up now.

"And here we are, Ms. Yorkshire. Oh, can I help you find something? You shouldn't be squirming about so much."

The nurse hurried over to Monique, put the float on the tabletop to untangle the helpless young lady before she screamed.

"I want to sit up, and I can't find the up and down remote! Where
is it?"

"Calm down, child; you can't find it because it isn't near you. The doctor didn't want you to sit upright, so we put it away. Now, take a deep breath and let me straighten your covers and adjust you in your bed. After that, I will help you raise up a bit. Is that good with you?"

Monique took a deep breath. She had acted like an ingrate and owed this sweet old nurse an apology.

"Sounds good. I apologize. I'm not irritated with you. It's just, I hate being an invalid."

The nurse worked on the bedclothes and fluffed the pillows. Monique asked for a second pillow for her head. There was already a pillow under her right shoulder and one to elevate her right leg. When the nurse finished arranging supports, Monique was cocooned in pillows, a comfortable place for now, but only if she could sit up. The nurse took the remote and pushed the button. They both waited for the bed to rise. Monique paid attention to her lower body and the strain of sitting up, while the nurse watched Monique's vitals. She stopped the bed at the same time Monique said stop.

"We agree then that this is high enough. I see you know how to read your body well. That's a good thing because I don't expect to have to tell you when to quit working or when to stop resting. Physical therapy will begin first thing in the morning. Now, enjoy your ice cream soda before it completely melts!"

The nurse was gone before Monique could make another sound, so she did the only sane thing she could do. Picked up her ice cream float with her left hand. How was she supposed to eat the darn thing?

"My, my what have we here? Sitting up and having what? It looks like a float. I thought they quit making those years ago."

Steve walked in ahead of Constance. She stopped to check-in at the nurses' station. He was pleased with what he saw and knew "mom" would be too.

"Yes, a Dr. Pepper float, and I want to devour it now! But I'm only one-handed. Can you help?"

Constance walked in.

"Monique. What a pleasant surprise. You look so much better than you did when I left."

Constance went to Monique and surveyed her vitals as she went.

"Your blood pressure is up. Probably because you moved around some. Did the nurse brush your hair?"

Constance studied her daughter once again and noticed the tangle at the back of her neck.

"Oh, I guess not, you still have tangles. I'll be happy to comb the tangles out if you like?"

"Thanks, but no thanks. If I happen to quit hurting, and I miss the pain, you'll be the first to know. Then you can torture me with fixing my hair."

Steve and Monique laughed at that statement. Constance pretended to be annoyed but couldn't pull it off very well.

"To answer your question, I'm better. The nurse rearranged my covers and me, fixed my pillows, raised my head, and brought me this wonderful Dr. Pepper float! What more can one ask? Except for a suggestion on how I'm supposed to eat it one-handed."

"Would you like me to feed it to you? It's been years, but I did do that once upon a time."

"Really, Mom? Can't we come up with a more inventive idea? I don't want someone to feed me. Steve, help me out, please."

"I liked your mother's plan but let me evaluate your dilemma. You have an ice cream float staring at you, but if you hold it with one hand, it's difficult to maneuver. Constance, roll Monique's tray over here. I've become an expert at lowering these things to accommodate most patients. Okay, now the straw is too high for you to be able to drink while the glass is on your tray, so—open this cabinet over here and voila, a pair of scissors. A little snip here and—perfect. The tray is low enough to leave the glass in place. You can either hold it in your left hand and drink from the straw or leave it on the tray and drink. But, most importantly, you can use your left hand to dip the spoon and get every last morsel of the ice cream while the glass remains on the tray. No need for a second hand."

"Thanks, Steve. I knew there had to be a better way than someone feeding me. Now, if you two will excuse me, I'll be busy for a short time!"

No one spoke while Monique finished her float, content to enjoy the peace of the moment. Of course, no one thought for a minute that the break was long-term or widespread.

Monique slurped the last of her soda with a satisfied sigh.

"That was great. I hope the soft food they give me will be mashed potatoes and cream gravy, cream of potato soup, or even cream of tomato, yogurt – strawberry of course, another serving of mashed potatoes with cream gravy and another ice cream float for dessert. Or maybe chocolate pudding for dessert, and I'll have the ice cream float before bed."

Constance removed the tray away from the bed to give her daughter room to move.

"Thank you, I was feeling kind of claustrophobic. How about watching some news? I want to catch up to the world, and Steve, are there any old magazines around?"

"Do you really want old ones? I'm sure we have more old magazines than we do new ones, but we do have some new ones."

"Old is great because I want to look at the world events from the days I was out if it. I thought about asking for my laptop, but as handicapped as I am right now, I think the old-fashioned way, read hard copies, will be easier for now."

"Then, if you're sure, I can do that for you."

Steve looked at Constance to make sure she was settled and appeared good with watching the news. He knew she typically stayed away from watching the news because it upset her. He also knew, since Monique asked, she would deal with it."

"Ladies, if you can't think of anything else I can do for you, I'll go find those magazines."

Chapter Seventy-Seven

The teams gathered back into the main conference room. Without preamble, Jack started the meeting.

"I can tell you guys, from my perspective, the magnitude of this operation is unprecedented. Thank you for your compilations. I combined all of your research into a single document and reached out to the Joint Chiefs. We had a three-hour discussion about the report. As it turns out, they've monitored chatter which hinted to this kind of event for several months. It wasn't a complete surprise, but everyone was grateful for our research. Our information was the final confirmation the intelligence community needed to go forward with a plan to stop these terrorists. The president has been advised and approved of the campaign to stop them before they can launch. Operatives and agencies in France, Afghanistan, and Brazil have orders to take out the three corporate CEOs of Global Resources."

Reed scratched his head.

"How is that going to stop the terrorists? The CEOs are only the money people. They probably weren't even in on the planning."

"Be patient. I'm not finished."

"Sorry."

"These extremists planned three different attacks to take place at the same time. If we took them one at a time, we could possibly disrupt two attacks and the rebels most likely would complete the third attack. Even if only one of the three attacks were successful, it would be catastrophic for us. I was told that there is data from as far back as 9-11 which supports the idea this has been in the works for years. These ISIS extremists took the time to recruit allies from our own country. They are not only devious and bold, but patient as well."

Robert was concerned about false leads.

"Were they able to confirm the logistics?"

"That's an honest question. The CIA and FBI stumbled into this long-term plan because of the mistakes of people like Connor. When I brought our information to the director with the details, all agencies agreed to share research material and work together."

"Who performed that magic?"

"It wasn't easy, but once I mentioned the other alternative, which would likely be a third world war, it wasn't too hard after that. Once the various agencies shared information, the Joint Chiefs had enough data to go forward with a plan. The president was updated and authorized emergency action to use our special forces, black ops team, military, and secret service. But we have to hit them fast and hard."

Reed ventured another question.

"So, what's the plan?"

Jack continued to outline the plan.

"There is a three-phase strategy in place. The first phase of the operation is to organize and plot a course of action. Even as we speak, the masterminds of the Pentagon and Joint Chiefs are working on a coordinated attack on all three fronts. The second phase is to arrest the CEOs, followed immediately by the third phase, which is to take out the terrorists who've infiltrated the target areas."

Craig did research thoroughly but liked action much better.

"A lot has happened in a short time. So, what's next for us? How do we fit into the plan? I'm ready to get into the game."

"Guys, we've done our part and have the casualties to show for it. At this point, we can watch each move as it happens. As soon as a plan is formulated and approved by all branches, the arrests will be ordered, and at the same time, our forces will move in and take out the bad guys."

"How soon will all of this happen?"

Barbara was just as glad to be able to watch this sitting in the war room.

"Not sure, but we don't want too much time to pass. We've witnessed the long arm of the enemy. The Pentagon wants to take action no later than midnight tonight, about six hours from now. We can take a break and come back here at ten o'clock to fire up the satellite and watch the action. Anyone who wants to be here is welcome. Of course, I don't have to tell you, nothing out of your mouths to anyone! Understood?"

"Jack, I want permission to update Monique on this operation. She has a right to know, and to have all of this go down without telling her anything—well—I don't think it's fair."

Reed wasn't sure why he reacted the way he did, except that Monique had become important to him, something that rarely happened. He had to decide what to do about it.

"Okay, Reed. You may brief her. Only her, not her family or friends, or sister or mother – her. The others don't need to know."

"Who do you think you're talking to? I know what is at stake. This will not get leaked from me."

No one spoke after that. Everyone was glad Reed had volunteered to talk with Monique. The various pieces of this massive operation were in place and in process. The chances of success were significantly increased because it had all happened in less than twenty-four hours, and the opportunities of reporters getting wind of something this big was much less. By the end of the week, the world should be a little safer, and they could move on to another threat to the freedom of our country, or a larger threat to the world.

"If there are no further questions or concerns, you're dismissed. We've worked hard and proved inter-agency cooperation is not only possible, but we've done it successfully!"

Everyone got up to leave except Jack and Robert. The two adversaries looked at each other. Jack grudgingly said,

"Robert, thank you for the assist. Your information was important to the case. If you're interested in watching the operations from our satellite room, I'll be happy to meet you and walk you through later this evening. Right now, I want to go get a beer and pretend I live in a safe world."

"Nah, thank you anyway. I wouldn't mind joining you for a beer though. You have an excellent team, and you have the makings of a great CIA operative. You can come over as your own team, and before you say anything, I don't make these comments lightly."

"You will have to feed me a lot of beer to get me to defect.
I'm willing to drink and listen, though."

The two gentlemen left the building together and agreed on where to meet for a drink. Reed happened to see them talking as they walked to the garage, and all he could do was shake his head. He would have thought those two would have separated with haste. Now they acted like best buddies.

The next stop for Reed was the hospital to talk to Monique. He had to decide if he intended to pursue something other than a professional relationship, and the drive wasn't that long.

Chapter Seventy-Eight

Monique turned off the television.

"Well, the news didn't give any clues about pending attacks or a terrorist alert or anything. I sure wish someone would update me on the world."

"Sweetie, can't you just take time to get well and let them handle it? After all ..."

"Knock, knock. Is anyone here?"

"Torrie! Please come in. Monique and I are discussing the news, life, and stuff."

"Pretty heady for hospital talk. How are you, sis? Did you ever get your fill of ice chips?"

"I did, and guess what my first meal was? You'll never guess."

"Let's see. You are probably on a liquid diet or maybe soft foods by tonight. I bet it had something to do with Dr. Pepper and ice cream."

"Mom! You told her. Not fair."

"It didn't take too much imagination to figure it out. Those are your two most favorite foods, and you've not had anything for several weeks. It made sense to crave your favorites."

"I may have to enlist you into ..."

"Knock, knock. May I come in?"

Torrie went to the door.

"Reed? What in the world are you doing here? How did you know I was here, and well, I'm on leave? Why are you ...? I don't understand."

"It's kind of complicated. May I come in?"

"Of course, there's still a chair left."

"Hello, Monique, and you must be her mom. It's nice to finally meet you. I have to commend you on raising such extraordinary women."

"Thank you, Reed, is it? You know both of my daughters? That's strange; they are from two different worlds."

Constance looked at both of her girls in confusion.

"Monique, do you want to explain, or should I?"

"Mom, Torrie, I'd like to introduce you to Reed Thomas. He is the FBI agent who rescued Connor's family and bullied his way into the CIA's investigation."

"You mean you knew about Connor? You weren't a marketing intern? But you were so good."

Reed gave a chuckle. "That's why I was put in. I have a marketing background but moved into the world of crime later when I got bored."

"This is bizarre. And you and Monique worked together?"

"Only after Robert and I attempted the rescue. Robert was injured, and I joined with the FBI team. We conducted separate investigations on the same case and thought it best to pool our resources. Reed, I need to speak to you about a thought I had before I was injured. I want to know what the status of the investigation is."

"That's one reason I'm here."

"And I bet whatever it is you are here to say is not for anyone's ears but Monique's. Torrie, I think it's time for us to leave these two spies alone."

"Mom, do you mind too terribly much? I know you think I shouldn't talk about work, but my work is really my life, and I want to know what's happening."

Constance had already gathered her stuff and was on her way to tell Monique goodnight.

"Goodnight, I love you and will be back in the morning. Meanwhile, Reed, don't keep her up too late. The body heals only when it's at rest."

"Yes, ma'am. Not late at all, I promise."

Torrie wouldn't be satisfied until she knew the entire story but realized it didn't matter.

"I'm leaving under duress, and I expect a full report from both of you whenever the top-secret stuff is over. I mean it!"

"I promise, and thank you, Torrie. We'll catch up with each other soon."

"Can't wait. Love you, sis."

Torrie and Constance left for home.

"How are you, really? You look like you hurt. Or maybe I hurt just to look at you. – I'm so angry with you, Monique. Why would you put yourself in such a dangerous situation? It was foolish and unnecessary. You could have …"

Reed stopped and took a deep breath.

"But I didn't come to yell at you. I'm sorry. You do look like you're in pain, though."

"Pain? Yes. I won't deny it. Foolish and unnecessary? I doubt everyone who escaped injury or worse because I waved them away thinks I was foolish. It was what had to be done. I'm glad you came, Reed, because I want to discuss a thought I had right before our attack. I'm sure about Kansas, but I think we need to change our focus. What is the status of the investigation?"

"Before we go there, I've something to say."

"Sounds serious. Good news, or bad?"

"I'll let you decide."

Now that Reed was here, he couldn't think of the words to say.

"Well, I'm waiting?"

"Okay, give a minute. I can't seem to remember what I want to say."

"If you don't hurry, I'll be discharged before I find out."

"All right. Here goes. The moment I saw you taken down by a door and knew you were seriously injured, the realization hit me full force. I care a great deal about you. And not only as an agent. You intrigued and fascinated me, and I connected to you as a person when we first met."

"Oh, my! That's a huge confession. You must have used every bit of your courage to say that."

"I stopped and purchased some more courage on the way over. But I'm serious. I want to help you and spend some time with you, and then, well, you know, see what happens …"

Monique stared at Reed in disbelief. She looked around for Gabriel, thinking maybe she had gone off into another alternate world. She opened her mouth, but nothing came out.

Reed started to back away and prepared for a quick getaway, expecting the worst from the silence that followed his announcement.

"No, wait. Reed, don't leave. I'm sorry, you just— I never—I don't know what to say."

"I guess you don't have to say anything right now, as long as you don't say I'm a jerk."

271

"My goodness, why would I say that? I never imagined in a hundred years that you thought of me as anything but a CIA agent who invaded the FBI. I—actually..."

"What? I understand if you can't say anything right now, just please think about it."

"You don't understand. Reed, I like you, really, but I would never say anything to you because why would someone who works for a rival agency want to, well, be friends."

"Really? Then it's okay if we are friends? At least to begin with. I didn't know if I would ever find someone so comfortable to be around."

"Are you sure it's me and not my sister? After all, you worked with her first."

"Oh, I'm sure. I like Torrie, but she's too, uh, serious. Yes, that's the word. Of course, I don't want to rush in and do something that isn't good for both of us. We haven't known each other that long, and we've been on high alert and focused on terrorists. Maybe we won't have anything else in common after this."

"Oh, I think we have more in common than you think. Reed, thank you for your honesty and for taking a chance to say something. You've proved you really are brave."

"Maybe not brave. As Jack tells me all of the time, I can be reckless."

Monique giggled.

"That's such a Reed statement!

"Now that we've got the serious stuff out of the way, may I change the subject?"

Reed was ready to move on. This conversation had been more difficult than he suspected.

"By all means, Monique. You said you had some thoughts about the terrorists?

"I've not been kept in the loop, and I don't care what Jack said about protecting national security by not telling anyone what is going on. Please, can you fill me in? I don't want to beg."

"My dear, you don't ever have to beg!"

Reed and Monique discussed love and war and the connection between the two. He sat by Monique's side until she fell asleep, then he went to FBI headquarters to watch the salvation of the United States. He looked forward to life after the save.

Monique hobbled into the kitchen as Constance finished up with the last of the dishes.

Six Months Later

"Well, I got here at exactly the right time! Where did the rest of your help go? Why didn't Steve help? He usually can't leave your side, or rather usually doesn't leave your side."

Constance turned toward her amazing daughter. She was still on crutches, though physical therapy strengthened her each time. Monique had invested three or four months of physical therapy on her broken arm before she ditched her wheelchair. Confinement to a wheelchair challenges most people, but for those as active as she— let's just say Constance was grateful for Reed during these six months. His attentiveness to Monique kept her sane.

"I imagine, my dear, that Steve is in the same place Reed is. In case you haven't noticed, they are both missing in action. Have a chair. Torrie will wander in soon. I'm going to get the Toastettes and cocoa so we can all have Toastettes and chocolate milk and talk girl talk!"

"Hey, Mom, Monique. Where are the menfolk? Yeah! How did you know that was exactly what I wanted! You always amaze me."

Torrie couldn't get over how her life had changed in the last six months. The largest clients of McGregor, Bright, and Anderson, went out of business and forced the marketing company into bankruptcy. Torrie was obliged to recreate her future. Several companies, ready to snatch up her talents, made generous offers, but she was burned out and not interested in that world anymore. Beginning with the day Torrie accepted the Lord, her interests changed. She took weeks to investigate programs that lined up with her master's degree, but nothing materialized. Unless a second master's was in the cards, the only option available was to continue in Marketing. Then she talked with Steve. He suggested she go to a seminary for now and enroll in theology classes. She could take the first semester to check out the other programs available. There were several routes she could take and still utilize her experience but transfer her skills to work for the Kingdom. So far, that made the most sense. She had yet to tell anyone, but now with Toastettes and chocolate milk, this would be a perfect time.

Life for the Yorkshires is good for the moment, but they understand that tomorrow the wind can blow in adversity. The pattern is much the same for us, and as they did, we have a choice to make. Will we choose whether to let the adversities get the best of us? Or will we overcome our adversities? Which will you choose?